CHASING KATE

Kelly Byrne

Two Pens Press

Los Angeles

Two Pens Press
PO Box 931121
Los Angeles, CA 90093
www.authorkellybyrne.com

Chasing kate: a novel/Kelly Byrne
ISBN 978-1-469-91105-2

For Tony, my Magic Man

They should prosecute people for inner child abuse.

—LINDSAY BROOKS

ONE

The first time I kidnapped Sadie Beck was an accident. In my defense, the second time was too. Initially. Having a little perspective now I can see how there might have been a better way to handle the situation, but at the time my perspective was in the toilet.

It was Halloween night and I blazed down State Street, the main drag in Salt Lake City, with little regard for the laws of traffic or decency. The air was moist and thick with fog. Neon signs on the storefronts flew by like Jackson Pollack pieces wrapped in gauze. Everything dull and blurry.

I was at the helm of The Green Beast, a '78 Jeep Cherokee three decades past its prime. I'd bought it in Big Bear a month before for the move to Salt Lake City. It got exactly 6.8 miles to the gallon, but it was cheap and had lots of space. Space still filled with paperwork, clothes, and miscellaneous irreplaceables packed away in boxes in the back. I'd sold all my electronics and furniture before I moved because Adam said we could use his when we found our own place. Turned out we didn't find that place. Turned out Adam was a big fat liar.

I blew through two pinkish lights and almost impaled Batman on a BMX as I hurdled the curb into the grocery store parking lot. He swerved into a lamppost on the sidewalk to avoid me. I would have gone back to help him but a furious, prepubescent voice wound a "Fuck you!" out into the universe telling me that wouldn't be necessary. I think he was just pissed at himself for not having better skills.

I parked and carried on with my mission: shove a bottle of vodka and whatever goodies I could fit down my pants and get the hell out of Dodge. It was a perfect plan and partially why I wore the oversized hoodie sweatshirt and baggy boy jeans. They also hid the pudgy spots and I needed to feel good about something.

But where the hell was the liquor? I stood in aisle nine surrounded by bottles of pink Boone's Farm malt liquor on one side and forties of Old Milwaukee on the other wondering who the hell stole all the good stuff in between. Had there been a mad rush for Long Island Iced Teas on Halloween?

"Where the fuck is the vodka?" I asked the shelves, expecting a response.

"At the liquor store."

For a second I thought I *was* living in a universe where smartass shelves spoke, but then I looked around and saw the pimpled stick figure at the end of the aisle, stocking the corner display with chips.

"What?" I said to him.

"Grocery stores in Utah don't sell liquor."

"What?"

"Yeah, oh, and, uh liquor stores aren't open on Sunday. You must nur ben fwomin hare..." My brain couldn't process what he'd said so I tuned him out. What kind of a grotesquely aberrant state doesn't sell alcohol in its grocery stores?

Panicked by my dearth of choices, I grabbed a bottle of Strawberry Boone's off the shelf in front of me and slipped around the corner. I waited till all was clear then stuffed it down my pants and moved on with my mission.

Already derailed, I was put out even more when I realized I'd have to pay for a few things. Trying to cram four pounds of Oreos and M&Ms, a family size bag of Hershey's Miniatures, a fourteen-inch brownie cake and two pints of "Chocolate Therapy" in with the Boone's was a silly expectation of the capacity of my pants.

I like my ice cream soupy, so I kept the cold stuff and the two bags of M&Ms down there ('cause they melt in your mouth, not in your pants) and stocked my arms with the Oreos, Miniatures, and brownie cake.

I glanced around to make sure no one had seen what I'd done. The aisle was empty. But what were those pricklies tickling the nape of my neck? I could feel it. Someone was watching me. Suddenly I was overcome by the urge to put everything back. Moving to Salt Lake had absorbed most of my finances and I couldn't, with good conscience, afford myself any luxuries. And I definitely couldn't afford to be caught.

But this wasn't a luxury. It was necessity. And I'd find work soon. Very soon. And I'd go to college and earn my degree in English and teach at U-Dub, where my mother had taught. My life would be brilliant. I would be brilliant. Tomorrow. Today I needed chocolate.

The only cashier open was a geriatric with rigor mortis and a comb over. The line from his register snaked halfway down through the frozen foods section and wasn't moving. When I reached the end of it I was certain I'd developed frostbite on very specific parts of my body, but I was a champion and not about to let a bit of dead flesh stand in the way of my fix. I left the ice cream in place and contemplated how much it would cost to install a vending machine in The Beast. I'd never have to open my door to the outside world agai—

"Sadie put them bubbles back. I told you, you ain't getting nothing."

The man in front of me cut my musings short. His voice was loose and irritating, like a dump truck had deposited down his throat. The screechy little thing attached to him wailed and squirmed from his grip. She dropped the blue bottle of bubbles on the floor and her gingery pigtails flew away from the line, bouncing toward the sliding glass doors. She was a quick one. The bells on her jacket strings were on crack; neurotically jingling with each step she took toward the exit.

"Sadie git back here." He didn't unclench his teeth and he didn't move out of line. From the side he looked like the weathered love child of Harrison Ford and Robert Redford. Good bones. Hard skin.

Sadie kept tinkling toward the door. I watched her go and reminisced about how I used to wear my hair in pigtails when I was that age. Whatever age that was. Kids were all two or ten to me.

"Dang it, Sadie. You little..." Lovechild glanced back at me and opened his mouth to speak. Nothing came.

I'd had that kind of effect on a few strangers in my time.

Though, normally, I'd be drunk on a dance floor working the hell out of a new bra.

"Save my spot," he finally said.

What happened to asking nicely?

"Sure, I guess." After all, he was my type. I'd noticed his ring finger, shiny with gold, when Sadie threw the bubbles.

He chased after the little monster and I felt a cold rivulet of cream oozing down my leg. I slid my hand into my pants to handle the situation without drawing anyone's notice. Instead of that, I drew everyone's notice.

The Boone's came loose and I tried to hoist it back up with my elbow but it kept sneaking down, like the sweat on my forehead. The whole situation was impossible to manage with my arms full, so I deftly remedied that by slipping in the puddle of bubbles the little brat threw on the floor. Oreos and brownie cake went flying into Darth Vader's basket behind me, and the Miniatures sailed behind him into Gandalf's beard. Finished with my stunning tribute to Martha Graham, I gathered all my limbs only to have the three-dollar bottle of Boone's slide down my leg and clunk on the floor. It sat there, peeking out, like an unexploded bomb.

I froze. Everyone in line stared at me. I bowed my head and squatted to pull the bottle out of my pants leg. Harry Potter snickered. *Asshole.*

I'd had a plan. It was simple. But apparently, so was I.

I left the Boone's in the middle of the floor. Not really a loss. If I'd had any sense I would have just snatched a bottle of Anbesol instead. Smaller bottle and it cures more than toothaches.

It would be like swallowing sun, but once it was down I wouldn't have felt a thing.

I waited for a citizen's arrest as I lurched away with my soupy ice cream and M&Ms. I thought for sure the cops with plastic guns and rubber handcuffs would tackle me as I neared the exit. Taking their costumes way too seriously, they'd shout, "Stop thief! Unpant those pints!" But that didn't happen.

Darth Vader wheezed after me, "Hey, heeeekhoooo, you want your snacks? Heeeekhoooo."

I didn't answer him. On my way to The Beast I passed Lovechild still looking for Sadie. The cold night air accentuated his aura of steel, cigarettes, and gasoline. Smelled great. I don't question my taste.

"Sadie, git back here now. I've had it with your crap." His impatient, angry voice echoed across the parking lot and made me shiver. I found him sexy. Maybe I should question my taste.

When I got to the jeep I stuck my key in to unlock the door then noticed it was already unlocked. A minor oversight. I pulled the mangled swag from my jeans and climbed up in. The passenger seat was cluttered with candy wrappers, Burger King bags and empty 711 Slurpee cups, so I swiped everything off onto the burgeoning pile of garbage on the floor to make room for my new one.

I emptied both pints in record time and exactly one minute later my pulse thumped in my forehead. *Everything's going to be just fine. I'll get Adam back, I mean get back at Adam, get a job and a place to live, and my world will be right again.* Sugar was my heroin. Good shit.

When my head stopped vibrating enough to focus on tasks, I drove to Ninth and Ninth and parked across the street from Adam's. The Beast's idle was loose and loud so I turned it off. Didn't want to garner any unwanted attention.

The porch was dark like the rest of the house. The perfect family within had gone off to bed to dream. Something about the idea of that and the way the house sat on its foundation, steadfast and strong, pierced me with an unwavering sadness. Even through the sugar. It was like the old Victorian had puffed out its chest and proclaimed, "Too bad, bitch. You're never getting what's in here."

I grabbed a bag of M&Ms to salve my fresh wound, silly as it was to be affronted by a house. Stubborn things, those pound bags. Like trying to rip open a bag of skin. I tore at it with my teeth and nearly broke a few molars loose, but not the seal. So I squeezed it, trying to pop it like a balloon. Didn't work. My passion for an open bag escalated quickly and before long I was sitting on it, hoping my weight would outsmart the plastic, but the seat cushion was too soft and my ass just sank into the lumpiness. It was toying with me and after being insulted by a house I was having none of it.

"Come on you goddamn mother-fucking cock-sucking piece of shit piece of shit piece of shit!" I screeched, bouncing up and down.

The irony of the situation struck me later. I think the trick-or-treaters standing outside my jeep, gawking at me in their Spiderman tights and Wolverine claws were in shock. All red in the face, veins popping out in places, I looked constipated and pissed off about it. Also, I might have looked like I was trying to use my seat as a toilet because I was yelling at my shit.

Spidey whispered to Wolverine. They giggled and ran away. I pulled the warm bag out from under my ass and thrashed it on the console and the windows and anything else that might serve to break the miserable process of opening it. And break it did.

The bag popped on the steering wheel, exploding in an orange and black hailstorm. If I'd been sane I might have found humor in it, instead, I screamed and flogged the steering wheel with my forehead. I was a big, red, thrasher bobble-head doll.

I would have kept going with that but it hurt so I stopped. Pain was not on my menu any more that night. I was stuffed. An hour before, Adam had dished up a serving of his own zesty, "I'm really sorry, Katie, but Hannah and I are going to work things out," curry. Left me with merciless heartburn. Spicy foods didn't agree with me. They didn't agree with Adam's face either. That was the impression I got after I threw his plate of Chicken Korma at him.

It went like this:

Him: "I know this leaves you in a bad position financially speaking. Do you need some money?"

Me: "You're an asshole."

"What can I do to make this better?"

"Develop AIDS."

He smiled. I wasn't kidding.

"I'm glad you can still joke. Hannah's pretty serious most of the time, but you know, we're going to try and work on that."

Then the Korma happened. Adam. What a shit name.

I sat still, listening to my body thump, coming down from my M&M tantrum. Then I heard something from the back of The Beast. Crunching. Someone was in there with me.

My head still gyrated from the onslaught of sugar and I couldn't form one coherent thought. Not one. Maybe one. Bat.

I'd been on a co-ed softball team when I lived in Los Angeles, after Portland and Atlanta, and before Bangor. I hadn't played in years, but I kept my bat because it reminded me of a simpler time. A time I was good at something. Couldn't hit a ball if it was on a tee, but my bat handling skills were exemplary. So said the majority of my male teammates.

Whatever. Everybody has a thing.

The bat was on the floor under a pile of trash behind my seat. I twisted around and inched it out. The crunching from the back continued, but the wood felt solid in my hand so I was a little less frightened of what I'd find. A little.

I nudged my door open, slipped to the pavement, and crept around behind the jeep. The misty air cooled my hot, pulsating face. Crouching down beneath the window, I snuck my fingers up and grabbed the rusty back door handle. The street was silent; I'd frightened all the children away with my fit. It was just me, The Beast, and the demon inside. On the count of three I'd swing the door open and face it. My mother had always encouraged me to tackle my fears. At least I think she had.

I took a deep breath and exhaled. I took another for good measure. You can never have too much oxygen right before you die. I counted to three, raised the bat, and swung the door open.

Then my world got weird.

She sat scrunched up on the floor of The Beast munching an M&M and stared back at me with enormous green eyes. There wasn't an ounce of fear in her. I was stunned. It was like looking into a mirror as a child.

She glanced at the bat behind me, still raised and ready to swing. I brought it down and used it as a cane.

"I'm Sadie," she said, like she wasn't camped out in the back of a stranger's jeep. She had a teeny voice to match her teeny body.

"What are you doing?"

"Eating emems."

"Why are you in my jeep? Your dad's really worried about you, you know."

She searched the floor for more M&Ms, found an orange one and popped it in her mouth. I suppose I should have stopped her, the five-second rule no longer applied, but I wasn't in the mood to play mommy.

She peered into me like she was studying my soul, then asked in her vile little voice, "Why awe you sad?"

Was she going to ask why I masturbate and chase married men next? "Listen, little girl—"

"Sadie."

"Whatever. I'm taking you home now."

"My mommy eats chockyit when she's sad too. But she doesn't thwow it."

Right. I wasn't about to be psychoanalyzed by a two-year-old Tater Tot with a speech impediment. Her little pink lips curled up into a grin. She must have been older than two. More like twenty or thirty-two.

"All right, let's go." The bells on her jacket tie strings jingled when I lifted her out of the back and put her on the ground. Her mother probably sewed them on thinking they'd help her keep track of the future little Jackie Joyner, like the jingle bells people attach to miniature dogs so they won't squish them by accident. I got the impression her father would have preferred her to be bell-less.

"Sadie, where do you live?"

She stood in front of me, arching her head back to keep track of my eyes, and advertised a gaping hole on the left side of her mouth when she smiled. I didn't see the top of another tooth sprouting so it must have been a fresh loss. Before I said anything else she stepped forward and hugged me. *Why the hell would anyone do that?* I gave her a couple polite pats on the back then removed her from my legs.

She jingled around me to the passenger side, stood on the running board pipe, opened the door, and climbed up onto the seat as if to answer any question I had about how she got in earlier. She turned and took the seatbelt in her tiny paws and with a little effort coaxed it down across her body. The seat was her throne. She was so small only her feet dangled over the edge like a doll. A meddlesome little Raggedy Anne who was quickly becoming a liability.

"Sadie, are you going to answer me? Do you live near here? Up in the Aves?"

Since my arrival from California I'd been living in the Avenues, a nice area set up on a hill overlooking downtown Salt Lake where people actually mowed their lawns every once in a while. I was staying with Randy, one of Adam's friends, a sports photographer whose disregard for personal hygiene was matched only by his astounding lack of couth.

"So you're the one banging Adam, huh?" he'd asked, as I stood shivering on his porch the night I arrived.

"Yep, that's me. The banger." I tried to diffuse the insult with humor. That was when I was still capable of humor.

"That's cool. His wife's a twat." Dirty though he was, at least he was concise.

I'd been at Randy's for two excruciating weeks waiting for Adam to extract himself from his current situation. Unfortunately he'd extracted himself from me instead. I couldn't wait to go back and sleep on Randy's couch, what a comfortable situation that would be now.

Sadie sat still, staring at the crooked latch on the glove box. I watched her chest just to make sure she was breathing. She knew I was waiting for her to tell me where to go. I felt like she was testing the limits of my patience or my devotion to the idea of actually taking her home.

"Sadie, if you tell me where you live I'll let you have the rest of the M&Ms." I meant the ones on the floor. I think she knew that. "Come on. You need to tell me where you live. It's getting late and both of our families are going to be worried."

She looked at me and obviously saw through my bullshit. Weird.

"All right, I'm going to take you back to Smith's then. Maybe your dad's still looking for you there." I started The Beast and clunked it into gear. It sounded a little angry at me for that.

Didn't get up and go right away. "Come on..." I floored the pedal and the engine swore at me then jerked into motion. "Good Beast," I said, patting the dash. A broken jeep was the last thing I needed.

"What's your name?"

Okay. Maybe not the last thing. I didn't need this.

"Esmeralda Ruthaninny Poppycock."

"That's a silly name. Ninny Poppycock is silly."

My mother used to call me that when I was upset and it made me giggle too. The tickling also helped.

"Can I stay with you, Esmelda?"

Funny how a question can feel like a bomb. The only children I'd experienced in my twenty-eight years were my landlady's when I lived, ever so briefly, in Bangor, Maine. She had a pasty little boy named Waldo and a girl whose name I can't remember but whose crusty eyes and snotty nose I'll never forget. Those two were relentlessly ill with some disorder or disease that had them expelling viscous green phlegm out their heads on a daily basis. I had no intention of bringing that kind of mess into my life. It was messy enough.

"Some other time. Tonight I have to take you home. But I promise, you can come see me and we'll play soon." If you're starving you'll say anything to get some eats. "Besides, your dad's probably going nuts."

She whispered something I couldn't hear. I didn't ask her to repeat it.

"So tell me where to go and we'll get you home."

"How old are you?"

"A hundred. How old are you?"

"Five."

"You're pretty small for five."

"You're pretty big for a hundred."

Touché. Quick little strawberry.

I pulled into the Smith's parking lot, this time the proper way, and cruised through the lanes looking for Sadie's dad. There were only a half dozen cars there now and the fog had thinned so it would have been easy to spot him if he were there. A few un-costumed people wandered out through the sliding glass doors but there was no sign of Lovechild anywhere.

"Now can I stay with you?"

"No, Sadie. You can't stay with me. You don't even know me. What if I turned out to be—" I stopped because I'd have to ex-plain words like pedophile and pornography. "Hey, why aren't you wearing a costume? You're a kid. That's what kids do on Hal-loween." Seemed like a logical segue to me, but Sadie sat still, studying her lap. I'd asked the wrong question.

"Okay, well, I just need to know where you—"

"My mommy didn't come back and pick me up."

Crap. Now I'd have to engage in some form of Concerned Conversation with Little Red.

"Well, you're here with me now, so I'll take you. Just tell me where—"

"She made me pretty like Tinker bell with wings but she didn't come to school. She never came back for a long time."

"Well, maybe she's back now. Let's go check."

"I don't like Chris. He's not my daddy."

Oh dear. Here we go.

"He seemed nice enough." No he didn't.

"I need a map."

"Why do you need a map?"

"I want to, I want to go someplace."

"Well, I have a map, but it's at my house. If you let me take you home I'll bring it over tomorrow."

"Pwomise?"

"Pwom—promise." I'd always had an ear for accents and now I had one for impediments as well.

"You can meet Matewda." It was almost an order.

"Who's Matilda?"

"My special friend."

"Where is she?"

"In my woom."

I was struck by the idea of some imaginary person hiding out in Sadie's uterus.

"All right. Let's get you back to Matilda then. Where to, Captain?" Finally, we were on our way to Sadie's house. Soon I could get back to obsessing over Adam. I had to admit though; the time I'd spent with her was a nice distraction because I hadn't given him one thought. Not one. Maybe one.

I wasn't suspicious of the directions she gave me. Didn't think much when she told me to turn left on Park Street. And I didn't question the right at the second stop sign onto Eighth Ave. It was a strange coincidence, but I didn't fully realize where she was taking me until I pulled up outside Randy's house.

"Sadie."

How did she know where I was staying? I barely knew. Then I realized the only way she could know was if she lived somewhere close by. Which meant she'd seen me before and climbed into my jeep on purpose.

I killed the engine, marched around to her side, and opened the door. "All right, we're home."

She didn't move. I unfastened her seatbelt and helped her down to the ground. When I tried to let go of her hand, she held tight to me. I wondered what highly contagious diseases were being transferred from her hand to mine. Children are filthy, scheming beasts and she was a prime example. As a miniature person of my gender she was off to a spectacular start.

"Let's go for a walk," I said, hoping to trick her into revealing which house was hers. The fog had lifted and the cold really set in. Aside from a dog barking in the distance, the street was still, quiet. All the trick-or-treaters had gone home.

"We've got to get you back to Methuselah. And it's probably way past your bedtime."

Sadie stopped and looked at me.

"Matewda."

"Right."

The wind picked up and the clouds above us separated. The moon poked its full, round face out of the hazy curtains like a nervous stage director on opening night and made Sadie glow as she squealed. I wanted to squeal for other less innocent reasons.

"It's the mooner," she said, letting go of my hand. She laid herself down on the dirty sidewalk, and stared up at the moon.

"Sadie, what are you doing? It's cold." I wondered if I could leave her there and run away. Would that be bad?

"I want to see the kisses."

"You can see the kisses just as well standing as lying down, you know. Want to try?"

"Mommy says you have to be down to see the kisses."

I didn't want to lie down on the cold, wet concrete. I didn't want to see the kisses. I wanted to crawl into Randy's couch and accidentally stop breathing.

"Sadie, I won't be able to see the kisses either way."

And then Sadie stopped breathing. The night paused. Above us, the clouds halted and hung sturdy, like locked doors, on either side of the fat moon, leaving it naked and luminous.

There were no lights on in the houses that were filled with them a moment ago. Everything was dark, devoid of life. The lamps had fizzled out. The lonely dog barking one street over was mute. Even the air smelled different. It was sweet like fruit. Manufactured fruit.

I looked down at Sadie lying on the cold slab of concrete and it struck me that she might be dead. Lil' Strawberry Shortcake, lit by the brilliant bulb in the sky, had expired right there in front of me because I couldn't see the kisses on the mooner. Her eyes were wide and unblinking, just like Shortcake's. I knelt closer to her and the sweet scent of artificial strawberries grew stronger.

Odd.

"Sadie, this is all very nice, but we really do need to get you home. It's getting late and I have to go to bed. I have a job interview tomorrow." Not a complete lie. I planned to look for a job the minute I regained the desire to live again.

Strawberry gasped.

"What is it? Are you all ri—"

"They changed colors! Mommy said they would and they did."
Her face held so much joy it was as if she'd just seen Santa fly by
with his eight tiny reindeer against the backdrop of the moon.

"What changed colors, the kisses?"

"You have to be down to see them."

"I don't want to. It's cold."

"Not down here. It's cozy warm."

I knelt down beside her on the sidewalk. Maybe it was a degree or two warmer.

"If you come down I'll show you Matewda."

"Fine. I'll give you a minute."

Unbelievable. I was bargaining with a Tic-Tac.

I stretched out next to Sadie and looked skyward. My head
still swam in the sugary pool of Ben & Jerry's, which was odd and
out of place because everything else was different than it had
been moments before. Maybe that was the point. Everything was
different, but I was the same.

It *was* warmer down there. The sidewalk felt like it had been
baked by the summer sun and smelled distinctly like fresh cut
grass. I didn't question it. After all, the world had somehow
stopped for me, so who was I to be skeptical of a hot, fragrant
sidewalk?

At first I stared at the moon so Sadie would let me take her
home. But somewhere in there the kisses became a challenge.
They taunted me because I couldn't see anything but fuzzy gray
craters, so I decided to park it till I saw one.

"What do they look like, Sadie?"

"Like kisses from my mommy."

Oh, okay. That clears it right up then.

I gazed, I gaped, I gawked. I ogled that damn rock, but those kisses were elusive little bastards. They wouldn't reveal themselves to me no matter how long I stared.

"See. They're big, huh?"

I felt like I was nine again, sandwiched between my mother and sister in the Dali Museum in St. Petersburg, Florida, glaring a hole in *Slave Market with the Disappearing Bust of Voltaire.* Everyone else could see the philosopher's face but me.

"Come on, Katie. We've been standing here for like, ever. Look," my darling, sensitive sister said, pointing her witch thin finger to what she was describing, "his eyes. They're made from the two chick's heads, here. See? They're right here."

But I didn't see. Therein lay the problem. And I hated that she could because, though she was a full six years older, she was never the cleverer of my parent's offspring. So *this* disturbed me to a spectacular degree.

"Right there, Bits," my father chimed in from behind.

I groaned and pulled my sweater (a twelve pound tablecloth large enough to cover a riding lawn mower) out from my chest. He'd nicknamed me Bits right after I was born and it stuck like a tongue to a frozen pole. I had small hands, small feet and big ears. I was a month premature and that's why I'm at least twenty minutes late to everything to this day. I had to rebel somehow.

By then I'd grown from the teeny preemie into a reasonably sized nine-year-old and I was at that precarious age when girls began to notice their parts. What I and most of the boys in my class noticed was that I'd already developed a set of nuclear reactors by the middle of fifth grade. So all I heard when my father called me Bits was tits. *Come on down for dinner, Tits. Did you clean your room, Tits? Jo, I think we need to buy Tits a top that fits.*

I found out much later how jealous this made Chloe, since she turned out to be flatter than bubble wrap.

"His nose is built by their collars," my father said, ever the architect. "See? His chin, look, his chin is held in the forearm of the lady pulling away from the beggar. She's holding her sister's hand."

He pointed to the painting too, showing the growing crowd around us how his daft, frumpy daughter couldn't see that damn face. I looked at my father and sister and wished they were just paintings too. Not long after that trip I learned to be careful what I wished for. They would eventually become as distant and frustrating as Voltaire's Bust had been for me that day. A broken puzzle I could never put back together.

"Do you see it?" my mother asked, resting her warm hand on my back. There was no impatience in her voice or her touch, nothing indicating she might want to move along and see the rest of the museum before our spring break was over. Nothing indicating she might *need* to move on because soon enough she wouldn't be able to see anything at all.

Lying on the sidewalk with Sadie I opened my eyes, but couldn't process what I saw. "What the..." I squinted. Maybe that would help make sense of it.

"Do you see them now? They're pretty, huh?"

I didn't see the kisses. "What color is the moon, Sadie?"

"It's pretty!"

"Yes, but what color is it?"

"The kisses are blue now."

A blue moon.

"Sadie, what're you doing down there? Hey, what in heck are you doing to her?" The tense tone of Lovechild's voice sent a jolt through my body like I'd touched a frayed wire. "Who are you?" he asked, staring down at me as he had at the grocery store. This time there was more anger less stunned curiosity happening. "Answer me. What're you doing to the girl?"

Trying like hell to get rid of her.

"I'm...we're...uh..." What could I say? There was no explanation here, at least not a good one, especially for a missing child whom I was sure he thought I'd taken on purpose.

"We saw the kisses on the mooner," Sadie said as he pulled her up into his thin arms.

Speak for yourself.

The way his L.L. Bean jacket hung on him I could tell he hadn't been to the gym in years. But he seemed to be the kind of man with a reserve of strength. He lifted her like he would a loaf of bread.

I stood and noticed how everything was back to normal now. The lights were lit, the dog barked, the clouds flitted past the moon, landing us in alternating darkness and soft cool light. Cool white light.

"Please, I'm so sorry. Let me explain."

"Let me explain," Sadie repeated.

"You hush."

I didn't appreciate how he talked to her.

"Did you take the girl?"

I didn't appreciate how he talked to me.

"No! God no!" I must have hurt Sadie's feelings because her head slumped down to her chest. "No, I—she—when she ran away from you in the store she hid in my jeep." I smiled, hoping to provide facial evidence of how much I wasn't a child molester. "She was probably just, you know, playing hide-and-seek or sardines or whatever games kids play."

"We got to go." His eyes were not kind, neither was his breath, it reeked of dead flesh and stale coffee. Apparently his level of concern for Sadie's welfare didn't preclude him from eating a solid meal.

Sadie was apoplectic as he strode away with her. She beat her tiny fists into his back trying to convince him to let her go, but he was unmoving. "Esmelda. I want Esmelda Poppycock!"

"It's all right, Sadie," I said to her disappearing silhouette. "I'll come play with you and Matilda soon." I would have said anything to stop that howling. She was like a baby wolf mourning her dead mother.

I'd wanted to be rid of her, but now I suddenly felt like I was sending little Strawberry Shortcake off to the stocks. That was disturbing.

TWO

When I opened Randy's front door I could still hear Sadie crying two houses down as Chris took her inside. It was eleven o'clock and Randy hadn't come back from his Halloween party yet, so the house was empty. I sat on the yellow Rent-A-Center couch in the dark and listened to my stomach grind away at the ice cream. *Why couldn't I see the kisses? What the hell* are *the kisses? Why do I care?*

I wandered into the kitchen, doing exceptionally well to stub my toe only twice. I didn't need to turn the light on to find what I was looking for. In fact I preferred darkness. It was familiar.

The weight of the frosted bottle was a relief in my hand. I let the freezer door close on its own and picked my way back into the living room, happy about one thing in my life. At least Randy had good taste in vodka. I'd figure out how to repay him for it later.

I took a few extended swigs of the Grey Goose, sauntered out to The Beast and headed back to Adam's after a 711 detour. A few hours later, I sat in the driver's seat and finished off the last gulp of vodka. I couldn't even taste the Suzy Q's or Oreos, but I shoved them down my throat anyway.

I'd parked around the corner from Adam's house this time. That would stop me from doing something unwise. A few hundred feet of lawn and a curb were my defense against all idiocy.

But Adam was a vortex sucking me in. He was a chronic insomniac. I'd just go take a peek around, see if he was still up. I wanted one more look at him. Just one look and I'd be on my way.

With a wavering hand I lit a cigarette and took a long drag. The smoke slunk down my throat, soothing and warm, like my mother's hand on my back saying everything was going to be all right. Except nicotine isn't my mother's hand.

I crammed the cigarettes in my sweatshirt pocket with the matches and wobbled across the lawn, doing my best to wind up at Adam's back door. Almost there, I caught myself on a tree to avoid falling headfirst into the manicured hedges in their backyard.

"Bitchery Hammah-rama cut these. They're juss perfec." I moved closer to the shrub, closer to the house. "Perfec hair, perfec teeths, perfec shr—ohhhhh. Look at that. She missed spot. Big fat stick sticking out. Bad Hammah-rama."

Hannah was Adam's wife and a lovely person, or maybe not, but either way, there was no reason for me to ridicule her pruning. Especially considering how I'd been an integral part of a plan to dismantle her life. Or so I'd thought. Funny how things work out in the end.

My brain sloshed around willy-nilly in my head, so I found a soft stretch of grass under one of the small trees by Adam's back porch and lay down hoping to soothe my vertigo.

The clouds danced and spun over the moon, parting to let it peek down at me through the skeletal branches of the tree. Most of the leaves had drifted away already but a few still clung to it hoping to be spared the Great Fall. There was a time I would have been able to identify all the trees in Adam's backyard. If they flowered I'd be able to describe what the blossoms looked like and how long they'd be around. But that was in another life. I worked hard to erase everything I'd known about trees long ago because then I wouldn't be reminded of what I'd lost every time I saw one my mother had taught me about.

Joanna Denai was an arborist masquerading as an adjunct English professor at the University of Washington. She began my green education the summer before I turned five. We planted her favorite tree, a Crepe Myrtle, on the south side of our house in Seattle. She explained that these particular trees didn't flourish in the Pacific Northwest because of the amount of moisture in the air and ground. They were susceptible to powdery mildew. I didn't know what mildew was then, but I knew powder. She'd pat it on her belly and around her neck with a furry puff pad and when she'd pick me up the soft floral scent would engulf me like a thousand velvety rose petals. Anything powdery was all right by me.

She said the Myrtles grew and bloomed the best in the southern states like Florida, where she'd grown up, but she was determined to make it blossom. It had been her favorite tree from childhood and she wanted her daughters to experience its powers. It was special, she said. Magical.

"Does it do twicks?" I asked, scooping the last bit of dirt out of the hole that would house the seed. I wanted to see a rabbit come out the trunk someday.

"Sort of. But not in the way you might think." She placed the seed into the earth with such care it seemed fragile, like a baby bird. "It rains," she whispered in my ear, our secret.

I didn't understand. Rain wasn't magical. Wasn't even special, particularly in Seattle. Who was she trying to fool?

"I don't like wain, Mommy." I stood up, dirty arms akimbo, waiting for her to stop messing around and get to the good stuff about how the tree would spit bunnies from its bark.

"Well, maybe someday you will, Bits."

A light came on in Adam's kitchen. There he was, loafing around in his robe. It was scraggly and blue and riddled with holes. I'd offered to get him a new one when he visited me in Big Bear the last time, but he explained about the robe. How it was good luck; how he'd opened more accounts and sold more snowboards on the days after he wore it. Bunch of hooey, superstitious crap. I didn't believe in luck. I hadn't seen any evidence of it in my own life, so why would I?

He even had a name for it. Lucky. The man had the imagination of a stick. It was difficult to remember what I saw in him. I never did like his legs. Too skinny. Like a Whippet's, you could almost see through them if he was backlit. The way they fell out of the bottom of his robe made them look like they'd been stuck on his body as an afterthought. And his forehead. The thing was nearly spherical. He must have just taken a shower because his hair was wet and it lay up there like a rattail. A rattail on a round rat ass. He carried a cup to the sink and looked out the window at his neighbor's house.

I sat up to get a better view. When I pulled my soggy sweatshirt from my back the motion sensor light on the porch clicked on. Uh oh. I scrambled on my hands and knees under the porch just as Adam and his legs stepped out. He scurried across from one rail to the other, shuffling his slippers over the uneven wood. The sound grated on me like his snoring used to. When he came over to my side I looked through the slats and saw straight up to his barely dangling junk. With his helmet snuggled up in his pubic hair he was, what is commonly referred to in locker rooms across the globe, a "grower."

"You bastards better not be trying to filch my boards again."

As assertive as a sock. Still, the shock of his voice rattled me. It splintered the silence. All thoughts of his stuff dissipated as I watched his feet scuffle to the steps.

Here we go. He's coming for me. He's going to press charges and I'm going to spend the rest of my life in some new-agey correctional facility for brutally depressed women trying to find the Meaning in life after being dumped-yet-again. We'll all stand around in our Birks and our tie-dyes holding hands, chanting ma-lee-ma-lee-uma-ma, or whatever it is they do to regain some kind of Clarity in their lives.

He tore out into the yard heading straight for the garage. The belt from his robe came undone and the sides fell open as he strode nearer to the door. He didn't notice or didn't care because he left it alone, inspecting around the perimeter and through the windows for intruders.

"Yeah, you better run, you little pricks."

I struggled to hold my tongue. Was he that much of a tool? Clearly there was no one out there. He made his way back to the porch, with his parts now in full view, and something unexpected surfaced in me. He was exposed and vulnerable and suddenly I didn't want to lash out at him anymore. I wanted to escape from under the porch meet him on the steps and stop him with my embrace. I wanted to feel his skin against mine again, breathe in his scent. He always smelled like cocoa butter and that was just fine with me.

I knew none of that would ever happen when, as if sensing my eyes absorbing him, he gathered the robe around his waist and skittered back up onto the porch and inside.

I'd had my look (frankly, more than I'd bargained for) so now I could go. Except, I couldn't. That's the tricky stuff of being human. The capricious nature of emotions.

The moment Adam closed his robe my heart sealed itself again. Something in the motion of it set me off. The way he jerked the tatty fabric around his middle like a two year old throwing a fit. *You can't have this anymore. Nanny nanny boo boo.*

I could have been reading a little too much into it, but that's how it felt and I used it to fuel my reinvigorated rage. And my new plan. It's not enough to suddenly be clear about why you're better off without the moron who just annihilated you; you have to get back at him somehow. Because no matter how much you don't like his blue-white pin-thin legs, or his unruly forehead, you still fell in love with him and he needs to feel some little bit of the pain he inflicted upon you.

I slithered my way out from under the porch on my stomach, dirt filling all my crevices. With the help of the railing I hauled myself up and began the formidable trip across the lawn again. Just when I thought I was making good time, my unsteady foot caught the top of the tree root next to Hannah's shrubs and I careened headfirst into them.

A clear-cut case of karmic retribution. The part Hannah missed didn't miss me. I rolled onto the protruding stick, tough little bastard, and it pierced my jeans. Impaled them, actually. It went straight through at the seam of my right leg near my knee.

In my state of drunky drunk I thought falling into her shrub was the funniest thing this side of Adam's package, until the kitchen light flicked back on. I'd been furtive enough in my lawn crossing not to engage the porch light again, but if Adam stepped out, the entire back yard would be illuminated. *Ah, there's Kate, skewered to my wife's bush and oddly happy about it.*

I couldn't let him see me like that. I still had a scrap of dignity left. But I couldn't yank the stick out of my jeans either, so I tore into my zipper, spun myself on my head and wriggled out of them. Sometimes, desperate circumstances require relinquishing the ego. Or at least setting it aside to be retrieved later.

Free and half naked, I scrambled upright and scurried off behind the garage. Fleeing through the shadows, I watched for any movement inside, but no one came. Part of me felt like one of those demented stalker-slash-streaker-crazy-jilted-ex-girlfriend types who...

Oh.

I made it to the garage, panting and spinning, and threw myself up against the side to rest. The peeling paint on the old wood was hostile to my unprotected ass, but I stayed. I'd decided revenge was the path I was going to take and the idea of backing out now was absurd. Even if it meant I could be caught and thrown in jail for any number of transgressions. I wasn't afraid of jail. Well, maybe a little. But I was more concerned with Adam getting away without a scratch, unaltered.

If only I could remember where he kept the key. The garage door was locked as were the windows because inside was his precious vintage snowboard collection. He'd spent years amassing these boards, but the unique thing about most of them was they'd never been used. This made them tremendously rare and valuable. They were pristine, brand shiny new, waiting to be defiled and disfigured by yours truly just as soon as I could find my way in.

I peeked around the corner of the garage. The house was dark again. Everything was. Somewhere in the middle of my adventure the moon had disappeared behind a thick shroud of clouds. Sorry, Sadie. Can't see the kisses. Not that I could when it was big and full and staring me in the face.

I tried to get her out of my head. She wouldn't have approved of what I was about to do. How would I know that? Why the hell did I care? Focus. If I were a key where would Stickly hide me?

My fingers groped around the top of both window frames on the outside of the garage and came up dirty and empty. There was a collection of old glass milk jugs sitting next to the wood pile. I chose the cleanest and tipped it over. Nothing but a drizzle of muddy water.

Undaunted, I went to the woodpile and wrestled with the tarp, trying to free it from under the logs without tipping over. Finally, I pulled it off and grabbled underneath the bottom row of wood for a key box or secret holder. A splinter pierced my left palm. I yanked my hand away and shoved it in my mouth to stop the bleeding and the screaming. Something about the metallic taste of blood sparked a memory. Magnets and metal.

I lurched around to the front of the garage. The grill of Adam's Toyota 4Runner stared me down like a bull ready to charge as I approached. It sat in the driveway and I got the feeling from its scowl it was pissed because *it* should have been in there instead of all the pretty, perfect snowboards.

I swayed over and squatted down next to the driver's side door. Holding on to the frame for support I fingered around up underneath. I should have remembered this was where Adam had stowed the key because this was the only place he would. Hannah never drove the 4Runner, she had the Subaru wagon to haul the kids in, which meant no one could get into the garage unless Adam was home. This was not a mistake. He was a control freak, especially when it came to his boards.

My fingers found the little magnetic box and plucked it from the undercarriage of the truck. When I opened it and saw the key snuggled inside, relief swept over me. I tipped it into my hand and ran my thumb over the jagged edges of the teeth. I had no idea that innocuous strip of steel would open the door to a whole new world for me.

With great effort I slogged back to the garage, wading through a pool of sludge. The lock gave me trouble. Like trying to fit a flounder into a buttonhole. After a few misguided and slippery attempts, I prevailed. The click of the deadbolt was a shot of adrenaline. I jumped into mission mode.

I'd never been in Adam's snowboard shrine; it was overwhelming. The entire space was covered with every brand of board imaginable. Burton, Winterstick, Sims, Salomon, Ride, Morrow, Gnu, K2. I was standing in the middle of a fourteen-year-old's wet dream.

Hell, I was standing in the middle of my own. I loved snowboarding, had ever since I'd strapped in two years before. I considered taking a couple to start my own collection, but first things first. I pulled the cigarettes out of my pocket, blew the dirt out of the pack, lit one and went to work.

The Burton Performer was poised on the back wall, wooden, regal. A vintage swallowtail, it was shaped like a fish. That whole wall was reserved for the spotless boards that had never been used. The boards he'd paid through his bony nose for. It was obvious by the position and placement of The Performer that it was Adam's prize possession. The way he displayed it, far above the rest out of anyone's reach with padded supports, this was his Hope Diamond.

I didn't know how I was going to get it down because there was no stepladder or chair to stand on, and the room swirled like an eddy every time I looked up, making things a bit more challenging.

I worked with my handicap. Cigarette still in hand, I staggered to the corner and threw up on the stack of boards waiting to be mounted.

Fate pulled me over there because when I finished I noticed a hockey stick hiding behind the boards and yanked it out. Now it was just a matter of finagling the Performer off the supports without it crashing down and splitting my skull open. I'd be lying if I said it was easy going. I swear there was a force field around the bastard. He must have paid extra for that.

After much irrational wrangling, I won out over the board and got a solid hold on the tail end with the curve of the stick. I gave it a flick and jumped back out of the way. Good thing too. It caught the tail of the next board down, a spotless Burton Backhill, and created a domino effect. All ten boards came hurtling down to the concrete floor. It was more than I'd hoped for. Not only did they scratch each other up in the tussle on the way down, the floor gouged a few edges as well as they bounced off it. I was worried the noise would wake someone in the house so I checked the door again. All was quiet and clear for dirty deeds.

I put my cigarette out on the face of The Performer; nice and slow just to make sure it was fully extinguished. Smoking was such a nasty habit, all the tar and chemicals, the ugly scars they could leave. I lit another cigarette and went to the workbench to find the perfect tool for scraping and found it under one of Adam's old t-shirts. After closer inspection I realized it wasn't an old shirt at all, though it was ripped and torn and smelled like cleaning fluid. It was the one I'd given him the last time he visited me at Abbey Rose, the snowboard shop I'd worked at in Big Bear. An old goat with a long white beard rode a snowboard on the front and on the back it said, "Still just a kid at heart." Corny? Absolutely. Absolutely Adam. He said he loved it. He said he loved a lot of things.

Adam. Such a shit name.

I grabbed the screwdriver from under the shirt and, with renewed disgust, disfigured his babies. I can't imagine what I looked like from any normal person's perspective. Half naked, hunched over a pile of snowboards with a cigarette dangling between my lips, slashing and slicing away like I was trying to rescue someone entangled in a web of wires or her own labyrinth of crazy. I was coiled up so tight, lashed by my anger, I couldn't see how it was destroying me with every breath. Sure felt good at the time though.

Until my chest started smoking.

The air turned acrid. In my vengeful frenzy I didn't notice that my cigarette had tumbled down inside my sweatshirt. When I saw the smoke rising from below, my fingers instinctively flew to my mouth, groping for the cigarette. I didn't believe it could be where I knew it was, stuck between my boobs.

I hopped up and did my best to peel off the sweatshirt, but I ran into trouble pulling it over my head. Hoodies can be tough to navigate over a wobbly, drunk noggin, or even a sober one. They're just tricky in general.

My nose wrestled that hooded monster and I felt the cigarette dump some ashes deeper into my cleavage. My bra started smoking and my arms were caught, flailing up in the sleeves behind my head. Then the opening got stuck over my forehead, yanking my head back. I was almost doing a back bend.

I leaned forward, thinking I might have better luck in this direction with leverage or balance or maybe I'd just seen my sister Chloe do this when I was younger. Hooded sweatshirts should be banned. They're health hazards. I hauled on it one last time. Felt like it might take my ears off just for spite, but it finally acquiesced and my head was free. I flung it onto the workbench and searched my bra for the cigarette, brushing the powdery ashes off my skin, but it wasn't there. I scanned the floor; it wasn't there either.

The sweatshirt landed on top of the shirt I'd given Adam. The shirt that was on the corner of the bed when he'd asked me to move to Salt Lake City with him two months before. The shirt that had just erupted into a fireball on the workbench. That shirt.

Shit. Shit. Shit.

Before I could think about tending to the burgeoning fire I saw a light flick on in the house. Then another. Quadruple shit. A figure strode through the kitchen and I knew he was coming for me. Then someone else showed up. Hannah. Even from a distance and through my fuzz I could see her hair was perfect. Every one in place. She was the Barbie to his Ken. On paper anyway. I don't think Barbie screams or throws fits and ceramic bowls.

I used their argument to my advantage, but before I escaped I tried to do the right thing. It wasn't my intention to burn the garage down, I just wanted to desecrate some of its goodies. So I took the jug of water sitting on the floor next to the workbench and doused the fire with it.

It wasn't water.

I got a little preview of Hell and I'm here to say: Be Good. I was sure my eyebrows, all of my hair, had been incinerated, but I was too busy peeling myself off the floor to take inventory. My bra smoldered so I patted it to make sure it didn't spontaneously erupt.

I stood and saw Adam stumble down the porch steps coming straight for me. Instinct took over and I flew with otherworldly, or what some might call average, dexterity behind a surfboard in the corner next to the door. When it flew open three seconds later I was protected behind both. I still stopped breathing just in case he could hear me through the rush of flames engulfing part of his reason for life.

"Fuuuuuck!"

I'd like to say I didn't enjoy that. I'd like to. I really would.

He didn't try to douse the flames with anything mostly because there was nothing to douse them with. I handily discovered that. Instead, in a fit of childish optimism, or selfish prickism, he dashed to the pile of boards in the back and retrieved as many as he could. I noticed he went for his Burton Performer first. Arms overloaded with scorching boards, he about-faced and sprinted out the door.

"Hannah! Hannah, help me!" He plunged back into the garage to save more of his boards. It was getting too hot; he burned himself when he picked the first one up by its edge, so he had to leave them.

Sweat poured from my body as I watched him dart out again. Felt like I might be melting. Like I was experiencing the physical manifestation of my complete mental meltdown that night. Or maybe I was just standing way too close to a fire.

When Adam didn't return I figured he was on his way to retrieve the hose from under the porch. I'd been squatting on part of it during our previous close encounter. I used this opportunity to slink out, but there wasn't enough time to bolt across the lawn without being caught, so I scampered to the side of the garage near the woodpile away from the house. It was dark there and he was too preoccupied to go hunting for the perpetrator. I peeked around the corner and watched him unravel.

"Hannah! Goddammit, call 911!" He crouched near the porch, seething as he tried to disentangle the hose from itself. The more frustrated and frenetic his movements, the more jumbled it became.

I could relate. This night was one gigantic snarl of bad intentions I'd be years untangling. I almost felt remorseful about the whole thing.

"How many times do I have to tell Carson not to knot the goddamn hose?" he said. Carson was Adam's son. I'd never met him and I was pretty sure I never would.

"What the...what is that?" He'd spotted the jeans on the hedge and stomped toward the bush yanking the hose over with him. It wouldn't quite reach that far so it wouldn't reach the garage yet either, but he got close enough to see what he needed to.

Those jeans were special and ever so incriminating because they were his. His favorite pair. I'd taken them from him on his last trip to Big Bear with the intention of giving them back when we moved in together. My premature return had just given us both away. He'd have to figure out a handy story for Hannah about why his special jeans were run through on her hedge.

"No way. You...Oh, you...bitch."

Remorse gone.

He dropped the hose and marched over toward the garage, straight in my direction. I leapt under the tarp, squatted down, and nestled up next to the firewood on the frigid dirt. It was musty and smelled like animal droppings. Probably mice. In which case, on top of everything else—jail or the women's correctional facility where I'd be coerced into Birkenstocks and talking about my feelings—I was in for a healthy battle with the Hanta virus.

I held the tarp and my breath as Adam rounded the corner of the garage.

"Kate? Are you here?" His whisper was the hiss of a snake. I'm not a fan of snakes. He searched around, breathing right over me as he checked both sides around the woodpile. "I can't believe you did this. I knew you were crazy. I didn't think you were this fucking crazy."

Excuse me? I felt like he'd just punched me in the gut with a ten-pound weight. Crazy? Me? I wanted to lash out. I wanted to leap up with a slivery log and scrape it down his bare chest. Hell, why stop at the chest? But I didn't do anything. Just crouched there holding my breath and the broken pieces of my ego, waiting for him to find something else to do.

"Fuck, Kate! Fuck!"

When he finished throwing his good-Mormon-boy tantrum, he went back to the hose. I heard the approaching whine of sirens and Hannah's voice and knew it was time to go. I'd used the vast stretch of lawn as an excuse not to leave but, really, I just needed to be near Adam one last time.

When I stood up from under the tarp my left bra strap, already weakened by months of continuous wear, got caught on a piece of wood and snapped in two letting loose a mountain of breast. What next? Would a pack of wolves attack and devour my underwear? Was I destined to get naked in Adam's backyard?

This whole night had seemed like a bastardized cleansing ritual with the fire and the naked and the proclamations of crazy.

I went with it. Since my bra was now offering more pain than support I took it off and stowed it behind the woodpile. Hopefully someday soon, Hannah would find it and have a few more questions for the man of the house. I gathered the tarp around me, checked to make sure the coast was clear and took off at full sprint, crinkling in the opposite direction of Adam and the life I was hoping to have with him.

The next day I woke to the pop of Randy's flash in my face and a vicious little man chiseling inside my skull.

"What are you...?" I couldn't finish my question. "Oh God." Bad things were happening inside me. It felt like somebody had hammered my head on a granite table then wrapped me in a lead blanket. I didn't know who would do such a thing, or why, but I'd set to the task of finding them as soon as I could properly identify my own nose.

I was sprawled on Randy's couch, still naked, tangled in the blue tarp with a rubber chicken between my legs.

What the ever-loving hell?

That excellent question prompted me to scramble into a more realized state of consciousness and untangle my limbs from the tarp. No easy thing, that. I was so entangled at one frightening moment I thought it had somehow fused to my skin. The more I moved the more it crumpled and crunched its way around me like a living thing. A python sliding in for the big squeeze.

Glancing south to get a better overall view of my situation I was pleased to find I'd at least kept my underwear on. Small mercies. Writhing and wriggling around on the couch, I looked like I was trying to make love to the tarp with all my parts to view. And all to the amusement of Randy, the swine, who'd put the rubber chicken on my crotch for the pictures.

"Holy God!" I stopped as a stabbing pain shot through my butt. A splinter the size of a Sharpie had lodged itself in my left cheek. Randy was delighted by this new development and click, click, clicked away.

"Stop taking my fucking picture, you moron."

He tittered like a teenage girl till his digital card ran out of memory. "Damn," he said. Then snickered again as he sat checking his brilliant work.

"I'm delighted you find this funny," I said.

"Dude, lighten up. This is good shit."

"No really. I'm happy you're getting pleasure from my pain, because I'm going to return the favor and beat you senseless in a minute."

Meaningless waffle? Sure. But it sounded good.

After careful extraction of the woodchip I reengaged in my tarp battle with great zeal. I'd been humiliated beyond retrieval of grace by that point, so I lost it all. Looked like I was having a seizure. Or being exorcised. I wished for an exorcism. Or a 9mm. Shoot that blue devil dead. Or me.

Ah, freedom!

In a flash of divine energy I was finally free of the malignancy. I wanted to stand, pound at my chest and shout, "Hah. I am

Kathryn Olivia Denai and I am smarter and more cunning than a square of plastic." But in the pit of my exposed, white belly I couldn't help feeling that statement lacked a bit of truth.

Besides, I had business to tend to. Before Randy had time to react, I grabbed the rubber chicken from between my legs and flogged him with it. He did his best to fend me off, but hell hath no fury like the wrath of a woman wielding rubber poultry.

"What (thwack!) the (thwack!) hell (thwack!) is (thwack!) wrong (thwack!) with (thwack!) you?"

"Wait, it was—ow. It's a jo—shit that thing—ouch. Dude, ease—"

Thwack! Thwack! Thwack!

"Ow. Ow. OW! Hey, watch the hair." Randy dropped his camera on the couch and stumbled to the mirror to fix his coif. For a man who so obviously disregarded standard hygiene—the only time I saw him use his toothbrush was the night he had a date with Adam's babysitter—he showed remarkable concern for his hair. The dichotomy of Randy. I suppose he was no different than every other person on this planet. We all have two sides (some of us many many more). I was about to see his scary one. And mine.

"You need to learn there are boundaries you don't cross, you do not cross, with people. Especially other people's people," I said, throwing that last part in for myself rather than as any kind of threat. I knew I was no longer anyone else's person; I just needed to feel a little armor over my nakedness.

Every word I spoke was punctuated inside my brain by that wee loathsome chap. He'd now upgraded from his chisel to a sledgehammer. Tore my head apart, but I soldiered on.

Randy spun around when he heard the camera latch open.

"No! That's irreplace—"

"Ooops," I said, biting his memory card in two.

He lunged at me, wheezing like an asthmatic, trying to rip the card out of my mouth.

"Crotch!"

I became acutely aware of my own business then, but instead of being self-conscious, I steeled myself to his challenge. I dodged him, spit the pieces out on the floor, then held tight to the camera as he grabbed for it. There I was, still drunk, wrestling dirty Randy, with all my naked bits a'bouncin'.

I didn't have to of course. I'd destroyed the pictures. I could have let it go and scurried off to the bathroom to become decent, but something in me wanted to, needed to, fight back.

Why was he so distraught over a silly memory card?

"You owe me a grand, bitch."

Boy, prices sure have risen. He tightened his grip.

"You going to tell those Burton dicks you jacked their shots?"

Was that a rhetorical question? Would they mind if I was nude?

"I can't re-shoot what I had, you cun—mother fu—"

I'd had enough of the two-step so I put my unshaved knee in his crotch. He crumpled to the floor screeching like a rat. If I'd been feeling generous I probably would have left him there and gone to get dressed.

But he had violated me.

So I took the chicken to him.

"I'm sure you couldn't give a shit, you misogynistic mongrel," thwack, thwack, "but just in case you were curious," thwack, "in some circles it's not considered acceptable behavior" thwack, "to take unsolicited photos of a naked woman with a rubber chicken in her crotch."

Thwack, thwack, thwack. My insides started groaning and creaking like they wanted to be outside. I stopped. But the room didn't. It swirled around me like one of those hideous round-and-round-till-you-lose-your-eight-dollar-hotdog-on-the-person-in-front-of-you rides at amusement parks.

"Oh my God." I dropped the decimated chicken on Randy's head and shot straight for the bathroom. I didn't think I'd make it in time. A self-fulfilling prophecy.

The chocolate-vodka tsunami rushed my throat, burning it. It was so forceful I didn't have time to open my mouth before the wave escaped anywhere it could. Mostly out my nose onto the filthy bathroom floor. It was slick linoleum made slicker by the contents of my stomach and just before my face made contact with it I had a vision of Sadie. She was sitting on the toilet with her hair pulled up in lopsided pigtails like she'd put it up herself. Her hand reached through me as I fell.

Also, she had wings.

I decided to blame the wings, hell, the whole damn thing, on my current state of health and disregarded it altogether. I was good at ignoring things I didn't understand, especially when they pertained to me.

Sadie disappeared when I lifted the seat, just in time to eject more. I was covered in my own filth from the slip-n-slide on the floor. The smell wasn't nauseating. It had surpassed that and went right into a distinct level of vile I have never smelled the equal to since. A mixture of bile, road kill and a hint of Roquefort cheese.

Randy's cell phone rang in muted tones in his pocket. I couldn't see him from where I hung on the toilet, so I didn't know if he'd moved off the living room floor or not, but I could hear him like he was next to me. His voice sounded maybe half a note higher than it had before I wrecked him. That was nice.

"Hey dude, I'm busy. I got—right now?" Then silence.

I held back my dire urge to purge so I could listen to what he said. I thought it might have been Adam calling to tell him what I'd done.

"Really? How many you got? No shit. Seriously? Fuck yeah, dude. I'm there." The house shook a little with each step Randy took toward me. Slow, heavy footfalls down the hall.

In a move that was part fight, part flight, I wiped my mouth, sprung to the door and slammed it shut. My slimy fingers fumbled with the lock after it closed. The handle jiggled. Then nothing. Then three thick thumps. "You and your shit better be out of my house by the time I get back."

I'd held out as long as I could. In between retching I heard him mutter, "...sick, man, God...the last time I'm letting Adam's chicks stay here," as he lumbered back down the hall.

The implications of that statement took about three seconds to sink in which, considering my state at that moment, was decent. I wasn't as dull as I felt after all. Then, something weird happened. I laughed. Not a dainty little chuckle, but a full-blown floor-pounding tear-inducing session of guffaw. At one point I was sure I'd lost my mind. *Well, Kate, you've finally crossed the line. The weather's nice here in Loonyville. I wonder if they have donuts.*

But after the laughter came the inevitable silence. I propped myself up on one knee, hunched over the toilet. A thin trickle of water tinkled inside its belly. It was barely loud enough to exist. I felt a strange kinship with that tiny waterfall. Some might find emotionally connecting with a toilet odd. I was just happy to feel anything at all.

I scraped myself off Randy's ruined floor and staggered to the mirror. It wasn't as bad as I thought it would be. My face was a battle zone, dirty and scratched, but I was happy to see I still had my hair and both eyebrows.

I'd broken the habit of seeking myself in mirrors years ago. Couldn't stand witnessing how everything faded. My eyes used to be bright emerald, like my mother's, but they'd dulled to a lazy hazel and my hair was no longer a vibrant sunset like it was before my tenth birthday. Life had leeched the color from me.

People talk about hitting rock bottom and then bouncing back. I stared at the mess in the mirror and wondered if my bottom was made of anything hard enough to bounce back from. Seemed like mine was quicksand and I kept twisting and winding my way into its murky depths.

Thing about quicksand is: you'll float. You just have to stop flailing around and get still. Thing about me is: I don't know how to do that.

THREE

After a quick shower I went to the living room and discovered most of my clothes had been peed on. Like an angry cat, Randy had defiled my pile of shirts and jeans. As an added bonus, he'd eaten asparagus. Everything reeked like paper mill sludge.

I gathered the pissy clothes, almost everything I had, and spread them out on his bed under the fitted sheet. I hoped he wouldn't notice till right before bed. Give the odor time to really permeate the mattress.

After a furious bout of hand washing I threw on a pair of his jeans and a sweater and took an extra outfit for later. I wasn't sure what I was going to do but I knew I'd never go back there. Never. Funny word. Holds tremendous potential to make a liar out of you.

I packed the rest of my clothes that had been spared the spray—a pair of underwear, a top, and a few socks—and grabbed some cheese sticks and chocolate pudding from the fridge. I was starving and they were the only appetizing things he had. I considered eating the rest of his asparagus and doing damage to his couch, but I just couldn't bring myself to it.

Not wanting to stay any longer than I had to, I made a cursory check of the house to make sure I hadn't forgotten anything. The rubber chicken tripped me on my way to the door. I bent down and squeezed his scrawny little neck. Devious thoughts of chucking him in the microwave swam in my aching head. I threw him in my bag instead. He would serve as a memento of my life in Salt Lake City.

The Beast was parked diagonally across Randy's lawn almost touching the bottom step of the porch. I put my things in the back and pulled myself up into the captain's chair. The clunk of the door closing was a gong in my head.

I glanced at Sadie's yard two houses down. It showed no signs of a five-year-old living there. No toys, no bike with training wheels, no dolls forgotten from the day before. Just a neglected patch of grass, similar in shape to our old lawn at 519 Willow Way in Seattle. I knew every inch of that lawn because I was the only one who ever took care of it. It was el shaped like a hockey stick with the largest part—

"Hockey stick. Shit."

I was sure I was a wanted woman.

It's not an easy thing to be inconspicuous in a mammoth green 1978 Jeep Cherokee so I knew I'd have to slip out of town pronto. It was pathetic and needy but I wanted to see Adam again, just once more. I even considered leaving a note before I left, apologizing for what had happened:

Dear Adam,

Sorry I toasted your garage. I only meant to wreck your boards.

Bygones, eh?

Be well,

Kate

P.S. You're still a mighty prick.

But something stopped me. Plain old common sense, maybe? Not the best idea to return to the scene of a crime you've just committed. Accident or not. Where would I go now, though? I didn't know anyone in Utah and I didn't have anything to go back to in Big Bear.

"Chloe." I'd stay with my sister in Portland. Make a fresh start. It would be just like after graduation without the meth lab and the junkie boyfriend who got her thrown in jail. Last I knew she was on parole and couldn't have anything to do with her people. It had been two years since we'd spoken and she only called then because she needed money. I didn't even know if she was in or out of jail. Sadly, she was my only choice.

I stopped at a Quik-Mart on my way to the freeway to pick up a couple things. Couldn't take a trip without road snacks. Bag in hand, I opened the door to leave and my heart skipped a thousand beats, sitting limp and still in my chest as a Salt Lake PD cruiser passed by. In no hurry, they moseyed like they were taking their car for a little stroll. But they didn't stop. After they moved on, my heart wound back up like a record coming to full speed and I ran to the jeep. If I'd bolted at first sight, it might have seemed a bit suspicious.

Maybe Adam hadn't reported me yet. He'd have to explain everything to Hannah if he did. Then again, he probably wouldn't tell her the truth. He'd already proven himself an expert liar when it came to me. So, maybe those cops just hadn't received the information yet. Maybe they were on break. Maybe there wasn't a warrant. Maybe I'd send myself into convulsions speculating and should just shut up and drive.

I'd never heard a sweeter sound than The Beast's loose, rough idle. I really needed to hold on to that bliss moments later when the obscene thump thump thumping came from the rear as I pulled forward.

I wanted to drive out anyway, but I knew that would decimate the tire and ruin my rims in the process. There'd be no shoplifting auto parts of that size, no matter how baggy Randy's pants were on me, so I pulled to the side of the building, away from the main lot, and parked it.

A swift, cleated kick to the head would have been preferable to emptying out the back of my jeep to get to the spare. Miserable business on a good day, but having the nastiest hang over in the History of Mankind added no joy to my experience.

I kept an eye on the road, making sure I wasn't going to get any unwanted help from the Men In Blue. Thankfully, they remained out of sight while I unloaded all my boxes.

Down to the last one. It was a sad little thing, busted up. I dragged it toward me and something silvery slipped out the bottom. It was my Italian link charm bracelet, a gift from my mother for my fifth grade graduation. She'd gone to Rome with my father to attend an architectural conference and returned with all sorts of goodies for her daughters who'd suffered through an entire week with "No Sweets" Aunt Janet.

I told her I liked it more than the regular charm bracelets girls wore because the links laid flat instead of dangling off the bracelet to get caught on earrings and pantyhose, even though I hadn't begun wearing either of those things yet. I'd always wished to be older. Couldn't wait to grow up.

My mother had only put one charm on the bracelet: a sapphire butterfly, my birthstone and favorite creature in all of creation.

"We've got plenty of time to fill it up. I just wanted to start you out with something special," she said when she put it on my wrist. But we didn't have plenty of time.

I don't know what possessed me, I hadn't done it in eighteen years, but I put the bracelet on. It felt cool and comforting around my wrist. My link to a different time, a different life maybe I could have again someday. But that day, I had business to handle.

And business wasn't good. I searched every inch of The Beast and discovered I didn't have a jack or a tire iron. Under those circumstances changing a flat could get tricky. Unless my name was MacGyver. Then I'm sure I would have been able to work it out with a stick of gum and a handy wipe. But my name was Denai and probably would be for the rest of my life.

The good news: I had a big beefy tire in the well underneath the floor. The bad news: it looked flat too. That was The Straw. I didn't care who saw me, or what they thought. I was too crazy with rage to even care if the cops caught me.

Before I stumbled from the back of the jeep I let loose a bone shattering wail that even shocked me in its ferocity and desperation. All the heartbreak and humiliation I'd suffered since coming to that awful place surged forth like a coach throwing a fit in an umpire's face.

I hit the ground running and gave the flat tire a good thrashing. It thrashed back. I jammed my right big toe in the middle of my tantrum, inducing more shrieking. Hopping around on one leg, screaming a cornucopia of obscenities that would have dismayed Hell's Angels, a thought popped into my head: *I wonder what normal feels like.*

"Are you okay?" His voice was timid. He seemed torn between being the Good Samaritan and good common sense, which dictates you never bother anyone who is obviously off their gourd.

When I looked up at him I stopped hopping for exactly two seconds. I counted one Mississippi, two Mississippi. It was all I could allow myself. I thought I'd disintegrate or turn to stone and grow moss on my nose if I stared any longer. Sunflowers grew in his hazel eyes and his skin glowed as if the moon had rented out an upstairs room inside him.

"I'm fine. It's good. I mean it's not good. I'm good. It's...I stammed my joe. Jammed, I jammed my toe." All this was directed to my shoes. I tried to ignore his perfectly defined soccer legs standing right there in front of me, screaming to be fondled from inside his cutoff sweats. "I'm flat. I mean my flat is...I have a flat. Tire."

This degree of verbal incontinence surprised me. I'd never experienced it at such a prodigious level before, so I decided to shut myself up before I said something really stupid.

"Yeah, I saw your flat." He smiled. Good Lord! How long was he going to torture me with his freakish perfection? "I thought maybe the jeep fell on your foot when you were jacking it up. Just came over to see if I could help."

"Oh, no. No. See what happened was I, well; it's a long story actually."

A chunk of his tousled black hair fell down over his distinctly non-spherical forehead. He ran his hand through it pushing it back out of his eyes. Was everything he did going to be disturbingly sexy?

"Boy, my toe really hurts. I think I'm just going to—" I sat on the steel bumper of The Beast and leaned my foot up against the open door to keep it above my heart. The throbbing settled a little.

"So can I help? I'm pretty handy with a tire iron."

"I'm pretty handy with a pick ax."

Oh-My-God, what did I just say? I gathered from his expression he was not on the same humor plane with me. Most people weren't. "I was just being ironic." Moronic more like, but I was hoping that would pass by Pretty Boy's notice. So much for staving off stupidity.

"Right. So where's your jack? It's not under the jeep." He wasn't messing around with this Good Samaritan shit. I had zero other options at that point, so I let him help me. Normally not something I'm keen on.

"I don't have one. Or a tire iron. I have a spare though."

"Yes you do. But it's flat too." He inspected my spare inside the well behind me. I liked him being that close. He smelled like cedar chips and a hint of sweat. "I'm Patrick by the way. Patrick West."

"Olivia Kinross." Olivia was my middle name and I took Kinross from my best friend in high school, Trindle Kinross. I hadn't spoken to her in ten years.

"Good to meet you, Olivia Kinross."

A calm came over me the moment I felt his grip. He had a strong, sturdy handshake.

"I'm going to go get my jack so we can take that tire off. I think your spare might just be out of air. We can take it to the Chevron down on the corner and fill it up."

"Yes. Good. Super."

"So I'll just go get my jack now." He smiled again. I was still holding his hand.

"Right. Sorry." I returned it. "Do you need help with the jack? What am I saying? I'm sure you can handle it. Strapping young man that you are. I'll just let you get to it. Boy, I've got a lot on my mind right now. You ever have two monumentally bad days in a row?"

"Seems like they multiply when you focus on the junk."

With that sweet nugget of wisdom he was off to fetch the jack. I watched him stride away and it struck me that I wanted to make Patrick West my confessor and spill all my dirty beans.

"Have you ever done something that started out being innocent, but really stupid then snowballed into a complete disaster?" I asked, peeking around the corner of the jeep while he took the tire off.

"I guess my first marriage could be put in the complete disaster category. I was too young to know I didn't know anything, ya know? We've all done regrettable things."

"That's putting it nicely."

"Well, that's me, the nice guy."

"This is a curse?"

"Sometimes. Guys down at the station razz me a lot. Call me

Dutchy, 'cause I'm always going around sticking my thumb in things to keep them from falling apart."

"How very literary of them."

The guys at the station. I knew it. He was a fireman and a darn good guy to boot. Could have been worse. Could have been a lot worse. Of course Adam was a nice guy too, at first.

He loosened the last lug nut with the tire iron. Patrick West was definitely a handy man.

"I hope I haven't made you late for work," I said.

"No worries. My day off."

"You only get a day?"

He removed the offending tire and laid it on the ground next to the jack. "We've been a little short staffed lately with that flu that's going around. I'm trying to stay healthy and keep it at bay. Just stopped to get some peanut butter on my way home from the gym. Sorry if I'm a little ripe."

He was ripe all right. Ready to be plucked and eaten. He took the spare tire out of the jeep and put it on the ground so he could roll it away.

"I really appreciate your help. These days it's unusual."

"Yeah. Too bad isn't it? The Jeepers though, we've got to stick together. Right?"

"Absolutely." I had no idea what he was saying to me.

"Sure would be a better world if we would all just be good to each other. I believe it's possible."

"Definitely." I was going straight to Hell. Not only did I think he was full of shit, I lied to him to boot. I lied to the fine young Christian firefighter who believed in the Good in us all.

"It's not about getting into Heaven and all that, 'cause I don't believe that's how it works. I just think God put us here to love each other. Unfortunately, a lot of people don't agree with me."

I wanted to tell him I'd be thrilled to take part in his great love project, but I figured that might seem forward. He smiled at me like he knew what I was thinking and his whole face brightened like a sunrise.

"Sorry. Didn't mean to get up on my soapbox. I'll put it back in my hip pocket where it belongs."

"No, I think you're exactly right." What were we talking about again? It was hard to concentrate when his person was close to my person.

"So, you want to wait here and take care of that toe while I go see if this can be salvaged?"

"No, I, I'll go with you. Nothing to be done about a wounded toe, really. Just suffer through it, right?"

"Guess so. My jeep's over there. You need a shoulder?"

"Thanks, no. I'm good."

He rolled the tire away. I hopped down off the bumper and hobbled after him wishing I'd said yes.

"I have a confession to make," I said, leaning out of Mr. Patrick West's blue Jeep Wrangler. He pumped air into the tire at the compressor and bent over listening for leaks. "My name's not really Olivia Kinross."

"Oh?"

"Nope. Sometimes I use a fake name when I'm not sure about

a person. I mean you could have been a serial killer or something."

"If I was a serial killer, giving me your name would be the least of your worries."

"Good point."

Finished blowing it up, he pulled the hose off the nozzle and laid the tire flat. "So what's your real name then?"

It felt more like a challenge than a question. He stood on the tire and started jumping like a kid on a trampoline.

"I don't know. Maybe I shouldn't tell you. Maybe you're some psycho who goes around helping women. Then, when you've gained their trust, you take them to your creepy basement where you do awful things with a garden hose and a spatula."

"You watch a lot of movies, huh?"

"Mhmm."

"I'm just trying to help you. I think this'll be fine." He rolled the tire to the jeep, threw it in the back and himself in the front.

"Kathryn Denai. Kate. Katie. Whatever you like." I never let anybody call me Katie. Of course, I would have let him call me Satan if I'd thought it would get me somewhere with him. Those eyes.

He started the jeep and turned to me. "So where are you off to now, Katie Denai?"

"Funny story, actually." Then, right there in the front seat of the beautiful stranger's jeep, I unloaded my shit. I told him my side of the story and went easy on the stolen goods and nudity sections. After all, we might bump into each other in another life. By the end, I'd even convinced myself I was the victim in all of it.

When we got back to The Beast he wasted no time putting the spare on and helping me load the boxes into the back. He was a machine: strong, efficient and quiet. Too quiet for my liking. I knew I shouldn't have told him.

I held the driver's side door, preparing to hop up in as he approached. "Thank you, you know, for all your help. And listening to my stuff. I shouldn't have...sorry I...you really saved my butt. I, I appreciate it. I've just had a rough couple days. Couple weeks, actually."

"I have a confession to make too."

Great. He *was* a serial killer. Always go with the first instinct.

"Oh?" I glanced inside The Beast to see if I could locate my bat.

"I should arrest you."

His words rushed me like a linebacker. I gripped the armrest on the door for support so I didn't fall on my face. There it was. I was going to jail. I'd get out when I was fifty, miles past my childbearing years and a foot from menopause. No one would ever marry me and I'd spend the rest of my miserable life playing Scrabble with my cat and talking to a shopping cart.

"You're not a fireman?"

"No. Why would you...?"

"Good Samaritan. The guys down at the station. Station could be either, but you know, we go with what we want to believe."

"Right. Anyway, that's not my confession." He studied his feet like he'd forgotten what he was going to say and they held the answer. "Damn it, I'm...well, I'm torn. Never experienced this before. I should take you in, but I also want to take you out."

I exhaled. "Well, that's quite a dilemma. I'm fond of the latter, but I don't mean to sway you one way or the other."

He smiled and the world was right, at least for that moment. I tried to play it cool, but my whole body was taffy melting into my jeep. Under different circumstances this would have been a real ego booster, but now I just wanted to bolt.

"You didn't mean to do it, Kate. Turn yourself in and I promise I'll do everything I can to help you."

I believed him but I said nothing more to Officer Patrick West and did my best not to get captured in his gaze again.

"Here, take my number. If you change your mind in the next twenty-four hours, call me. Otherwise, someone else will be knocking on your door tomorrow. I got to walk away now." He turned and did just that. But then he stopped and said, "You have a good life, Katie." It was a statement, not a farewell.

I stood in the deep sparkling pool of that idea watching him move away. When I put his card in my pocket I found a wad of cash in it. I'd forgotten I was wearing Randy's pants and welcomed the extra money. The extra four hundred and thirty-seven dollars. Who the hell carries around a chunk of change like that? It didn't even occur to me to give it back. It was payment for my spoiled clothes. Now we were even.

Patrick left and I felt an unfamiliar tug inside. Part of me wanted to stay, believing in the good in me like he did. But the other part, the doppelganger, shoved me up into the seat and sped out of the parking lot, leaving my good side and my good life behind.

FOUR

It's funny how sometimes you are your own nemesis. Funny, like watching a thousand pound wild boar devour you from the leg up.

Just when you think you've got things figured out, an innocent oversight derails you. Like when you're leaving Salt Lake City for good, cruising north on Interstate 15, headed for your sister Chloe's in Oregon when you remember you haven't talked to her in two years and don't even know if she's a citizen of the free world or not. So you reach into your purse and search around for your cell phone. You know, the one with all your Important Numbers in it. The one you'd be lost without because technology has afforded you the luxury of becoming a mental slug. The one you forgot this morning because it was still charging in Randy's office.

"Shit! Shit mother shit! Why? Why does this always happen to you Kate? You fucking moron." I slammed the brakes without any regard for the people behind me. Somehow, they managed to swerve around, narrowly avoiding the opportunity to integrate their car with mine, and went on their angry honking way.

Most normal people would have driven to the next exit to change direction. Tedious. I took a shortcut through the center divider, a shallow, swampy half-pipe filled with long grass and odd bumps, none of which were any match for The Beast. It was an all-wheel-drive monster equipped with posi-trac. That jeep could have forged a path through the Louisiana Bayou.

I turned onto Randy's street at dusk and sandwiched The Beast between an Escalade and an Armada. It nearly disappeared between the two behemoths, exactly what I'd hoped for. Randy's truck wasn't in the driveway, but just in case he came home while I was in the house it was good for me to be hidden, have the element of surprise.

A pair of headlights flashed in my side view mirror when I killed the engine. The car passed me then turned left into Sadie's driveway across the street. I ducked when I saw her climb out of the passenger's side, afraid she'd make a big deal about seeing me. I wasn't up for that scene again. But curiosity prevailed, so I peeked a little.

Lovechild was already on the porch unlocking the door. He seemed perturbed and distant. Sadie was still at the car struggling to pull something off the seat. I wanted to go help her. Not as an altogether altruistic deed, but to see what was so important she'd rather struggle than ask for help. But then I saw as she finally dragged it out into her tiny arms. It must have taken all her strength to hold it. She stood still, like she was afraid she'd drop it if she moved.

I ducked down onto the seat. Not because I thought she would see me, but because I couldn't watch her. I suddenly realized why she'd hidden in my jeep the night before. Why her mother never came back to get her from school. I wanted to race over and sweep her up in my arms, tell her it would all be okay someday, but I couldn't do that because it wouldn't.

She was holding her mother. But her mother wasn't holding back. That's the thing about urns.

I was shocked to find myself crying for her. There would always be a void in her life from that point on. Especially because her stepfather was, like my own father had been, on the fast track to indifference.

I absently fingered my charm bracelet. It felt cool under my touch just as it had the evening my mother gave it to me. I couldn't stop stroking it.

"Bits, you're going to rub it clean if you keep that up."

"Sorry, Mom."

We were in my parent's bedroom and she was getting ready for dinner, my dinner, to celebrate my fifth grade graduation. My father and Chloe were ready and waiting downstairs as usual, continuing their chess game from the last time we went out. It was their ritual. And me helping my mother get ready was ours.

It was no secret I was my mother's favorite and Chloe was my father's. Like the clouds settling in over the Emerald City every fall, it just was.

"I'm teasing, honey. In fact, the man I bought it from in Rome said it was a special Good Luck charm bracelet. There are only a few in the whole world. You rub it and make a wish and it'll come true."

How silly I was. I followed her directions, but I made the wrong wish. Just a few short months later I would have given anything to have a do-over. I understand now it wouldn't have made a difference, but at the time I was consumed by guilt because I'd wished for a new bike instead of my mother's life. When she died I ripped the bracelet off and threw it in my underwear drawer where it stayed till the day I ran away eight years later.

Joanna Denai was a finicky woman. My father used to call her "particular", but I realized as an adult he was just being kind. Her fussiness made it difficult to be on time for anything unless she started to prepare three hours in advance.

Partly to speed her process, but mostly because I loved watching her, I'd help her get ready whenever we went out. She wasn't high maintenance to the point of ridiculousness, but she did like to put herself together before she left the house. Especially for extraordinary occasions. And this was one of them. It wasn't every day her baby girl graduated a year ahead and at the top of her class.

"I'm so proud of you, Bits."

"Mom, stop calling me that," I complained, well on my way to becoming a whiny tween. "And can you please tell Dad to stop too? It's so embarrassing."

"I'll work on him. Now, which one?" She held a shiny blue satin dress up to her chest. It was a sexy low cut V-neck. Then she switched it with a more conservative black cotton turtleneck number. "Oh, wait. There's—" She dropped both dresses on the bed and strode to her closet to pull out another. "What about this one?" she asked, holding another dress up for judgment and I knew this would go on for an hour if I didn't do my job.

"I like this one," I said, dunking my hand in the middle of the shiny dress splayed on the bed like a deep sapphire pool. I reveled in watching her transform from mother to Goddess.

"That's right. You like the satin." She hung the dress she was holding, came to the bed and held up the one I'd chosen for closer inspection. "As usual, you have impeccable taste my darling girl." She slipped it over her head and it became a waterfall shimmering down her breasts and belly. I couldn't wait to grow up and wear waterfalls.

Almost on cue, Dad yelled up to us.

"Joanna, I have no doubt you are even more gorgeous than usual right now, but your eldest is going to run away and never return if you don't choose something soon."

If only he could have known how prescient that statement truly was.

In the mirror, she pressed her lips together to solidify the lipstick. She turned to me and smiled when she saw me pressing mine together too, even though I wasn't wearing anything but my own lips.

I headed down the stairs first; she trailed right behind me. Her heels were a comforting sound on each step, sure, confident. Like Marilyn Monroe, the woman knew how to walk in a shoe. Just as we rounded the last curve of the staircase something went wrong. My memory was suddenly clouded and the air turned cold and heavy. Dense silence met me when I touched down on the living room floor. I glanced back to find an empty staircase.

When I looked across the room I saw my father, already an effigy, in his chair, but neither the chessboard nor Chloe were anywhere in sight. He was wearing a black suit and a vacant stare. I'd fallen into the day of my mother's memorial. Thanks to Sadie, my stay was short.

I didn't see her go into the house, but the slamming of the

door pulled me back to the present. Sadie would begin her new life now and I could continue on with mine, both alone, both struggling not to drown in the wading pool of humanity without any guidance.

I slunk over to Randy's front door and used the key I'd forgotten to give back to open it. It was dark now and there weren't any lights on in the house. I wondered if he'd been back since I'd left. The bathroom floor was my answer, although, I wouldn't be surprised if he left my mess for days.

Randy's office was directly across from the bathroom. I'd had to plug the phone in there the day before because the outlet in the living room by the couch didn't work. This was going to be a simple in and out kind of thing. Simple. An ordinary word imbued with wicked irony in my world.

The phone wasn't there. I checked in all the drawers, on the floor, underneath the desk. It was gone.

"Looking for this?" Randy flicked on the light. I stopped crawling around on all fours and looked up at him standing in the doorway holding my phone and charger. So much for my element of surprise.

He wore a grotesque smugness that distorted his face like a funhouse mirror.

"May I have it please?" I said, standing. I wanted to stick my knee in his balls, grab my phone, and run like hell for the door, but I thought civility might be the wiser choice in such a supercharged situation.

"No, you can't. But thanks for asking." He tittered like the little girl he was and dangled the cord in front of my face. Wow, talk about tough. My hackles raised and I felt every cell in my body ready itself for attack. It took all the self-control I had not to send him screaming into next month.

"Randy, give me my phone. I'll leave and you'll never see me again."

"It's interesting how calm you can be considering you burned down somebody's garage last night."

"It's interesting how calm you can be considering you have a collection of kiddy porn in your closet I'd be happy to tell the cops about when they come get me. Feel free to use my phone to make the call."

"You got nothing. They're all legal."

"They'll investigate regardless. It might get sticky to have the son of Salt Lake's D. A. under investigation for child pornography. It'll be in all the papers. You might even find it a little hard to get work for a while. But I'm sure they'll eventually exonerate you."

He furrowed his brow, made him look like a Neanderthal.

"Sorry. I know that's a big word. It means to pardon. Now if you'll pardon me, I'd like to get my phone and be on my way." I reached for it, but he pulled it back. Diplomacy, also known in some circles as extortion, was not working as well as I'd hoped. More drastic measures might need to be implemented.

"My dad would crush that shit in a heartbeat. But I'm going to be nice. I'll let you trade me for it."

My gut and the look that came over Randy's face told me this was not going to be good. His eyes grew dark, like the sky just before it let's loose a shitstorm.

"Adam says you're good with your mouth. Prove it and I'll give you your shit."

I had a choice. As the last day and a half had proven, I was keen on making the wrong ones. Maybe it was time for a change.

"Call the cops," I said.

"What?"

"Call the cops."

"What're you talking about?"

"Call them. Turn me in. It's all you've got, so do it."

"Listen, I'm trying to make it easy on you."

"This might come as a shock, Randy, but I don't consider blowing you the easy way out."

"Fine. You want it, I'll give it to you."

"Do you talk like that because you can't even bribe people to have sex with you?" That one flew straight over his head, parting his hair on its way.

He flipped the phone open and stared at it like it was the first time he'd ever seen one.

"I think 911 might do the trick." I couldn't believe I had to help him turn me in. I felt a little sorry for the guy. He was like a child, but not in a good way, and it made me sad. "Listen, Randy, I'm sorry about what happened this morning." I had no idea where the words came from, but they were on the shelf and there was no taking them back. "I didn't mean to ruin your pictures or beat you with the chick—actually I did mean to do that, but you pissed me off. You know?"

"Dude, no need to apologize," he said, dialing. "The look on your face when they drag your ass out of here will be enough for me. Besides, I'm not missing out. Adam said you were shit in bed. Said a sock puppet could've sucked him off better."

I'm not sure which part of me broke apart first. It was all a blur. What I do know is my foot found its way into Randy's crotch just as someone answered on the other end of my phone. Fortunately, they put him on hold so no one heard him scream. I grabbed the phone and charger from his hand as he crumpled to the floor.

"Thanks for the clothes. I figured you wouldn't mind trading some of yours since you had such a fine time defiling mine. Thanks for the cash too."

On my way out, the adrenaline subsided and my toe began to throb. I'd used the wrong foot. I hobble-skipped out to The Beast, pissed at Randy for making me kick him in the balls again. When I got back on the road I called Chloe but her machine picked up, which meant she was alive and more than likely a real citizen. I had to take a chance she'd let me stay.

I was thrilled to be mobile again. It felt safe, comfortable. Since the day I'd left home in Seattle I'd been on the move. Always looking for something new. Always starting over again.

I'd left Salt Lake with the intention of never returning. Intentions are all well and good, but sometimes a bit of life gets in the way like a sliver under your thumbnail, causing great pain and frustration. My mother used to tell me they'd come out on their own if you left them alone. That night I wondered what she would have told me about a five-year-old sliver with red hair and a penchant for stowing away.

FIVE

I learned two very important things during my time with Sadie: 1) always, always, always lock your damn doors, and B) once you've crossed the line to the dark side, it's much easier to keep tiptoeing back and forth. If you're not damn careful, someday you might just forget to leap back to the light altogether.

It was one in the morning and I decided to get off at the Bliss exit in Idaho when I mistook a couple of deer running alongside the highway for Randy and Adam. I thought they'd found me somehow, put a GPS tracker on the jeep before I left, or tasted of my tailpipe like old school bounty hunters. It occurred to me halfway through my musings that the brown things springing through the air on all fours were, in fact, just deer and I needed a rest. My blood sugar had plummeted and I was ready to eat my gas pedal so I pulled off on exit 22 and stopped at the Shop-N-Go for snacks and a pee.

I got a whole lot more than that.

"Goddammit, you sneaky little mo-fo," I mumbled to myself hobbling, bag o'goodies in hand, back to The Beast. My co-pilot sat stick straight in the passenger's seat. A Dora The Explorer backpack was splayed across her lap and she was holding a scraggly red-headed doll under her arm. Her eyes were heavy from the nap she was still surfacing from. If I hadn't just been through a tumbler of shit I might have found her beyond adorable, but at

that particular moment adding kidnapping to the long list of no-
no's I'd cultivated in the last thirty-six hours was not a choice I
wanted to make.

She studied me and flicked her smile on like a light when I
opened the door. "Esmelda!"

There it was again, that damn plastic strawberry scent. Too
strong to be a coincidence. I had nothing in the front that would
even remotely smell like manufactured strawberries. Two-week-
old remnants of yet-to-break-down-because-it-isn't-really-food
fast food, yes. Fake fruit, no.

Sadie pulled the doll from under her arm and sat it down on
her backpack, making sure its plaid skirt was uncrumpled. It was
fascinating. I'd never seen a little one take such care with anything. Then she unbuckled her seatbelt and held her arms out to
me.

"Sadie," I took her hands and brought them down to rest on
top of her doll. "What are you doing here? This is bad. We're
going to get in a lot of trouble. You shouldn't have come with
me."

I used my stern babysitter voice. It worked because the smile
light flicked off as quickly as it went on. Lights off, water on.
Tears instantly gathered in the bottoms of her giant green sau-
cers. I'd have to teach her a thing or two about energy conserva-
tion.

First, I had to plug the leak. Crouching down I tilted her face
up with my hand. She had the biggest eyes I'd ever seen. Except
for every time I looked in the mirror.

I wasn't any good with kids when they were perfectly happy

and whole, what was I supposed to do with one who was damaged? "No Sadie, it's...crap. Don't...I'm sorry. I didn't mean to make you sad."

"Finemymommy!"

I wasn't sure what she'd said, but I knew we were in for a struggle in a minute and one of us would be disappointed in the end.

Her face turned a lovely fuchsia and I thought for a moment I might need to perform some lifesaving technique I knew nothing about, but she started breathing again so I didn't have to dive into her mouth.

"Sadie, why did you get in my jeep again?"

"Nee...uh, uh, uh, map."

Here we go again with the map. She picked up her doll and held it close, gasping and snotting into the messy red yarn hair. She was so careful not to throw it around but she thought nothing of gushing snot on its head.

I reached inside the glove box and pulled out a Kleenex for her. She didn't take it when I offered it so I did what needed to be done. "Blow." She blew. Oh. My. God. Are children just miniature snot factories? And why was it pea soup? That couldn't be good.

I retrieved another Kleenex and set the plastic pack on the center console. She blew when I put it up to her nose. The tissue nearly covered her entire face. She was a living doll. I didn't know anything about children, but this one seemed smaller than the average five-year-old model. A subcompact.

Except for those eyes. They were moss colored silver dollars and every time she looked at me I felt like she was tiptoeing into my soul to have a peek around. I didn't appreciate it then, but at least she was respectful and took her shoes off when she came in.

"Why do you want a map?"

She was finally done leaking. I wiped the green guck away so she could speak. She sniffled a couple times, then gazed up at me without a word. Man, that kid had a way of burrowing in.

"Come on, Sadie. Why did you come with me? Why do you need a map?"

"You said you, you said you had a map. I-want-I-want-to find my mommy."

Oh God.

"Well, where do you think she is?"

"Sister Margaret said that, that, that, she's in, she's in Heaven."

"Do you know where Heaven is?"

"Which one?"

"Which one what? Which Heaven?" I was intrigued by the notion that there might be more than one in Sadie's world.

"The old people one is up there." She pointed to the ceiling. I noticed two Band-Aids on her fingers. I'd address them in a minute. Right now I had to switch tracks before my train derailed.

"Is there another Heaven Sister Margaret told you about?"

"The one Mommy and Daddy are at."

Right. Nothing better than a family reunion. Except when it's Just Not Possible. And was I supposed to be the one to tell her this? Where the hell was Lovechild in this scenario? What did she think was in the urn? This was ugly.

"Do you know where that Heaven is?" I asked.

"No, that's why I need a map."

And it was my job now to ruin this child forever. To tell her the truth about her parents. The truth about her life. Sadie, your mom and dad aren't in heaven. There is no such thing. Your mom's a couple pounds of dust in a jar up on your mantel, if you have one, and your dad's a pile of chopsticks six feet under somewhere.

Yeah, I'll pass.

It was too late to start back to Salt Lake then, so I decided to get a room in Bliss. We'd sleep and head south in the morning. On the way down I'd figure out what to say to her stepfather. Or maybe I'd just dump her at the curb and screech away like a bank robber. Even though she was the one who'd stowed away I still felt a little dirty, like I'd done something wrong. I blamed it on the state of the world, all those randy pedophiles making a bad name for the good fine folks who just wanted to move to Oregon and start over again.

Shit. Did he call the cops? Did he know she was with me? Are they out searching for a mammoth, green, wanted-in-connection-with-lots-of-indiscretions jeep right now?

The reality of my situation landed on me like Dorothy's big ole black and white farmhouse. Driving down the barren Route Six into town both sides of the road were suddenly illuminated. Everything clear and Technicolor bright. It was like someone had turned the lights on in the middle of the night.

The trees and grass were a vibrant shade of green like The Wicked Witch of the West and the cows, well, the cows were all electric blue. They dotted the fields on both sides of the road like plastic lawn ornaments. Blue lawn ornaments. Blue plastic cow lawn ornaments.

"Where we going?" Sadie asked.

The more appropriate question then might have been, *Do you see those fucking blue cows, Kate?* but I suppose some part of me was happy she didn't ask that. I wasn't in the right frame of mind to answer her or accept this as my reality so I stopped. In the middle of the road.

Maybe they weren't real. I was tired and wonky and just needed to rest a bit. I'd been pretty stressed the past couple days. And now I was wanted for kidnapping. That might add to the stress. It could do many bad things to a person. Make you fat, raise your blood pressure, even kill you. Was hallucinating blue cows so far off?

Maybe they *were* real. Maybe Sven, the feisty local avant-garde artist, skulked around late at night with a bag full of spray-paint *creating* his livestock masterpiece. Called it "Once In A Blue Moo." It was all the rage here in this burgeoning metropolis, population 324. Or maybe, as suspected earlier, I was just nuts.

"Sadie, I'm going to ask you a question and I want you to answer me honestly. Can you do that?"

"Yes." She was thrilled to have an important job.

"Good. Now, I want you to look at those cows over there and the ones across the road over there."

My headlights sliced into the night in front of us. Bugs and moths danced in the beams like they were at a disco, but I was more concerned with the other light on the side of the road. The cows were being lit by something else.

"Sadie, what color are they?"

An enormous smile crept across her face as she examined the blue beasts. "They're pretty!"

"What does that mean? Why are they pretty?"

"I like them."

"But what color are they?"

She didn't answer me; instead she started singing Blue Moon.

"Blue Moos you saw me standing along..."

No. No. No. This can't be real. How the hell did she know about that?

I jumped out of the jeep. The air was surprisingly warm for November first. More like a summer night in August. Halfway across the pavement I stopped and looked up. There it was dangling in the black sky like a glowing yoyo. Another freaking blue moon. I could have blamed it on dust particles from Mount St. Helens or the wild fires spreading across Southern California, but I knew exactly why it was blue this time and it had nothing to do with science. Or any logical thing in this world. I knew why, I didn't know how.

There was a dip on the side of the field where the grass met the pavement and I had to jump over it to get to the fence near the cows. I heard her open the door but I didn't want her to see me like this. "Sadie, stay there." My voice was full of emotion, which could easily be mistaken for anger. What the hell was happening to me?

When I turned back around I found a cow looking me straight in the eye. Nose to nose. We stood there for a moment, barely breathing. Then I brought my hand up to touch her face.

She didn't flinch or try to back away. She didn't speak either. I thought she might.

The cow was real, her fur felt coarse under my hand. Short puffs of breath rushed from her pink nose onto my cheeks and her mouth smelled like grass. She was black and white. No blue anywhere.

"Can I pet her?"

"God Sadie, you scared me." She'd crept up beside me and I hadn't even noticed. "I told you to stay put. Now go back to the—"

"But I like cows."

"What?"

"Can I pet her, please?"

I was too jumbled in the head to be mean.

"Yes, you can pet her, but quickly. We have to go." I picked Sadie up to pet the cow and she chirped with delight when she touched the furry face.

"Sadie, why did you start singing that song in the jeep?"

"My mommy sings it sometimes."

"Oh." Maybe it was just a coincidence.

"Blue Moos, you saw me standing along—"

"It's not Blue Moos, Sadie, it's Blue Moon. You know, like, well, like what we're looking at right now."

I put her down and we walked back to the jeep.

"I know. I like Blue Moos though. It's funny."

"Right. Funny."

"You like it too, huh?"

"I like what?"

"Blue moos."

I squatted down in front of her gripping her shoulders. "How do you know that, Sadie? How do you know about that?"

"Don't be mad."

"I'm not mad. I just want to know how you know I like blue moos."

"Idonknow," she said to the ground.

Little liar. Did she go through my things? Who knew how long she was in the back of the jeep before I got in. She could have rummaged through my boxes and found it. That still didn't explain the actual appearance of the—oh god. My head was spinning somersaults. I was too tired to think about it anymore.

"You know what? Never mind. Let's just go."

I helped her into the jeep and crawled in to buckle her up. When I stepped down and turned around to look at the cows one last time, it was too dark to see them. The one we pet had moved off, disappeared. They'd all gone deeper into the pasture. It was like they'd never been. And the moon was ghostly white.

SIX

I woke to the sound of my father crooning along with Frank Sinatra down in the living room. His voice was muffled because of walls and distance, but I'd had a bad dream and just hearing him comforted me. I crawled out of bed, nuzzling my Strawberry Shortcake doll, and padded to my door. It was always kept open at least an inch to let the light from the hallway in because I was terrified of darkness. My mother giggled like a teenager downstairs and I knew they were doing it again. Being nomandtic. I was five and my parents were in love.

Without a sound I crept to the top of the stairs to watch them. Chloe was already there and when I approached she told me to go back to bed, but I sat down next to her on the top step. It was a hot August night and all the windows in the house were open. The crickets on the front porch were Dad's backup singers and the moon his candlelight.

It was exciting spying on my parents. Like we were privy to something top secret and important. I stuck my head through the railing to get a better view. They seemed joined together as they danced. His left hand held her tight against him and his right cupped hers close to his chest. They were perfect together. The Auburn Queen and her Steadfast King. Like actors behind the TV screen, untouchable.

I used to think the people I saw on television actually lived in there and I felt bad because they were so tiny and didn't have normal lives like the rest of us. I worried about how they ate and went to the bathroom and where they lived and if they had a mommy and daddy who loved them. I didn't worry about my parents. I knew they were loved.

My father's voice melted with Sinatra's and filled the room with *Blue Moon,* the delicate melody that would stay with me for the rest of my life. It was my parent's twelfth anniversary and they slow danced in the moonlight to their wedding song, a tune I would come to loath when the reason for playing it ceased to exist.

I sat on my legs on the kitchen stool feverishly coloring a picture I'd drawn with my set of Crayolas. The morning sun lit the kitchen like a spotlight, glowing through Shortcake's pink bonnet as she lay on the counter watching me. Her red hair was ablaze in the light, and tangled from sleeping with me every night. My mother prepared eggs as I sang and colored. The sweet scent of my plastic friend drifted in the air close to me, above the smell of breakfast.

"Blue moos, you saw me stamping along..."

"Morning, my lovely ladies." My father came in and kissed me on the head. "What's this?" he asked, about my picture. If he'd paid more attention when he came in he would have heard my song, but I realized sometimes grown-ups weren't terribly aware.

"It's Blue Moos like you sang to Mommy."

They glanced at each other then at me. My mother came over

to look at the picture I'd drawn for them. Giddiness swept over her and she giggled. I thought she was laughing at my picture and tears sprang up like Old Faithful. She saw my crisis and swept me into her arms immediately.

"No. No Bits. I wasn't laughing at your picture. It just made me so happy I couldn't keep it inside. Thank you, honey."

"That's right. I've never seen such colorful livestock," my father said.

"They're blue moos for your annverswing!"

"Well, they're just perfect," he said.

My father was good at fixing me back then. He took me from my mother and put me high up on his shoulders. We brought my picture in the living room and he set it up on the mantel. Later, they'd frame it and hang it above the antique Victrola that played their wedding song every year. And then I'd take it with me when I ran away after graduation. It was packed up in a box in the back of The Beast.

"Esmelda likes the blue moos."

My father turned around with me still on his shoulders and there she was, teeny as ever, standing in the middle of my childhood home. She held her backpack in one arm and Matilda in the other.

"I can't sleep. Show me the blue moos again."

Wait a minute.

She came toward us and my father put me down to face her. We could have been twins. She stared at me for a few seconds, stared into me more like, dropped her doll and backpack to the floor and hugged me. Her arms wrapped around my whole body, warming me like an electric blanket. When she let go I felt more alive. Like I'd just guzzled four Grande Lattes.

"Wake up, please. Esmelda I can't sleep."

I opened my eyes to Sadie, standing right next to my bed, picking her bag and Matilda off the floor.

"I can't sleep."

I sat up. "I'm sorry. Can I..." But I couldn't finish my thought because there was a halo of light, or energy, or, I don't know, angel dust, surrounding Sadie. It was shiny and distracting and I told myself it was just my eyes trying to adjust to suddenly being awake and the harsh glow of the florescent light from the bathroom. I'd kept it on for Sadie in case she had to get up in the night. But the truth was, I was as awake and alive as I'd been at the end of the dream. I reveled in feeling vibrant again. So I accepted that Sadie was glowing and left it at that.

"Can I sleep with you, Esmelda? I got scared." She sounded horrible. Like she'd stuffed two earplugs up her nose.

"Oh, I don't think so Sadie. I'm a bad sleeper. I mean, I kick sometimes and I like to sleep diagonally. Well, sideways. I drool. And sometimes I fart."

Sadie climbed into bed, backpack and all. She snuggled up with it facing me and closed her eyes. Resigned, I lay on my side and watched her. Her breathing was labored but she still smelled sweet, although the strawberries had faded a bit. Maybe she was like a scratch and sniff sticker. If I scratched behind her ear or on her belly would she give off more scent? I was tempted to try it.

I watched her fall asleep. Kept track of her breathing till it was slow and even, unlike my thought process. *Damn it, she's adorable.*

But she's not my problem. She's a little leech. But she obviously needs something. Someone. I'm not her mother. And I don't want to be. I can't even open a can of beans without making a mess, how could I ever be a mother to—what the hell is wrong with me? Hello? You're taking her home tomorrow. You can't just steal someone else's child. Good God get ahold of yourself.

About an hour later, just after I'd finally fallen back asleep, Sadie woke me with a coughing fit. She was sitting up clutching her bag and hacking away. Her poor throat sounded like it had been stripped raw. I sat up and felt her forehead just before another fit seized her. She was hot. Not ready to be plunged into a tub full of ice hot, but definitely feverish.

I jumped out of bed and scurried to the bathroom. I'd never taken care of a sick child, but I vaguely remembered what my mother had done for me when I was sick or had a fever. I grabbed a washcloth from the rack and ran the coldest water I could get over it.

"Lie down, Sadie. I need to put this on your head." I turned on the nightstand light and it cast a yellow glow over her face. For the first time, I saw a hint of fear come over her.

"S'it going to hurt me?"

"No, honey, it's going to make you feel better."

Did I just call her honey?

"What is it?"

"It's a washcloth. Let me put it on your forehead to help you cool down. It's going to be cold, so you have to be ready."

"Will you hold my hand?"

If I'd been a nicer person, one with a bigger heart, it probably would have melted just then.

"Yes. I'll hold your hand." I put the washcloth on her forehead, then sat down next to her on the side of the bed. She put her hot little hand in mine and I curled my fingers around it. "Does it feel all right?"

"Yes. It's cold," she said, her voice shaky and weak.

"That's good. It'll help you cool down."

"Can I have a washcwoff for my stingy burny too?"

"Where's your stingy burny?"

"In your hand."

I looked down to my hand but there was nothing unusual there. I turned it over to look at my palm. Perfectly normal hand.

"No, the other one."

The hand holding hers. Ah yes. The Band-Aids. I'd made a mental note to look into those when I'd first found her in the jeep, but with the blue cows and exhaustion I'd forgotten all about them after we checked in.

"What happened?"

"I got ouwies."

"Can I look at them?"

She nodded. I peeled both Band-Aids off. They weren't positioned with much care. Whomever had adhered them was still learning the complexities of the opposable thumb. The skin underneath was moist and white, the way it gets when it's not allowed to breath. There were two big blisters on the tips of both fingers, rimmed in red and full of liquid.

"How did you get these, Sadie?" Did I really want to know? I realized it was the wrong question to ask a half second after the last word escaped my lips. Now I had to care about the answer.

"Soup."

"Did you spill soup on your hand?" I could live with that.

"No."

"How did you get the ouwies?" I felt the washcloth. It was warm already so I took it to the sink and rinsed it under the cold water. "Are you going to tell me how you got them, Sadie?"

I watched my reflection as I spoke. I looked tired, but my hair looked brighter. Must have been the light. My eyes looked different too. Less gray, more green.

I brought the washcloth back and put it on Sadie's forehead. She didn't feel any cooler than she had before I put it on five minutes ago. Her skin was hot and clammy. Not good from my recollection of childhood sickness.

"Please don't tell him 'cause he gets mad at me."

She was struggling to stay awake now. Her eyelids tugged at her to let them fall, but she wasn't giving up without a fight.

"Don't tell who what? Your stepfather?"

"Chwis. He gets mad with stuff. He doesn't like the noise."

"But I don't understand how you burned yourself, Sadie."

"The soup was hot and doing bubboos and I turned the hot blue off so it didn't do bubboos."

"Bubbles. The soup was boiling and you turned the stove off? Did you turn the stove off by yourself?"

"Uh huh. But I got a, I got stingy burny first, but I shushed 'cause, 'cause he gets mad at me with the noise."

A grotesque fire surged in my belly. I wasn't sure where it had come from. I wanted to go back to Salt Lake then and show Chwis the backside of my fist. Or at least the front side of my knee. Indifference was one thing. But this was active and insidious.

Sadie's face suddenly scrunched up into a wrinkled mess of emotion. She turned a darker shade of crimson and let loose a piercing cry full of pure, innocent anguish similar to the night Chris had taken her away from me on the sidewalk.

"Wahmymommy!"

She took me off guard, sprung up to my chest and clung to me weeping and gasping for air. For the first time, I wasn't concerned with whatever disease-infested germs she was smearing on my clothes or that she probably just ruined my favorite sleep top. Well, I hoped it wouldn't stain, but it wasn't the first thing on my mind. I wanted to help her, but I didn't know how. So I just held her and let her cry and snot on me until she didn't have anything left. Her tiny body jerked and convulsed with despair and I figured she knew deep down her mother was never coming back.

"Shhhhh. It's okay."

No it wasn't. I had no right to say that. It wasn't okay and it would keep not being okay if, when, she went back. But what was I supposed to do? Take her to Social Services and report him? So then, not only is she taken from her own home, she's thrust into a new environment with new people she doesn't know who may or may not treat her better than he did. I couldn't imagine Sadie going through that kind of hell. Damn it. Why did mothers have to die? There should be a rule. Parents don't die before their children turn eighteen. I'll get that memo request out to God right away. Not that He'd listen to me. He never had before.

She pulled her head away from my chest and looked up at me. Like grass after a summer rainstorm, her giant eyes were even more vivid. They glistened with tears. She held me in them and I couldn't look away. I felt a question coming on and I knew I wasn't going to like it.

"Esmelda, will you—"

"Sadie, can you keep a secret?"

"Uh huh." She sucked a gallon of phlegm down her throat and I reached for a tissue.

"Blow." I held the Kleenex up for her. She blew. I think the entire contents of her head came out in my hand. I wouldn't have been surprised to see some gray matter in there somewhere. At least she was thorough. More than I could say for myself.

"If I tell you, you can't tell anyone."

"Kay."

She was excited to have a special secret just between the two of us. It took her mind off other things for the moment too, which was a blessing if you believe in such hooey.

"Actually I have two secrets. But one isn't so secret."

"I'll keep them."

"Good. Well, the first one is my name. It's not really Es-merelda Ruthaninny Poppycock."

She spit out a thick giggle, full of residual tears and phlegm.

"Careful. Don't hurt yourself." I rubbed her back until she

breathed normally again. It felt good to help calm her down.

"I like that name."

"You can still call me that if you want, but I just thought you should know my real name. It's Kate. Well, Kathryn. Kathryn Olivia Denai."

"Kathryn Oliva Denaio."

Interesting how she mispronounced my last name.

"Close enough. Call me Kate if you want."

"Katie rhymes with Sadie. I like Katie."

I had associated Katie with my childhood and I'd grown up so abruptly; I didn't feel it was appropriate anymore.

"Katie it is."

"What's the other secret?" She lay back on her pillow and yawned. I could see she was fading. A good thing. I felt her forehead with the inside of my forearm, the part you slice when you're trying to kill yourself. She was still boiling up.

"Damn."

"Damn."

"No Sadie, you're not supposed to swear. Only grown ups do that."

"You shouldn't too."

"Well, you're probably right."

I went to the sink and soaked the washcloth again. My little friend had a point. Maybe I'd try to stop swearing. It was, truly, the sign of a weak mind. Thus explaining my excessive use of colorful expletives over the years. As my mind dulled, my vocabulary devolved into the vernacular of an angry hooker.

When I went back to Sadie her eyes were closed and her

breathing was heavy but steady. I placed the washcloth on her head and sat on the bed listening to her. It was soothing to watch her like this. She was peaceful. Her face was dry again, no sign of anguish left there. Just clear, flushed ceramic skin. When I bent to kiss her cheek a small bubble of spit blew out of her mouth. What the hell was I going to do about her?

I took her wounded hand in mine and lifted it to look at the blisters. They'd probably benefit from being popped to relieve the pressure, but I didn't know if I should do it or not. I didn't know what to do about a lot of things. So I kissed them one at a time and put them back on her rising belly, turned the light off and climbed into bed.

"My mommy went to Heaven too, Sadie. We're not going to find them," I whispered. My mind was blurry, like a window after a hard rainstorm. I rolled over onto my side and watched her sleep. Something in the way she breathed gave me a strange and sudden sense of hope. It was strong and steady and innocent, qualities I hadn't snuggled up with in a good long time. For a second I couldn't imagine myself without her. It was like letting myself down into a tub full of warm water. Everything felt good for that one moment.

"But maybe we can try someday." I didn't know why I said it. She was asleep, she wouldn't know. Then, as I turned over onto my stomach, I was shocked to realize I hadn't said it to her. Before I closed my eyes I was sure I saw her smile, almost a Mona Lisa smirk. Like she knew much more than she should at five years old.

I was thick with exhaustion from the last two days, so I fell asleep almost before my eyelids closed. And sleep kept me soundly for the remaining three hours of night. But around eight o'clock the sun crashed through the center of the curtains and hurled me back into reality. A reality I was not expecting. I rolled over on an empty bed. Sadie was gone.

SEVEN

"Sadie?" No reply. The tan sheet twisted around me like a wildly aggressive toga and I winced at having to untangle myself yet again from an inanimate object. The longer it took the more panicky I became. "Sadie, where are you?"

Having stowed my ego and conquered the sheet I ran to the bathroom. It was empty. The tan shower curtain stretched across the length of the tub. A knot wrenched in my belly. The image of Sadie's tiny bloated body floating face up behind it slammed into me. I whipped the curtain aside and let out my breath. Just an ugly, plastic motel shower.

Maybe she was playing hide and seek. But why would she play when I was asleep? I crouched down and checked under the bed closest to the bathroom anyway. It had a solid base. There would be no hiding under the beds.

See Kate? How could you possibly think about taking care of her? You can't even keep track of her for one night.

"I didn't ask for her to hide in my jeep. I didn't ask to be saddled with this. It's not my fault if—oh just shut the hell up."

Unfazed by my breathing life into the definition of crazy, I ran outside nearly naked. Of course I did. I enjoyed being naked in public. A troublesome condition I might look into someday if I can rustle up a dollop of give-a-shit.

Bursting through the door into the harsh light of morning I

couldn't get the thought of Sadie being kidnapped out of my head. Kidnapped from her kidnapper. They broke in after we'd gone to sleep the second time and took her right out of bed. I was too tired to wake up. Too tired. That's how I'd lived my life for the last ten years. I was a living, breathing, dead person. Couldn't take a nap without taking a nap first.

I was awake now damn it. Unfettered inside my thin cotton top, my breasts felt like they might detach themselves and bounce away on their own as I ran around the corner toward the jeep. There weren't any spots left when we checked in the night before, so I had to park it in the back.

"Oh God, please." I prayed I hadn't learned my lesson about the locks. That Sadie was a creature of habit. For this story to have a happy ending.

I sprinted through the empty gravel lot with bare feet. It could have been hot coals. I didn't feel a thing till I reached the passenger side door. Till I saw her sitting there, buckled up, sleeping. She hugged her backpack close and her forehead rested on the top of it. Adrenaline threw a party in my veins and my whole body trembled as I stood watching her breathe.

I was about to open the door when Sadie screamed. Maybe she'd heard me going for the handle and thought I was someone coming to take her away. I'm sure her mother taught her to scream holy hell if strangers approached her. Though she had disregarded that rule when she came face to face with my bat and me two nights ago. Damn, was it only two nights ago?

"It's okay, Sadie, it's just me. Sadie, it's all right."

She cried out blindly when I opened the door.

"Mommy!" She clung to me. "Mommy I got 'fraid! The count's going to get me! I couldn't swim!"

"Shhhh. It was just a dream. You're safe." I released the seatbelt and held her against my chest. She pulled her head away and looked up at me. It was then she realized I wasn't her mother. Disappointment washed across her face. For some odd reason, it stung.

"I couldn't get to my mommy. She was in the water."

"Uh huh. And you couldn't swim to her?"

"No, 'cause The Count was trying to get me."

"Who's The Count?"

"He counts stuff. On Saysme Street. He tried to hurt me. And, and I couldn't get to mommy 'cause I, 'cause I, I couldn't swim."

"It was just a bad dream, all right? The count isn't after you. He's somewhere far away counting buttons or something."

"He counts butts?" She was shocked.

"No, buttons. Buttons. Although maybe..." I decided to stop there. No need to suck this innocent into my warped worldview.

"Why did you come out here?"

"We're going to find our mommies."

So it *was* a Mona Lisa smile.

"Well, you shouldn't have come out without me. You had me really worried. I thought you...got lost or something. You scared me." This wasn't my stern babysitter voice, this was my worried mother voice and it surprised both of us.

Her face crumpled up again. "I'm sorry."

"It's all right. Just don't do it again, okay?"

"Kaaaaaaay."

When I picked her up the backpack and the doll fell off her lap to the floor. I thought I might go deaf from the piercing cry she let rip in my ear.

"Matewda! Katie please get Matewda and my bagpag! They falled on the floor!"

"All right. Settle down. Everything's fine." I picked up the doll and gave it to Sadie then bent back down for her bag. When I lifted it I was surprised by its weight. It was much heavier than I imagined it would be. Felt like she'd put a sandbag in the bottom.

The path back to the room was not as numb-with-panic or pain-free as the trip out. Felt like I was inching my way across a lot full of, well, loose gravel. The added weight of Sadie and her accessories didn't help. The adrenaline party had ended early; I was left with a nasty headache and lead for limbs. And my toe throbbed up into my ears.

Sadie rested her head on my shoulder as we made our way back. "Will you pet me, Katie?"

"What?" Was she a dog?

"Scoos me."

"Did you burp?"

"No, you're sposed to say scoos me, not *what*."

"Well, it is more polite." Was her last name Post?

"Will you pet me?"

"Maybe later." I'd have to research this. I thought that was a special bonding ritual reserved for the Garfields and the Marma-dukes with their doting owners. Was there an alternate universe where petting a child was the norm? Did they wear collars? And poop on the lawn? Now it was just getting weird.

"You'll have to show me how to do it."

"Kay."

"What's your last name, Sadie?" So I could look for it on those junk mail flyers and the sides of milk cartons.

"Beck. My mommy's used to be Garrett like carrot but then she got married. I'm Sadie Wizabeth Beck."

I wondered if Chris's last name was Beck, if he'd adopted her.

"Well, Sadie Elizabeth Beck, we've got to get going."

But which direction?

Back in the room, I set her down on the bed. She laid back clutching her bag, watching me pick up my dirty clothes and pack.

"What's in your backpack?" I asked, rifling through the pockets of the jeans I wore the day before, Randy's jeans, looking for the slightly diminished wad of cash I'd been using. I found Officer Patrick West's card instead. I thought about that last moment with him, the way his full lips rose up into a smile like a theatre curtain over his perfect teeth, and how those eyes careened into me. How positive he was I had a good life. I wondered what he'd say about it now.

"My stuff," she said, somewhere far away from my daydream.

"Uh huh. Like what?" I'd basically tuned her out after I found the card and waded through the memory of that last snapshot of Patrick; contemplating all the naughty things I wanted the good officer to do to me. I bet he wouldn't believe in my inherent virtue after that.

"My book. My teethbrush. My mommy's sand."

"Your mommy's sand?"

"It was in a big pot but it bwoke. I have to keep it safe for her."

The big pot snapped me out of my sex haze.

"What did the big pot look like?"

"It was round and white."

And filled with your mother. Oh God.

"Can I see the sand, Sadie?"

She rolled up and pulled the bag onto her lap. I threw Patrick West and his card in the trash and sat down on the bed next to her. My stomach was at once knotting into a pretzel and unraveling into a big gooey mess. Maybe it *was* just sand. Maybe her mother really liked the ocean and brought some home from their trip to the Virgin Islands. Maybe it was sand from the Great Salt Lake. Maybe the moon was made of crack.

I wondered if it was fantastically morbid of me to want to see the remains of this poor child's mother. To my knowledge most people didn't look at them. They just kept them in an urn on a mantel in the living room. Safe and out of the way. But in the way enough to remember the person they used to be a little every day. That's what we did with my mother. I never once looked at them.

Well maybe once. Or twice. Or nearly every day for several years. I don't know why but something about being that close to her helped me.

Every night after my father went to bed, between seven and eight o'clock, I dragged a chair from the dining room into the living room and took the urn down. I'd bring her up to my room and sit with her on my bed while I did my homework. Sometimes I'd put her on my great-grandma's old mahogany rocking chair next to my bed. She used to rock me to sleep in it when I was teething or colicky or just plain grumpy as a baby.

My mother died at two o'clock in the morning on my tenth birthday, September 22, 1987. I haven't celebrated the day of my birth since. A year later, on the night of my eleventh birthday, I bolted awake at exactly two a.m., shocked to hear the creaking of the rocking chair as it swayed back and forth. This used to be such a familiar and comforting sound to me, but it had been so long since I'd heard it I couldn't comprehend what was happening then.

My mother sat in the chair looking at me.

"Mommy?"

I knew she couldn't be real, but I wasn't afraid. When she smiled at me I couldn't hold the tears back. It was her smile. Her eyes shining. Her face lighting up at me.

"Don't cry, Bits."

She couldn't be sitting in the rocking chair and she couldn't be talking to me but I believed she was because my world had crumbled to dust without her. If I could only have a tiny bit of her back I'd take it.

"You have to be strong. Daddy needs you."

What about me? What I need? I need my mother.

"I love you, Katie. I'm so sorry."

The apology sent me into hysterics. That my mother apologized to me for dying meant she knew the hole she'd left in my life that would never be filled. She knew my heart, my pain. That gave me comfort and I reached out to her, hoping to be able to feel the warmth of her touch one last time, but she dissipated and I never saw her again.

Every night before I went to bed and every morning when I woke I would check the chair. Sometimes when I was feeling especially lonely or needy I'd slide the rocker over right next to my bed so I could rest my hand on the seat as I fell asleep. If she came to me again I would feel her and wake up. She never did.

Sadie sat mouth agape, dead still, gazing at me. Tears formed around the bottom edges of her eyes, but in every other way she looked like a doll. *Her* doll as a matter of fact. Matilda was cradled under Sadie's left arm, facing toward me. How had I missed that before?

"Hey, you okay?"

"Katie's sad again."

Damn it, am I that easy to read? The tears she was storing plopped onto her cheeks and plowed two wet paths down her face. I sat in front of her, my hands resting on the backpack. The tears fell off her chin and melded with them.

"How do you kn—" A peculiar feeling came over me. From nowhere the earthy scent of soil filled my nose. I looked down at my hands and I could have sworn they were covered in dirt. It had been one of my favorite aromas as a child. My mother kept a garden and I would always help her plant every spring for the summer harvest. Ever since the day we planted the Crepe Myrtle I'd been hooked on the scent of earth, but I hadn't gotten my hands dirty since my tenth birthday.

Yet somehow they were now. I closed my eyes and inhaled deeply against my fingers. Pulling the scent into me I felt invigorated and, for the briefest moment, happy. Like I was five again planting a tree with my mother and nothing would ever change.

When I opened my eyes I saw Sadie had closed hers. Who is this little Tootsie Pop? How does she do these things? The strawberries, the blue cows, the dirt. And how did she know what was in my head? And why did she—wait a minute, I *did* lock the doors!

I shot up from the bed and grabbed my purse off the nightstand. Somehow I knew they weren't going to be in there, but I had to check anyway. My clean, dirt free, hand rummaged around inside it, found nothing but a bra (I wondered where I'd put that one) my wallet, and a plethora of old gum and candy wrappers.

"Sadie, did you take the keys?" I checked the long table where I'd put my bag earlier that morning when we came in. The bag filled with Randy's clothes, a toothbrush, and a rubber chicken. But not keys.

"Sadie, did you unlock the door this morning when you went to the jeep?" I looked back at her on the bed. She'd opened her eyes; they were wide and filled with fear and more tears. She clearly thought she was in trouble, and frankly, she was if she'd left the keys in the jeep. What if someone stole it? Why anyone would want it was beyond me, but still, it housed my entire life, the pathetic remnants of it anyway.

"Sadie, answer me. Did you take the keys out to the jeep this morning?"

"Don't be mad at me. I don't want you to be mad."

"I'm not mad. Just tell me where you put them." I was pissed.

And the knot in my stomach continued to grow. I knew something was off.

"I put it, I put it in the icknijin." Her nose ran with thick green gook and I had to make an executive decision. Blow the kid's nose or go get my keys and hopefully the rest of my pitiful life with them. I grabbed some toilet paper from the bathroom and threw it at Sadie as I headed for the door.

"Blow your nose. And stay put. Do not move."

"Kay." She stared at the toilet paper lying on her hands and wouldn't look up at me. I wanted to pull her face up and tell her it was all right, but I couldn't do that until I knew it was. And I had the distinct feeling it wasn't.

Learning from experience, I put my shoes on this time and flew out the door. Unfortunately I didn't learn the lesson about loose boobs. They ached as I ran around the corner once more so I latched on and steadied them with my grip. When I saw it sitting there alone, the gentle green giant, I slowed to a walk and stopped fondling myself. At least one thing in my world hadn't been flipped on its ass. Yet.

So what was that nagging feeling about?

When I got back to the room Sadie was sitting in the chair by the door ready to leave. She'd put everything back in my bag and purse, closed them up and set them by her chair. I put the keys in my purse and hauled the bag up onto the bed she'd tried to make. I couldn't help feeling at five she had her shit more together than I ever would.

"Are you mad?

"No, sweetie, I'm not mad." Damn it. Who was this person

saying "sweetie" and "ouwies"? I'm pretty sure I meant to say Sadie. And I was mad, but it faded when I saw her on the chair. How could I be upset with such a teeny person?

"I'm going to take a quick shower and then we'll get going."

"Can I take my bath?" she said, her voice thick with emotion and phlegm.

Oh God. I forgot about that. The kid needed to get clean somehow. Was I supposed to undress her and wash her or could she handle it? Would it be pervy if I did it? She wasn't my child. When I got caught with her, because I would get caught, they'd automatically accuse me of depravity because her bits were clean. No, I decided, she was on her own. She'd be fine. I'd stand right outside the door, impotently waiting, in case she needed anything, like a chef or a spider wrangler. Two more things on the long list of people I couldn't be for her. Mother, of course, topping it.

"Um, sure. Let me shower first, then you can take your bath. Why don't you take a nap while I'm in there."

"I'm not sleepy."

"All right. Well, how 'bout some TV?"

"I only like Dora the Explorer."

"Well I'm sure we can find it here somewhere." I wasn't sure of anything except how goddamn difficult it was to entertain Little Miss Muffet. I turned on the television and surfed every channel. All two of them. "Sorry. No Dora." I assumed she wouldn't have much interest in rebuilding a truck engine so I turned the television off.

"Can you read my book?"

Was it a hypothetical question?

"Yes, I can read it, but not right now. We have to get going."

The idea of reading and books brought other things to mind.

"Sadie, do you go to school?"

"Yes. Sister Margaret is my teacher."

Right, Sister Margaret. She'd mentioned her before. So she's Catholic enough to go to an actual school for them and I stole her away. Good thing I'm not Catholic. I would have been wrestling with double the guilt.

"And Jenny Jacobs got a puppy. I like him. He licked my cheek. I want a puppy too."

And I wanted to be lying naked on the French Riviera with my Italian lover rubbing coconut oil on my parts. Some things might have to wait.

"Maybe someday you can have one, but right now I'm going to shower and I want you to stay put. Will you promise me you won't go anywhere?"

"I promise."

I didn't believe her. Something in those eyes made my stomach lurch and I knew she was hatching another devious plan to scare the hell out of me. So I did the only thing I could think of that would keep her safe.

"Do you take showers?"

"Big people take showers."

"Well, would you like to take one with me?"

I can't believe I'm doing this.

"But I'm not a big people yet."

"We can break the rules just this once 'cause we're in a hurry."

"Are we going to go to Heaven to find our mommies?"

"Something like that. But they won't let us in if we're not clean, so we have to take a shower now."

"Will I get soap in my eyes?"

"I'll make sure you don't."

"I don't like it when, I don't want, I don't like water in my ears."

"Then we won't let it get in them."

"Will you wash my hair pretty but don't let soap in my eyes?"

When did this become a negotiation? "I sure will. But we have to get in now. We've got a long trip ahead of us."

"Will you sing to me too?"

Now she was pushing it. The only songs I'd sung in the last eighteen years all had words she shouldn't be privy to at least until she could legally buy cigarettes.

"I don't know, Sadie. I don't really know any songs and—"

"Mommy and me sung row, row, row your boat gently down the stream in my last bath."

She had to do it. Of course she did. Played the Mommy card. How could I say no now?

"All right, but you might have to help me a little. It's been a long time. I don't know if I remember all the words."

My mother and I used to sing the same song in my baths.

"I'll help you. It's rowrowrow your boat—"

"Let's work on it in the shower," I said, herding her into the bathroom.

"Gently down the stream. Mary mary mary mary, life is butter dream."

She sat on the toilet and watched me disrobe. My body fascinated her. I could tell by the way her voice fell off when I started undressing. It was barely audible by the time I was naked. As always, my chest was the main attraction. She'd probably just finished breast-feeding a minute ago. I imagined she was drooling, smacking her lips, thinking, *yummy snack time.* Of course, like most things, I was dead wrong about that; I just needed to let my inner moron run wild for a minute.

I felt her gaze on my back when I turned the water on. The only people I'd been naked in front of in the last eighteen years (aside from Randy, and technically I wasn't completely naked) were men I was sleeping with. And only after we'd buried ourselves under the protection of covers or darkness. They were fascinated with me too, but for very different reasons.

Even in high school I didn't get naked in the girl's locker room. I'd always been self-conscious about my parts, especially the ones that could double as lifeguard rescue tubes.

I didn't feel any of that with Sadie. Her innocent curiosity put me at ease. I didn't feel any of the perviness I thought I might standing there al fresco in front of her. Her gaze was a mirror reflecting my imperfections as perfection. For the first time in anyone else's presence I felt truly beautiful.

I had no idea what to do with myself.

"Come on. Last one in's a rotten melon."

"Rotten egg."

"Oh, look who knows so much. Well, I'm going to win, rotten egg." I pulled the curtain back and put one foot in the tub, but stopped when I saw her face drop. She went red and crumpled up again. This whole pseudo-parenting slash kidnapper thing was hard work. All the coddling and requisite attention to feelings was exhausting. I kind of wanted a nap.

"What's wrong?" I wrapped a towel around myself and knelt in front of her on the floor. Tears streamed down her cheeks and I wiped them away. They warmed my hand and for some reason I thought of her heart. That it had been hurt. Why would I think that?

"Sadie, tell me what's wrong." I held her close to me and started feeling sick. My heartbeat became erratic and my skin turned clammy. I struggled to pull her away, but she clung to my shoulders. I needed to see those eyes though. "Are you hurt? Do you hurt?"

She shook her head no. A relief. Then I almost asked the question I didn't want an answer to. If I had the answer it would confirm what I was feeling was real.

"Is it something with your—"

"They fixed my bumper when I was little."

Well that wasn't exactly what I'd expected. My thoughts were more in line with a new engine. Maybe I was wrong after all.

"Bah-bump bah-bump. That's how Mommy says it goes. Bah-bump bah-bump."

Damn. I hate being right.

"Is that why you didn't want to take a shower?"

"Will it hurt my bumper door?"

"I don't think so. What's your bumper door?"

"Where they cut me."

"Oh."

We absorbed one another for a moment in the quiet. Two birds chatted in the trees outside the bathroom window, but all else was still, hushed. Everything was brighter than it had been a few minutes before and not because the sun had just come out. I felt lucid, in tune with Sadie. For the first time since I'd met her, I felt like I was in control of my situation.

"I won't let anything bad happen to you, Sadie. I promise." As soon as I spoke the words, my heart settled and beat its usual rhythm. She looked into me and her eyes sparkled.

"I promise too." Her whole face opened into a smile that could have swallowed the sky. She wrapped her arms around me with such force I almost toppled over backward. I was touched by her reciprocal promise. She knew exactly what she meant when she said it, though I had no idea. I'd realize much later just how true she would stay to her word. If I'd looked closer I would have realized her simple presence in my life was keeping that oath.

"Now, how 'bout we get in that shower?"

"Kay."

After we pulled her shirt over her head she looked down to her scar then up at me waiting for my reaction, so I smiled to loosen the tension we both felt. Relieved, she let out her breath and returned my gesture.

"My bumper door." It was a long line about a quarter of an inch thick that ran down the center of her chest from the base of her neck to the middle of her ribcage.

"Does it hurt?"

She shook her head no.

"Does your bumper hurt?"

She shook her head again. Then a thought struck me like a sucker punch to the gut.

"Ohmigod Sadie medication! Do you, do you have medication you take for it? For your bumper? Do you have it with you? Do you have the prescription with you? Ohmigod. I have to get your medication. Do you remember what it's called? What does it look like?"

I think I freaked her out a little. I certainly freaked myself out.

"What's a mebcation?"

"Pills. Your pills. Do you take pills so your bumper works right?" Yes, I felt silly saying bumper when I should have been teaching her heart, but she was going to die any minute from sepsis because she didn't have her anti-rejection medication, so it didn't matter anyway. She wasn't cooperating though. She just stood staring at me like I had a chicken leg sticking out of my ear. Great, it was already starting. She was in shock and couldn't respond to me.

I charged back into the room and went straight for her bag; she'd left it on the chair by the door. Matilda was propped up on top of it like a little yarn-haired sentinel. I checked the outside pockets for pill bottles but only found a crusty green Kleenex. When I started unzipping the big pouch part I remembered.

"Idontakepills!"

I gasped when I saw them and turned around to face her holding the bag open, making sure not to spill anything. I'd completely forgotten. The keys had distracted me before and she never got around to showing me her mommy's sand.

Human ashes do resemble it, especially to a five-year-old, but to the trained eye there's no mistaking them. There were small bone chips that brought me back to my own days of mother gazing. In eighteen years they hadn't gotten any better at expunging the human element from remains.

When someone you love dies you wish more than anything what's in that jar *is* a bunch of sand from their last trip to the Virgin Islands. Their bones, even tiny shards, are an unwelcome validation of your loss. A reality some people might not want to face. Especially tiny people.

I zipped the bag and placed it on the bed. We'd get to that later. Or never. Sadie held me in the vice grip of her gaze when I knelt down in front of her. I wore the truth about her mother on my face like a cheap foundation three shades too dark, so I tried to bring my thoughts back around to the matter at hand. But she was searching me again. Nibbling on my mind like a mouse on a big hunk of cheddar.

"You don't take pills?" I needed to find out if she was in danger. She'd definitely had a fever last night, but she looked all right now. Sepsis could be deceiving though. One minute you're recovering, the next you're dead. I felt her forehead; it was warm, but not blazing like it had been before.

She released her grip on me and gazed at the bag on the bed.

"It's all right. I didn't spill any of her sand. Sadie I need you to tell me if you have any special medicine you take for your bumper."

Maybe it was from my expression, maybe it was something else, but I realized when she brought her focus back to me her whole world had just imploded.

"That's my mommy?" Her voice was so small I could have fit it in a pinhole.

The tears came again. This time, they were mine. My whole body lurched, fighting against them, but it was stronger than me. Pain usually is. I couldn't answer her. Didn't need to. She knew.

I pulled her into me and held her warm little body close. She was still for a few moments. Shock takes time to wear off. And then it came.

"Mommy!" Sadie wailed and screamed for a mother who would never hear her cry. And I held her through it all. She clung so desperately it felt like she'd dissolved into me.

When we finally separated, she looked up and I could feel all the questions she had in her head. But she only asked one.

"Can I, can I, be...with you?"

I was shocked to find, at that moment, I wanted nothing else. How could I bring her back to Chris now after the soup incident and who knows what else? And the idea of a foster home was just cruel and unusual punishment now that she knew the truth about her mother. She needed to be with someone she trusted. Someone who would protect her the way I'd needed to be protected.

I wanted to run away with her, find a home in West Utopia, and bring her up as my own. People wouldn't question it; we were practically twins and I was the perfect age. It would all be perfect.

Extreme emotion is like heroin. It takes you on an incredible ride, high and happy as a duck flying free just before he's shot in the ass by some drunk hunter. But when the ground reaches up and you crash to reality like that poor quacking bastard, your first thought is to find your next fix, not fix your life. I'd been getting high on my own drama for years. It was time to stop.

I was too young and too broken to be a mother. And she was legally someone else's. And what would I teach her? How to drink herself into oblivion and set fire to her ex-boyfriend's garage? How to be an exhibitionist? I had nothing to give.

"Yes, Sadie, you can be with me."

Fuck it. I'd worry about my imminent plunge tomorrow. I knew the hunter was out there, I just didn't know how close he was.

EIGHT

She wasn't going to die. Not on my watch, anyway. Sadie hadn't taken medication for her heart in two years.

"I had a hole in my bumper when I was a little baby and they put a patch on it," she'd explained to me in the shower. But that patch was no match for the death of a mother.

We left Bliss different than we'd come. To be expected when you stay in a town synonymous with ecstasy. I wondered, though, if everyone experienced its antithesis or if we were the only ones. We headed north toward Portland on I-84 and, through my exhaustion, I pondered how the founders had grossly misnamed the town. It should have been called ShitStorm or WhatTheFuck? instead. Just a little heads up for the fools passing through to brace for the worst because ignorance is not in Bliss.

Poor Sadie. I'd be dissecting my unique relationship with her for years. I still didn't get how she understood about her mother, but I knew it had everything to do with me. And now my world had everything to do with her.

I'd deal with the details—food, shelter, life—later. Right now I had to concentrate on getting to Chloe's without being caught. I kept the radio on so I could hear the Amber Alert they'd be broadcasting about us, but so far there'd been nothing. Odd but good. I wondered if Chris even noticed she was missing. And if he had noticed, if he'd called the police. I wondered about what else he'd done to her and what we were going to do when we got to Chloe's.

My sister, the ex-con-crack-addict, would have all the answers. And they'd be perfect. And with those perfect answers I'd scrape my life off the septic tank it had leeched to, bathe it, pat it on the butt, and send it back out to the playground to start over. Everything would be great as soon as we got to Portland.

The Beast had been acting funny since we'd left Bliss. It had slipped out of gear, didn't shift when it should, and as we chugged up a steep hill it sounded like an old smoker suffering an angry bout of emphysema. I had the gas to the floor but suddenly we weren't moving any faster. In fact, we were slowing down drastically. The engine wheezed and whined, but gravity pulled us backward. That woke me up.

"Holy fuck!"

"You said the fick wood," Sadie said from her co-pilot's chair.

"I know, I know. Just, definitely don't listen to anything I say right now. I'm trying not to get us killed."

"Idonwannagetkilled!"

Perhaps that was the wrong thing to say to a fragile five-year-old holding her mother in a backpack on her lap. But in my rear view mirror the two eighteen-wheelers filling both lanes, barreling down the road straight for us, made me a bit jittery.

"I don't want to either." Although, it would solve a lot of problems. I took my foot off the brake and stood on the gas. The Beast roared and fell backward again.

"Motherfucker!"

I hit the brake.

"That's a bad word too."

"God, please don't do this. Please?"

"God, please don't do this. Please."

I wasn't sure whom we were talking to, but I was positive He wasn't listening. I shouldn't have wasted my breath.

"Why awe we stopped in the middle of the road?"

The trucks were going to feed on my back bumper in about five seconds. Somehow they didn't realize I was an immobile object. So much for being polite and asking nicely.

"Because the goddamn jeep won't move. It's broken."

I spun the wheel to the right, put it in neutral, and took my foot off the brake. We coasted onto the shoulder just before the two death ships roared by, blasting their horns. The Beast swayed in their wake. I eased it backward down the shoulder until we were on flat ground again.

"We moved. It's not broken anymore."

Oh, how I wished for that kind of sweet simplicity again. The jeep moved, therefore it's not broken. Your heart's beating, therefore life doesn't suck.

My hunter had come for me. And so soon. I wanted to buckle up and drive that grassy hunk of scrap metal off a cliff. Exactly five seconds of deep contemplation held me still before I erupted.

"WHYYYYYYYYYY?!!! God DAMN it! Fuck you and fuck you and fuck you again. Why is it always—what's the message you're trying to send here 'cause I'm NOT FUCKING GETTING IT! AAAAHHHHHH!"

I'd curb my swearing tomorrow.

I felt sorry for the steering wheel. And the door. And Sadie.

Poor Sadie. She'd heard me lose it before, the M&M Incident, but not this up-close-and-personal. I was sure the hideous face of my rage was too terrifying for her to comprehend. Guilt and shame over my inability to cope with anything in my life wormed its way in. I buried my head in my hands and wept.

She was so stealthy I didn't hear her unbuckle or navigate her way past the center console over to me. Her hand was warm on my back like a hot water bottle. I didn't lift my head; I didn't feel strong enough to face her.

"It's okay, Katie. We'll be okay."

Without looking up, I wrapped my arm around her back and pulled her into me. Her embrace sent a wave of energy through my body almost like a jolt of electricity. It was as if she was taking on the burden of my pain. The weight lifted from my veins; I felt light everywhere. Not just weightless, but glowing. I was a human light bulb.

Part of me felt bad about transferring all my shit onto her, but another part felt really great to be rid of it, if only for a moment. Selfish? Human. Like when you call a friend to find out how they're doing, but you spend the entire conversation lamenting your failed relationship and how your daughter got her head stuck in the banister again.

We separated and I felt mostly sane. "I'm sorry," I said.

"Don't be sad. You're my favorite people 'cept my mommy."

It was the nicest thing anyone had ever said to me.

"Thank you, honey, that means...thank you." I gave her a kiss on the forehead. She pulled my face down to hers and returned the favor.

"I want you to stay here. I'm going to go try to find out what's wrong with this hunk o'junk."

"Kay."

I pulled the latch to the hood and climbed out. This was the first time I'd inspected any vehicle's gray matter. Inky gook coated everything. I didn't even know where the dipsticks were. I'd always been more concerned with other kinds of dipsticks to bother finding out. Besides, the people attached to those usually did these things for me. Boy was I regretting that now.

Nothing screamed broken at first glance. There were no great plumes of smoke rising, no eruptions of toxic gases or liquids. I squatted down and checked underneath to see if anything was leaking. Not even a drop of oil. I felt some bit of pride at that. As old as The Beast was, it didn't leak. Good Jeep. But it didn't move either. Bad Jeep.

I checked the tires, hoping I was stuck in some alternate reality where a flat could cause a vehicle to lose its power of forward locomotion. All it would take to get going again in that universe was changing said tire. Although, I'd be screwed there too because I never bothered to pick up a jack. Maybe in that universe I wouldn't need one. Maybe Sadie could balance The Beast on her back while I unscrewed the lug nuts with my hands, since I didn't have a tire iron either.

In my world, plain ole reality, the tires were fine. But I worried we might not be. I went back to the cockpit and grabbed my purse.

"Is it fixed?"

"No," I said, pretty sure it wouldn't be either. I took my wallet out to check my finances. I'd filed Chapter 11 for my crushing credit card debt about six months previous, so there was no option of paper or plastic for me. I paid with trees only, but my forest was rapidly being cleared. It cost as much as a two-karat Harry Winston to fill the belly of The Beast so I'd taken a good chunk out of Randy's stash.

"Damn." I didn't have nearly enough to fix whatever disease The Beast had been afflicted with and I had no idea what to do next. It made me a little nuts. Generally I prefer not to know just how close to the edge I'm living. Jump blind and hope your chute opens.

Before I closed my wallet, I noticed a card stuck haphazardly in the back of it. When I saw Officer Patrick West's name I looked at Sadie for an explanation.

"Did you put this in here?"

"I saw you, I thought you threw it away and you didn't mean to."

"Well, thank you for that." I think. I stowed the card and put the wallet back in my purse. Not even Officer Patrick West's perfectly defined legs could keep me from focusing on our dismal predicament.

"I'm going to go make a leg. A call. I'm going to make a call. Sit tight. I'll be right back." I grabbed my cell phone and opened the door. I didn't want to take the chance of Chloe hearing Sadie yet. I'd deal with it later; figure out a story before she came to pick us up.

"I'm hungry."

"Right. Well, I think I have some, there should be uh, I think there's a Snicker bar in the glove box. If not there are some Doritos left in my bag. It's in the, uh, wow. That's, that's great Kate. It's in the back."

I was a paragon of health and wellbeing. Not only was I worth nothing, I was prone to violent outbursts of ugliness, and I ate like a ten year old on summer vacation. What the hell was I doing with her?

It's really noticeable how fast cars on the highway go when you're not in one of them. I jumped out and several trucks sped by in a black blur, engulfing me in a wake of cold, gritty air. I brushed the hair out of my eyes and dialed Chloe as I walked around to the safe side of the jeep, where the shoulder met the crunchy yellow grass of the dying field.

I didn't notice the lack of battery bars, but after I pushed send and listened to about thirty seconds of nothing I became suspicious. My phone had run out of juice and I'd forgotten to plug it in at the motel. "Yeah. Fine. Good. It's like this then."

A hand-me-down from my ex-boyfriend, Larry, the epitome of generosity, it was as useful as a walkie-talkie on a deserted island. Since I'd inherited it, the longest it had kept a charge was thirty minutes. I'd been too busy last night with blue cows and green gook to remember its incessant need to be plugged in. And I didn't have a car charger.

Instead of shouting obscenities and beating my fists about my head, I decided to show remarkable restraint and simply hurled my phone into the field. Excellent and adult-like. I hadn't thrown a fit. I'd thrown my phone instead. Much better. Except. Every. Single. Number. I needed was on it.

"Damn it."

"Can I help?"

"Shit, Sadie, you scared me." The kid would grow up to be a spy. I never heard her coming. She must have taken lessons from Randy. "I wanted you to stay in the jeep. It's not safe out here with all these cars flying by. Go on. I'll be back in a minute."

"But I want to help you find the phone."

Boy oh boy, what a fine example I set.

An ugly red Mustang with rust chewing away at its sides squealed off onto the shoulder about three inches from where we stood. It was the kind of quick maneuver that screamed wannabe NASCAR prick, or pubescent moron driving his dad's old 'Stang. I jumped back, pulling Sadie with me.

"Hey, you all right? You need some help?"

I waited for the dust to settle before railing him. He embodied neither of my preconceived notions.

"Sadie, you stay right here where I can see you. Do not move a muscle." Excellent mommy-speak.

"Kay."

I approached the car confidently. At least I hoped that was the impression I gave. "Are you trying to help us or hit us?" I tried to infuse my voice with a dab of sarcasm and a sprinkle of humor, but it just spewed out like a blob of bitch.

"Geez, I'm sorry. I thought you might need some assistance. You having car trouble?" His hair was salt and peppery, buzzed like a marine's, and he was the owner of the two brownest, beadiest eyes I'd ever seen on a human being. Hamster Man.

The ruddy birthmark on his right cheek looked like a wayward Rorschach test and as I leaned in closer to the passenger window, careful not to get too close, I saw creases around the mouth and an upper lip that had all but disappeared. I figured he was wading around in his mid-forties.

"We're fine, actually. Thanks." It was the lip. There was something genuinely creepy about it, like one of those flesh eating super worms. What little there was of it sort of wriggled around his upper teeth. That lip was smarmy. I felt like I needed a shower.

I marched back to Sadie and guided her to the jeep.

"I don't like him. He's funny," she said.

"Yeah, funny like Chlamydia."

"What's Kamyda?"

"Highly contagious. Now let's get up in." I opened the door for her and noticed Hamster Man was still idling ahead of us. I was going to have to be Mean Kate, I could feel it.

"Now you hold Matilda and stay put. I mean it. No getting out of this jeep, no matter what." Boy I was getting good at this. Before I closed Sadie's door, Lipster got out of his car. That sent me into overdrive. I hopped back up into the jeep, locked the door, and shot straight for the bat. It was turning out to be a handy thing to have kept.

"Whasamatter Katie?"

"Nothing. Everything's fine. Just, Sadie, I want you to come back here. Come on. Now."

She scooted to the back with her mother and Matilda in tow. Unlike two days ago, she was frightened to see the bat in my hand now. I tried to put her at ease. "It's all right. Everything's going to be all right. I'm just going to go bash his fucking skull in if he tries anything." Hmmm. I'd been doing so well. Sadie didn't see any humor in that at all.

"I don't want you to bash his skull! You might get hurt!"

How sweet. She wasn't worried about me going to jail; she was worried about him hurting me.

"I'm just kidding. Everything's fine, honey. I'll be fine. Now, I want you to sit behind the seat here. And don't move."

I'd taken care of myself since I was ten, I could handle this. If only I'd had a bat handy with Martin. But I couldn't think about him now. If I did, I was afraid I might just kill this guy. I'd tried for so many years to put that bastard out of my head. Expunge the breath that always reeked of rotting animal flesh and self-righteousness. I'm a vegetarian (chocolatarian) today because of Martin Flemming.

The only consolation I had when I'd heard he'd killed himself was his supposed piousness. He was a God-fearing man. Good thing, I'd thought. He had a lot to fear God for. Not that I believed in God anymore by then. I figured He was like Santa and the Easter Bunny. A nice idea in theory. Good for a few stories for the kiddies on Sunday mornings. If there was a God, and I was His child, why the hell would He take my mother away and throw me to the wolves? That wasn't a very fatherly thing to do. Of course the irony there is, that was exactly what my biological father did. So much for the Way Things Should Be.

The one beneficial thing borne of my experience with Martin was rage. I wasn't yet adept at separating the good kind from the bad, but at that moment I focused on the kind that made me jump out of the jeep, bat in hand, instead of locking myself in wondering what was going to happen to me this time.

The Lipster saw the bat and stopped. It's funny how a thin hunk of wood can make a grown man, a tall one fully unfurled, halt in his tracks. I held the bat in both hands and stood my ground. Wanted to make sure my message was clearly sent, no crossed wires.

"I told you we're fine. I'd really appreciate it if you'd leave."

"Well, now wait a minute. I don't mean you and your little daughter there no harm, I's just trying to help. There's no need for a bat, Miss."

He started creeping toward me. I felt like a caged lion. Like I was eleven again. If he didn't mean any harm, he would have schlepped back to his car and sped far away from the crazy lady with the bat. But he didn't. He crept closer.

And that fucking lip. I saw how it writhed on his gums when he said, *your little daughter*, like it wanted to jump off his face and into Sadie's pants.

Of course, I could've misjudged this whole thing. He could have been a Good Samaritan with an anorexic lip who really wanted to lend a hand. But in my experience, it's always best to be on the safe side.

Or at least the side with the better weapon.

That's why I hauled off and lambasted the front panel of The Beast. Hopefully he'd see I was intractably mad (what sane person would beat their own car?) and get that we weren't worth his trouble. Because he would. Have. Trouble.

Sadie screeched when I pummeled the jeep. I wasn't thinking

about how it would affect her. I'd definitely put that on the list of things to work on later.

"I'm practicing for softball. Think my swing needs a little work. You got any balls I could use?"

"Now, look, I told you, I'm just trying to—"

"I don't give a shit fuck what you said, you're still walking toward me. I promise if you come any closer I will use your head for batting practice."

He stopped. Not from my threat, but because someone else had pulled over behind the jeep. The purring engine of that silver Volvo station wagon saved him the tedious task of collecting his gray matter from the splinters of my bat.

"Well, Miss, I hope you get your problem solved. You have a good day."

If he'd just wanted to help, he would have stuck around, but now there was a witness. Another possible pedophile, but a witness nonetheless. He scurried back to his car, like the rodent he was, and squealed away. The tire marks on the road were the only scars left from that encounter. If only I'd always been so lucky.

"Katie!" Sadie opened the driver's side door, crawled down and latched herself to my leg as I bent over inspecting the damage I'd done to the jeep. I pulled her around in front of me. She looked up wide-eyed and concerned. "I got scared when you batted the jeep."

"I'm sorry. I just wanted to scare the bad guy away."

She stretched her arms out, my signal to pick her up. I dropped the bat and lifted her, holding her tight against me. We watched as the mustang crested the hill and disappeared. "No more bad dude."

"Dude" sounded funny coming from Dressy Bessy. Like hearing her give a dissertation on the dangers of mold spores, it just didn't fit. It was novel for me to be thinking about what sort of words were coming from her mouth. Like a parent would.

"Where did you hear that word, dude?"

"That's what the paperboy says. Hey dude, here's the paper. Hey dude, look at my new snakeboard."

The notion of an actual paperboy or anything so Norman Rockwell was foreign to me. I'd spent the last few years in the beds of married men and now I was an arsonist and a kidnapper. My destiny was not the white picket fence. I was headed for the electrical kind with the tunnels of razor wire on top.

"Hey dude, you have pretty hair."

"All right. I get—"

"Hi." A soft voice came from behind me. I nearly dropped Sadie when I heard it. I'd forgotten about the other car, the silver angel.

I whipped around and faced a woman with the longest, most stunning hair I'd ever seen. It was like autumn had exploded all over her head. Was there some union of redheads I was now suddenly part of? Her eyes were warm and inviting and she made me feel at ease without saying another word.

"Hi," Sadie and I said in unison. I wanted to drop to my knees thanking her for showing up when she did, but I thought that might be a bit much.

"I didn't mean to...well, I saw you with the bat when I passed by. I just thought maybe you needed—"

"Thank you. Yes, I did. I do, actually."

Wait a minute. *When she passed by?* She must have doubled back for us, gone out of her way to help. That was different.

"I never stop. It's really not safe these days. You just don't know what kind of trouble you'll find."

Amen to that, sister. I wanted to tell her to about face and run, run, run away because if she stayed one minute longer she would become an accomplice.

"Well, I can't tell you how grateful I am you decided to break your rule for us," I said.

"What happened?"

Did she want me to start from the beginning? She seemed like the kind of person who'd actually be willing to listen. Her voice was sweet and marshmallowy, like a Pinwheel. But there was extraordinary sadness floating too close to the surface in those hazel eyes. A kindred spirit.

"Broke down." Concise. Good job, Kate.

"Gosh, do you have triple A? Are you from this area?"

"You have pretty hair. I like it."

She looked at Sadie and I could tell she was holding something back. Her smile was genuine but she was in pain, and shit at hiding it. "Thank you. I like your ponytails." She turned to watch the traffic, suddenly, like she couldn't stand to look at either of us. It was the kind of thing a woman does to keep herself together in front of strangers when she'd much rather melt into a big puddle at their feet. I'd had much experience watching traffic.

"Actually, I don't have triple A," I said. What I really wanted to say was *cry. Scream. Rant and bitch if you want to. We all do.*

She turned back to us and I could tell she'd stuffed it away like a good girl. Whatever bubble of despair surfaced a moment ago had been popped. She was all business now.

"I'm sorry, you said—"

"I don't have triple—"

"Right. Are you from this area?"

"No, we left to go to Heaven to see my—"

"That's good, honey. I'll tell the nice lady, all right?" I almost put my hand over Sadie's mouth. The only way this would work was if she didn't talk. Not yet anyway.

"Carolyn. The nice lady is Carolyn," she said, holding out her hand to shake. I shook.

"I'm Sadie!"

"Well hello, Sadie."

"Hi Cowlin." Sadie threw her arms open hoping she would take her. Carolyn flicked a smile then busied herself with something in her purse. More traffic watching, I presumed. Sadie pulled back and rested her head on my shoulder.

"I'm Kate," I said, then gave Sadie a peck on the cheek.

"So, I can help get you a tow. I'll stay here till they come, but then I, uh, I have to get home." She pulled her AAA card out along with her cell phone, which was newer and looked much more useful than mine. It reminded me I still had some searching to do.

"Wow, that's really great of you. Where's home?" I tried to sound nonchalant, but it came out desperate and nervous like the high school pocket protector asking the beauty queen for a dance.

"Fruitland."

I remembered from my brief perusal of the map that Fruit-land was almost at the border of Oregon. Not ideal, but farther north than Mountain Home, where we were then.

"I'm still hungry and I have to go potty."

Right. Sadie may have had an old soul but her appetite and bladder were very much those of a five-year-old.

"I know, honey, we'll get you taken care of soon."

"There's a rest stop about a mile up the road. They have bath-rooms and vending machines," Carolyn said.

"Okay, great. Well, I guess we'll have the tow truck...we're...you know, we don't really...god. I've just had a real-ly hard couple of days. I'm sorry. It's just, it's been really hard," I said, acting my ass off.

"Take your time." It looked like she was holding herself back from patting my arm or hugging me, so it was working. She'd flipped a switch and rolled into caring friend mode.

"Our...my...mother, we're going to my mother's funeral in Portland and—"

"Oh, I'm so sorry."

So was I. I felt awful for lying to her, especially since I wanted to tell her everything, but this would be the better way to get help. Most people willing to aid balk when it comes to abet.

"*Your* mommy just went to Heav—"

"Yes, honey, my mommy, your nana, just went to Heaven."

"When is the, uh, when is it?" Carolyn asked.

I had to remember what day we were standing in first. Tues-day. Had I only met Sadie two days ago? It didn't seem possible.

"Thursday morning. I'm just afraid if we tow the truck now we won't get there in time for everything."

"Is your mommy with my—"

"Great granny? Yes she is, honey." Sadly, I was good at this.

"I can take you as far as Fruitland, if you have someone who will pick you up from there. Would you be open to that? I know you don't know me—"

"I'd be so grateful."

"What'll you do with your jeep?"

"Oh, I'll just leave it for now. My, I'll let my brother, Fred, worry about it. He likes to mess with things like that. Heck, he'll probably come down and try to fix it on his own."

I was officially OOC, Out Of Control. In twenty-eight years, the word "heck" had not once escaped my lips.

"Do you mind if I just, I need to grab a few things first. Is that all right? I know you're in a hurry."

"Of course, take your time. I'll be in my car."

Carolyn went back to the Volvo and we got to work. I enlisted Sadie to help me find my phone first. She was a good little tracker and spotted it lying dead next to a large white rock. If it had landed an inch to the left the rock probably would have shattered it, rendering it eternally useless. Life and her teeny mercies.

"When did your mommy go to Heaven?" she asked, marching next to me back to the jeep through the crunchy grass.

"Let's get our stuff ready to go and I'll tell you a story."

Back in The Beast Sadie gathered her things, Matilda and her mother, and kneeled on the seat peeking over the edge at me while I rummaged through boxes.

"My stuff is ready and I still have to go potty. Can you tell my story now?"

Kids.

"In a minute. I have to get my things ready."

I wouldn't be returning for the jeep. I'd decided that when I used it for batting practice. But I obviously couldn't take everything I owned, might seem a bit suspicious to Carolyn, so I searched through to find the irreplaceables.

I found my best friend Trindle's favorite candle, with handpainted dolphins, tucked in the corner of a box full of towels. She'd given it to me when I lived with her after graduation because she knew it was my favorite too. That was Trindle. I'd hoped someday I might be able to return it to her. Didn't seem likely now, though, so I put it back in the box and moved on to the next.

When I ran away from home the night of my high school graduation, I didn't take much with me: some clothes, the charm bracelet, and the "Blue Moos" picture. I'd lifted it from the wall above the Victrola after my mother died, so my father couldn't destroy it, and kept it hidden in my closet for eight years. Not that I had to hide it. I could have had an elephant in my room, he wouldn't have known.

A month after she died, my father took everything that reminded him of her and burned it all. Clothes, perfume, the blanket on the living room couch that would forever smell of roses, the paintings, and all of her photos. He couldn't bear to have her eyes watching him from the walls, or albums or anywhere else. I'd started to look a great deal like my mother by then, but he couldn't toss me on the funeral pyre too. Not literally anyway.

The traffic whizzed by outside and the sun told me to hurry up. It was falling ever closer to the western horizon, splashing the sky with deep tangerine and cherry paint. I'd soon run out of light.

Overwhelmed by everything, I stood up in the middle of the mess and decided to leave it all. Start new. At least that was the plan, until I saw the box squatting in the corner. The old decrepit thing my charm bracelet had slipped from.

I sat down on the floor and opened it. The "Blue Moos" picture was tucked in on its side, so I slid it out and put it on my lap to examine more closely. The Crayola colors had faded, but at least the glass in the picture frame had protected the paper from falling apart over the years. Too bad they didn't make frames for people.

"What's that?" Sadie asked.

"Come on, now. You know what it is. You looked at it before, didn't you? You can tell me. I won't be mad."

She poked her face down as far as she could without falling over the seat to take a look. "I didn't look at it, ever. Oh, I know, it's the blue moos! Just like we saw!"

Right. So much for my theory.

"Yep, just like the ones we saw."

I pulled a Zippo lighter out of the bottom of the box. It had belonged to Larry, my ex from Atlanta. I flicked it open, dragged my thumb over the coarse metal of the spark wheel, and a small flame leapt out. I was mesmerized by it, by its power. After Larry broke up with me for his size zero dog walker it lit the cigarette that started the fire that left him incapable of enjoying his penis for a very long time. Lots of power in that little lighter.

I put my picture and the Zippo back in the box and left everything. There was something to be said about starting over fresh, with no baggage.

"All right, I'm ready," I said, not entirely sure I was.

"Me too."

The hazy darkness of twilight settled in around us and Sadie's features got blurry. It was harder for me to see at night with astigmatism in both eyes and I made a mental note to look for my driving glasses after our talk. I climbed over the back of the seat with my bag, sat down next to Sadie, and found my glasses. Apparently, my ass received the memo before my eyes did. The pitiful crunch underneath me was my first clue to their whereabouts.

"Excellent. That's great. That's just—"

"What's great?"

"You. You're great."

No need to dwell. Certainly an improvement for me. I pulled the glasses out from under my left cheek and tossed them in the back with the rest of the life I was leaving behind.

"Now listen, that nice lady—"

"Cowlin."

"Yes, Carolyn. She's going to drive us up to her house so we can..." So we can what? I hadn't given that much thought. What were we going to do when we got to Fruitland if Chloe wouldn't come pick us up?

"So we can go potty?" she asked.

"No, we'll do that before we get there."

"Good. 'Cause I got to go bad."

If she weren't so adorable, she'd be really adorable.

"I need you to do something for me. I need you to pretend, just for now, just while we're with Carolyn, that I'm your...that you're my daughter."

"Why?"

"It's, well, it's kind of, I'll explain later. Just for now, we have to pretend. You know how to pretend, right?"

"Is this my story?"

"Yes, this is part of your story. You're going to be in your story so—"

"Why?"

This is why kids are so impossible. A grillion questions I didn't know how to answer.

"It's complicated."

"What's compucated?"

"Tricky, like...pantyhose."

"What's pannyose? Can you eat them, 'cause I'm really hungry."

"No, honey. I know you are, we'll get—you didn't want the snickers?"

"I want a cinnmin pretzel."

"Okay." I appreciated her specificity, even if I couldn't do a damn thing about it. "We'll work on finding one, but we're getting off topic here. You just...I need you to pretend I'm your mommy and we're going to my mommy's funeral."

"Who's my pretend daddy?"

Excellent question. I was thrilled she was taking this seriously.

"Well, he's..."

"My daddy's a hero. That's what my mommy says. She said he saved people from a big fire when I was a little baby. But he never came home after. Ladder sixty-two. That's what he used. The ladder number sixty two."

Right. So her father wasn't a pile of chopsticks. He'd been cremated, no doubt saving lives. Wow.

"So your pretend daddy can be your real daddy and that's why he's not around anymore."

She looked away. This obviously upset her. I felt horrible for not thinking about the trauma she'd just been through. Christ, she'd just realized she was carrying her mother around in a backpack less than eight hours ago.

"I'm sorry, honey, does this make you sad?"

She didn't answer, just inspected her shoes.

"Sadie, I know this is hard, but we have to do it so we can get to Portland. All right? Everything's going to be better when we get to Portland."

An eighteen-wheeler blew past and the jeep rocked like we were in water.

"Kay," she whispered.

"Besides, if you don't pretend just for now, your nose will turn purple." She giggled. The desired effect. Maybe I could do this. "One time, when I was your age, I didn't pretend I could fly and my whole face turned purple for three days."

She stopped giggling. "Idonwannapurpleface!"

Not the desired effect. What was I thinking? Purple face.

"No, you won't, it's not...don't...come here." I wrapped her in my arms and for the first time, since the night on the sidewalk, I couldn't smell the plastic strawberry scent. I should have been relieved. Excellent, I'm not crazy as previously thought. But I was disturbed. It was like her innocence had faded away.

"My daddy's in the old people's Heaven. I'm not going to see him either, huh?" she said into my chest. I looked down to answer her as she poked her head up, but I found someone else. Her body was the same, teeny and sweet, but in the dusky light her face had aged about forty years. She looked like a full-grown woman. Her freckles had disappeared and her eyes weren't mossy anymore. They'd faded to a dull gray and wrinkles clenched the skin around them. Her hair had turned the color of dead pine needles, like mine had after so many years of disappointment.

I sat there, stunned, not knowing if this was a blue cow phenomenon or a preview of things to come. When I blinked she was Sadie again. Vibrant and young, with the rest of her life ahead of her to become just like me, bitter and self-destructive because she was dealt a bum hand. It's funny how one moment can bring a lifetime of blurriness into focus.

"What's the matter, Katie?"

"I'm good. Fine."

I drew my thumbs across her cheeks, like windshield wipers, clearing the tears. "You ready?" She nodded.

We collected our things and headed for the passenger side door. When I opened it, my breath caught in my chest and I froze. I hadn't been monitoring the radio that whole time. Surely Chris had reported her missing by now. What happens when the cops find The Beast? No doubt they're looking for us. They'll know we went north and—suddenly, there was a little doll kiss on my cheek.

"What was that for?" I asked, turning to her.

"'Cause you needed it."

I smiled and returned the favor. The kid had a way of getting in. Like a heartworm, only much cuter and less stringy.

I helped her climb down to the pavement and she stood there, clutching her doll, waiting for me. She was a Lifesaver candy, tiny and sweet, with a little hole in her middle. I was a hula-hoop. It was time to start filling our middles back up.

I put my things in the trunk of Carolyn's car, buckled Sadie in the back seat with her backpack and Matilda, and climbed in front next to the driver.

"Thank you again for this," I said.

"Of course."

When we pulled out onto the road, my chest got heavy and I couldn't breath.

"Stop, please!"

Carolyn veered off to the shoulder, just ahead of The Beast, and slammed on the brakes.

"Did you forget something?"

"I'm so sorry. I'll be right back." I ran to the jeep and opened the back door. It was dark by then so I had to grope my way through the boxes to find it. It felt cool in my hand, solid. I pulled "Blue Moos" and the Zippo out too.

Back in the car I laid the picture on my lap and put Trindle's candle on the floor between my feet. Part of me believed something was still possible.

"Sorry. I made this for my mother a long time ago and I want to, I'd like to bury it with her." Again, my heart clenched and I felt like such a fraud for lying. I wondered what was happening to me. I'd never had a problem with it before.

We inched back onto the road. Carolyn was probably waiting for me to scream again, but I was silent. I watched the inky silhouette of The Beast become smaller and smaller in the side view mirror. Just before we crested the hill, bright orange flames licked at its roof.

My mother once told me Rangers set controlled fires to encourage the growth of new life in forest habitats. My motives had very little to do with nature, except my own, but I still hoped for something new to grow.

NINE

It was nine o'clock when we pulled into Carolyn's driveway. The frigid night air enveloped me when I stepped out with Sadie. We were both exhausted. The last thing I wanted to do was call my sister and argue with her about coming to get me this late. Frankly, it would be a miracle if she came at all at any hour. She'd rejected her sister gene at birth. Mine.

I stood by the car and looked up at Carolyn's home, a white clapboard farmhouse with a wraparound porch. A bay window in the living room sat underneath two smaller ones upstairs. They all glowed with the light from a fire and in the dark it looked like the house was smiling at me.

The whole perfect picture reminded me of those candles they carve scenes into at gift shops in Florida. When you light the wick your candle becomes a bright, warm world unto itself. Dolphins dancing in the waxy ocean. Flowers blooming in fake fields. Everything glowing from within. The heart of Carolyn's candle was bursting with energy and warmth. Everything looked so perfect and normal and inviting. But like the façade of any movie house, nothing is ever as it seems after you walk through the door.

Carolyn led the way up onto the porch. She walked like a woman carrying too much. Her shoulders slumped just enough to make it clear she was not comfortable with her height. I hadn't noticed how tall she was before, about two inches taller than me, which would make her just six feet. Her jacket hung over her bones like it would a skeleton. Nothing filling it out.

When she opened the door a bubble of garlic air floated out and burst around me. My head simmered in olive oil, wine, and herbs. It was glorious. I wondered who was cooking.

"Go ahead, Sadie." Carolyn nudged her forward. Sadie looked back at me as if to make sure, then Carolyn took her in. I followed close behind. My stomach growled and I realized I hadn't eaten any kind of home cooked meal in a very long time. I couldn't wait to get into that kitchen.

"That smells amazing. Who's the cook?"

"Oh, that's Martin, my husband, the erstwhile chef. He still likes to tinker around a bit every now and then. Please make yourselves at home."

Carolyn took our coats; the bells on Sadie's jacket tinkled as she walked them over to the closet. She was a good host, making her guests feel comfortable. A regular Martha Stewart in training. Her house was meticulous. A page out of House and Garden, like a dollhouse. My last apartment looked like a tornado had not only gone through, but actually stopped and raged in the middle of it for an hour or two.

A rocking chair in the corner caught my eye. The quilt hanging over it seemed two-dimensional, drawn on. The plants were flat too, like they'd been sketched and colored in. I glanced around the room trying to find more weirdness but my inspection was disrupted by Carolyn's marshmallow voice.

"Can I get you something to drink?"

"Vodka, straight, please."

Carolyn's eyes widened almost imperceptibly, but I saw the flash of shock in them. I wasn't even that fond of vodka, especially after my last encounter; it was more a default response after a bad day.

"Or..."

"Bodka straight, please." Carolyn and I both looked over at Sadie, standing in miniature next to a velvety red recliner.

"They just repeat everything, don't they?" Carolyn said. She knew of which she spoke. I was curious. There were no scattered toys in the living room. No pictures on the walls of tiny Tater Tots. No scent of children at all, yet I had the distinct feeling she had one. Or had had one.

"We'll just have water. Water's good," I said.

Carolyn disappeared through the hallway I assumed led to the kitchen. I moseyed over to the fire and squatted down in front of it. Sadie tailed right behind me. She was different here. Timid. Almost afraid. Of what I wasn't exactly sure. She crept behind me, nestling in my hair. It felt good. Like I was Mama Bear and she was Baby riding on my back.

"Kate, can I bother you for just a second?"

So much for quality bonding time.

"Sure. You stay here and get warm. I'll be right back."

"Can I go?"

"No honey. You can't go where I'm going."

"I don't want to be alone."

"You won't be for long."

I wasn't quite sure what I was saying or why. I saw no reason she couldn't come with me, but something put the thought in my head and the words in my mouth.

The moment I stepped into the dark hallway the snapping and crackling from the fire sounded far away, like it was behind a thick door, but the door leading from the hall to the living room was still open. I turned around and checked just to be sure it hadn't closed. When I turned back I was in the bright kitchen basking in the glory of garlic. But Carolyn was nowhere in sight.

"Oh, I'm sorry. I thought Carolyn was in here."

"She went upstairs for a minute. I'm Marty."

"Kate."

He put the frying pan and tongs down on the stove and offered his hand. I accepted. Something in me said not to. His hand was hot. And so was he. Erstwhile chef? More like erstwhile underwear model.

"She should be back in a minute," he said.

"Great." Was he staring at me?

"She's upstairs. She'll be back in a minute."

Was he daft? "Right. You said."

"She'll be back in a minute, so..."

Was that an offer? No, Kate. No. Your mind is playing tricks. He's your type, but handle yourself. You heard him; she'll be back in a minute. Step away from the beautiful man.

"I'm just going to go back out to—" And there he was as I turned to leave. In front of me, all six feet plus of himself. I swear I could feel him throbbing. Or maybe that was me. Either way, it was hard to tell who it was after he leaned in for the kill—the kiss.

His tongue was wet and warm and his mouth smelled like peppermint. Or spearmint. Or some mint. I'd never been a fan of mint. Not since I was eleven anyway. Martin Flemming had been riddled with muscle aches. He'd soothed himself with Bengay and little girls.

Must stop kissing. Must stop. There was a disconnect between my brain and my lips and arms because I didn't stop. I wrapped him in my embrace and dove in. Damn it. I thought I was done with this.

I tried to pull away, but his arms caught me and pulled me closer. His breath was labored and his kisses were getting sloppier. So sloppy he just drooled into me. His tongue darted in and out of my mouth almost like a snake testing the air. Other things on his anatomy were darting out as well. He pressed himself against me hard. Too hard. It felt like he was trying to break through me. The more I pulled away, the stronger he became.

Then I heard Sadie scream. I couldn't tell what she was saying, but she needed me. I struggled to free myself from his grip but the more I fought against him the more arms he seemed to have. He was an octopus sealing his dinner for the night.

"Let go of me, goddammit!"

Oh how I wish he hadn't. With a little space between us now, I saw the man I'd been kissing wasn't Carolyn's beautiful underwear model husband. It was Martin Flemming. I'd tried so hard to erase the memory of his puffy lips and potbelly, but there he was in front of me. His whole putrid self, standing there, still reeking of menthol and meat.

"You'll never get away from me."

Sadie's screams again. I couldn't move. I was paralyzed. Stuck there, inhaling his putrescence. The stench of rotting flesh permeated the air all around him.

"You're never going to stop running from me."

It sounded like someone was trying to kill Sadie in the living room. Her screams became more and more urgent. I had to get to her. When I tried to move, nothing happened. I was stuck in place. In front of him. So, I started small. Just tried to move my eyes. To my surprise, I could. I looked away.

"Look at me you harlot. You slut. You're a dirty slut and you'll never be anything else." He spat on me as he spoke. Just like old times. It took me longer than I would have liked, but I eventually found the strength and the words I needed.

"Maybe not. But you're dead and I'm alive so I guess I've got a shot in hell, don't I?"

With ample mobility now, I grabbed the sizzling frying pan off the stove and hauled it upside his head. Oil, garlic, and chicken went flying with him into the corner and came to rest next to a broom. A broom and my father's feet.

Where the hell had he come from?

"Kathryn why did you do that? He was a good man. He was just trying to fuck you. You should have let him."

It took great restraint not to take the frying pan to him too but I had to get to Sadie. I raced into the hallway leading to the living room and everything was different now. Sadie was still screaming, but the sound came from every direction. All echo and reverberation. I thought for a minute everything might just be in my head.

I chose a direction and ran. When I reached the end of the hall, the door was locked. I turned and ran to the other end. That door was locked too. I tore at the knob to no avail. Sadie was dying and I couldn't get to her. I was useless, just like Martin said. I'd never be anything but a dirty slut.

I pounded the door screaming out for Sadie and kept trying the knob, but it wouldn't budge. Exhausted, I fell to the floor weeping. Then two hands snaked their way around my waist and pulled me up. He hissed in my ear.

"Don't fight me, Katie. You'll alwaysssss loooooooossssse."

I grabbed the doorknob and held on with everything I had. That bastard wasn't going to take me again.

"No!"

"Kate. It's okay." His voice was higher, far away. I didn't recall kicking him in the balls, my signature move, but when I got a good shot I would be sure to. He yanked me loose from the door. I flailed to free myself from his grip, but found I had no more strength.

Martin dragged me thrashing down the hall past my father. I noticed how old he looked. How frail. All wrinkles and sagging skin. Gravity, in every way, had taken its toll on him. His eyes were devoid of color and his teeth were rotting. It didn't seem possible he was my father.

"Daddy, help me! You have to help me! It's what you're supposed to do. He's going to hurt me. Please, do something!"

I beat my fists against Martin and noticed how small they'd become. How small I'd become. I was eleven again.

"Why won't you do anything? Why didn't you do anything?" I

screamed at my father. He looked away. "I hate you!"

Martin stole me away down the hall and out into the frigid blackness of the night. My father watched him take me without a word.

I grabbed one of Martin's bony arms with both hands and twisted back and forth giving him an Indian burn. Chloe used to give me these relentlessly if I dared breach her sacred bedroom sanctum. I always wondered what she was hiding in there that would bring her to such violent measures. I realized after she left she wasn't hiding anything. She'd just enjoyed torturing me.

"Kate, please wake up, that, ow! Stop it. That hurts. God, I need my arm."

I was yanked out of the dark tunnel of my dream and deposited back in the warm front seat of Carolyn's car, twisting her arm. "Oh god. What am I...? What did I...?"

Carolyn jerked her arm back to her side. "I think you and Sadie had a bad—"

"My hand!"

Startled by Sadie's scream, I looked back to see her tugging on one arm with the other. What Carolyn must have thought of us.

"It's okay, honey. You're safe," I said. Still coming out of my own sleep/dream haze I hoped that sounded motherly.

"I'm so sorry Carolyn."

Sadie was agitated and wouldn't stop yelling, so I unbuckled my seatbelt and turned around, preparing to hurdle the seat into the back.

"Do you want me to stop?" Carolyn asked. I looked over at her, and in the yellow glow of the dashboard lights I saw the fear in her eyes. We'd done our best to freak her right the hell out.

"No. We're...fine. We don't usually...I'll just..." I couldn't seem to create a coherent thought so I stopped trying.

I climbed over the seat, headed for Sadie in the back, but halfway there my ass hurtled into Carolyn's face when she swerved to miss something in the road. It wasn't good for either of us and I tried to rectify it as quickly as possible. I wouldn't have blamed her if she'd pulled over right there and dumped us both out onto the pavement without looking back.

"I'm so sorry, Carolyn."

"It's...okay," she said. Her quiet, marshmallowy laugh belied her obvious frustration with having a total stranger's trunk up in her grill.

Sadie's screeching got worse, so I shot myself like a javelin over the seat into the back. A broken javelin. I crumpled into a pile next to her, crushing her half-eaten bag of pretzels.

"Mommymommy! My hand!"

When I sat up, her little arms wrapped themselves around my head. "Shhhh. Sadie, you're dreaming."

"It broke off! My hand broke!"

"You're fine, honey. It was just a bad dream." I finally gained full upright position and cradled Sadie to my chest. She was hot from her nightmare. So was I. We were both sweating.

"Is she all right?" Carolyn asked, her voice full of concern. She probably thought she'd picked up the spawn of the devil.

"She'll be fine. She's just, you know, we've both been having dreams since my mother passed. We loved her." I glanced down at Sadie, nestled into me. "You okay, now?"

"You left with Cowlin and I was alone and it got cold and my hand broke off in the fire."

"Well, it was just a...I left with Carolyn?"

"I told you I didn't want to be alone. He, he grabbed my hand and pulled me into the fire and I screamed and screamed and—"

"—and I couldn't open the door," I said, realizing exactly what it meant. She glanced up at me and we shared the recognition. "Who was he? Who grabbed you?"

"Chris," she whispered. If I had had any residual qualms about not returning her to him they were definitely gone now. I gave her a peck on her clammy forehead and scooped her onto my lap.

"It wasn't real." *Was it?* "We're going to be fine," I said and held her in the cocoon of my arms. I was thoroughly exhausted but I couldn't even think about sleeping.

"Please keep me safe, Katie," she whispered, snuggling up. It felt like she was trying to burrow her way into me. I didn't mind.

When I woke wringing poor Carolyn's arm I hadn't had time to think about anything but getting to Sadie, but now the dream was settling into my bones. I did my best to throw it out. I'd never been one for gleaning meaning from dreams and I wasn't about to start.

Martin was dead, and for all I knew my father was too. I hadn't seen or talked to him in ten years. But suddenly they were as real and present to me as Sadie's screams had been.

I tried to put it all out of my head, but my gut wouldn't leave me alone. I couldn't shake the nagging feeling our shared nightmare had been a premonition of things to come.

TEN

"Joe?" Carolyn called, setting her suitcase down. She made her way through the dark hall, but Sadie and I stayed by the door holding our things till she flicked on the light so we could see where we were going.

"Please, come in," she said. She switched on two Tiffany lamps on the end tables in the living room and everything was illuminated in a wash of soft yellow light. Toto, we were not in our dream anymore.

"Oh my God, Joe. I'm sorry it's...here, let me...Joe!"

Carolyn spun around the room like a top, whisking away dirty dishes and pizza boxes, dirty clothes and X-Boxes. Any qualms she might have had about us after the dream debacle were replaced by her obvious embarrassment over an unkempt house.

She cleared a spot on the couch for us to sit. "Please, make yourselves at home." We did, crouching close together. It was maybe sixty degrees in there, far from the sanctuary of light and warmth of our dream. I put my bag on the floor by the couch, but Sadie held tight to Matilda and her backpack.

"I'll have Joe start a fire. It warms up quickly. Let me go find him."

I spread my wings around Sadie, sheltering her in the warmth of my jacket. We both had a quiet look around the place; comforted it was nothing like the living room of our nightmare.

"Gosh, I'm not sure where he is," Carolyn said as she whipped back into the room. She gathered more junk and headed for the hallway. "I'm going to go look for him, but can I bring you back something to drink?"

I felt bad she was doing all this work for us. Felt like I should pitch in a little.

"Water would be great."

But then, it wasn't my house. And I wanted to stay as far away from the kitchen as possible. Carolyn was halfway down the hall when she called back to me.

"Oh, shoot. Kate?"

"Yeah?"

"I forgot; the phone in the living room doesn't work. You can use the one in the kitchen to call your family if you like."

Right. I'd kind of forgotten the reason we came here. What if Chloe wasn't home? God, what if she was? She probably didn't even have a license anymore. I think they take it away after the fourth or fifth drug conviction. I really didn't care to have my speculations confirmed or denied. But if Carolyn found us still sleeping in their guest room a month from now she might become a wee bit suspicious of my motives for coming there. The idea of falling into a coma for a month and letting this whole thing float away like a warm breeze appealed to me a great deal. Unfortunately I was headed in the opposite direction. Less zephyr, more category five.

"That's okay, I'll just plug my cell in out here. Thanks."

"You might have some trouble with that. We don't get very good reception here."

We were not entering that kitchen.

"All right. Well, I'll give it a go anyway."

I pulled the phone out and plugged it in. She was right. Not even a hint of a bar. Damn.

I took Sadie's hand and we approached the back of the house with trepidation. The dim hallway leading to the kitchen was like a birth canal, dark and cramped, with light at the end of the tunnel. We both came out unscathed, but I noticed Matilda had been squeezed into a little red yarn ball on the way.

"I'm with you. I'm not going anywhere." She glanced up at me. I smiled and winked, like I wasn't petrified too, and she loosened her grip on her poor doll's head.

The kitchen was empty. No Carolyn. No erstwhile underwear model husband. No lustful scent of simmering garlic and herbs, just a quaint farmhouse kitchen, everything cheerful and bright. The walls were a cool yellow and the cupboards were white with mint green trim. Mint. My stomach lurched.

"What was that?" I whipped around to face the doorway. Nothing there.

"I didn't hear anything," Sadie said, gripping my hand tighter.

In your head, Kate. Let it go. Breathe.

"Right. I'm going to stop being crazy for a minute so we can get on with this. Why don't you sit while I call?"

Sadie pulled herself up onto an old farm chair at the table while I plugged my phone in to retrieve Chloe's number. Nothing in the kitchen had a twin. Everything was mismatched and country chic. All aged and crackled. I liked the look. Used. Lived in. Like me.

I found Carolyn's phone sitting on top of an antique table near the back door. Like everything else, it was vintage. An old cherry red rotary. I liked Carolyn's style. She preferred sturdy over cheap, old over new. Things with a history, a past life.

The dial tone was a low buzzing hum. It always sounded different through that type of phone. Heavier, almost tangible. I cranked the one and listened to the dial whir and click quickly back in place. That sound returned me to a better time in my life. It was something I wanted to share.

"Sadie, do you want to dial for me?"

"Why?"

"Have you ever used a phone like this?"

"I don't think so. Is it magical?"

I'd asked my mother something similar when she offered first dialing privileges to me on our old black rotary. I thought maybe the *phone* would spit bunnies out its bottom if the damn Crepe Myrtle wouldn't.

"Not really..." But that wasn't true either. There was something magical about it. Something simple and easy that harkened back to a quieter time. Waiting for the dial to finish its voyage around the face of the phone taught you patience. Something I was lacking in almost every aspect of my life now. Something most people of my generation were lacking. Fast food and video games were to blame for it all.

"...but it is more fun to dial. Here." I lifted the phone and set it on the table in front of her. When it touched down the delicate bell inside whispered a faint high note. It made me think of ZuZu and her petals and the idea of angels getting their wings every time a bell rings. "I'll tell you the number and you dial. Ready?"

"Ready."

The homey kitchen helped relieve us of any residual dream-fear we had. We were comfortable now. There was still no sign of Carolyn, but I thought I'd heard some pointed whispering from a distant room, maybe the basement, when I was rummaging around in my purse. Low mutterings probably about our unexpected arrival.

"One."

Sadie glanced up at me wondering what to do. She'd obviously never seen a phone like that before.

"Just put your finger in the hole by the one, right on top of the dot, and pull down."

Whir, click.

"Good."

She squealed with delight.

"Wait for the big numbers. That's when it gets really good." She probably still hoped a bunny would make an appearance though.

"Nine. Oh, this is a good one." Whiiiiiiiiiiiiiiiiiir, click. "Seven." Whiiiiiiiiiiiir, click. Sadie's lips curled into a grin after each dial, like a lily blooming upside down.

"Big finish. Zero." Whiiiiiiiiiiiiiiiiiiiiiiiir, click. Somehow in the thirty seconds it took to dial my sister's phone number I went home again. But this time, I was Mommy. A silly idea that would have sent me screaming off into the hills before. Before Sadie.

"That was neat. I like dialing."

"Good. You'll be my official dialer from now on."

It was ringing. Oh boy. People talk about butterflies in the stomach. Those sweet twinges of nervousness, their little fluttering wings tickling your insides. My experience was different. Felt like two pterodactyls engaging in the Final Battle in there.

The cord on the phone was long enough to travel to Spain and back with a little left over for a short stroll through the park, so I paced the perimeter of the room while it rang trying not to get tangled up in things like chairs and the lies I was about to tell. Five rings and counting. Could it be possible she was screening? Was she a screener now?

Carolyn appeared from thin air just as Chloe's machine picked up. I smiled hoping she wouldn't suspect anything. How could I be guilty of lying if I was smiling at the same time?

"I'm not here. You probably wish you were since you're calling me. Too bad for both of us. Not. Leave a message."

Chloe. She'd always sounded an inch from angry, but this message wended along the path to just barely irritable. And it was a different one than the day before so that was positive. At least she wasn't in prison.

The beep. I'd made my way back to the rotary base just in time to hang up without being seen. Carolyn was busy at the fridge pulling out a water pitcher along with a carton of orange juice. I pushed the little white receiver button down and picked up the base so I could carry it with me as I strolled around the kitchen.

"Hey, sis. How's everybody?" Mmmm. Too cheerful. Take it down a notch, Kate. "Yeah. Well, did..." Shit. What did I call my brother? "Did he, did Fred! Did Fred get there yet? Good 'cause he's going to need to fix my jeep. We broke down on eighty-four. Yeah, I know, right?" Good God. Was I sixteen? "Well, luckily a very kind woman named Carolyn offered us a ride to her place in Fruitland, and that's where we are now. Yeah. So, I know you're kinda night blind, but could you come get us tonight? We've already imposed enough on this poor lady." The Indian Burn and Ass in Carolyn's Face incidents floated through my consciousness like two wet rags upside the head, one after the other.

"Oh. Huh. Really? Wow. Well, and nobody else has a car? Or a license? What about Uncle Harry?" I was having fun. Although, I did still feel a violent urge to slam the phone down and expose myself as a fraud. What was it about this woman that made me want to spill my shit? Maybe it wasn't her. Maybe I was just becoming more available to the idea of spilling it. Like with Officer Patrick West.

"When did he—hysterical blindness? Oh god. Because of mom? Wow. I mean, I know it was sudden, but—so no one can— right. Hold on. Carolyn, I'm so sorry to have to ask this, but no one can come for us tonight. I hate to impose—"

"You're welcome to stay. It's not a problem. I'm Joe."

Carolyn glanced over at him from the sink where she was pouring the water. It was like she'd just found out her kid had given back the wallet with all the money still safely tucked inside.

Joe sent a cursory smile and nod my way, then set his sights on Sadie. When his gaze met hers he softened. Catching himself staring, he dove into the refrigerator. Probably his way of watching traffic. He was a good-looking man but he was not, nor had he ever been, an underwear model. To my delight, he was nothing like Martin either. His deep laugh lines and the messy dish-water blonde hair tiptoeing on his shoulders telegraphed the impression he was a free spirit, loose and fun.

"Yes, Kate. Whatever you need. You're welcome to stay," Carolyn said.

"Really? Wow." Boy was I a shit.

"Chloe? What time will your car be done tomorrow? That late? Well, so what time—all right. Yeah. I'll see you then. Kisses all around. Right. Love you. Bye." I hung up feeling both proud of, and thoroughly disgusted with, myself.

"Well, I guess we should make some supper. You two must be starving," Joe said.

"Thank you both so much. Really. Thank you."

"It's no problem. We're happy to have the company," Carolyn said. I wondered if she spoke for Joe. But maybe I was wrong about what they'd been discussing before. Maybe it wasn't about us at all.

"That's right. It's not often I get to cook for four," Joe said. Erstwhile chef? Somebody hit the brakes in my head and my stomach smashed into the dashboard.

"Oh, do you do most of the cooking?" I tried to force a natural tone, but when I force it I end up sounding like Shelly Duvall.

"He's really wonderful. I told him he should've been a chef instead of an architect."

Architect? Like my father.

"I enjoy designing things. With food, it's just a different kind of designing. It's a meditative act, really."

"And I get to reap the rewards of his meditation."

"It's a win-win situation," he said.

Boy, they sure did seem happy. The way they were acting reminded me of a man I once met at an Overeater's Anonymous meeting. Charlie Dunkum. He'd come to every meeting wearing a huge grin and too tight pants to show how happy he was with his progress. He was the fake-it-till-you-make-it guy. If I pretend happy to everyone else, maybe it'll eventually rub off on me.

I'd always had problems with *genuinely* cheery people too. They were suspect. *Why are you so happy? Did you not have a childhood?*

"Would you mind if I took a shower before we eat? I just feel grubby from the road and—"

"Can I take one too, please?"

We all turned to her sitting in the chair, holding Matilda under one arm, her chin just clearing the tabletop.

"Of course you can, sweetheart."

"Thank you, Cowlin. You're Joe, I'm Sadie."

Joe smiled and squatted down in front of her.

"Well, yes I am. Pleased to meet you, Sadie." He held his hand out to her and she put hers in it. They shook and she giggled. It felt like some unspoken deal had just been made.

"What's your friend's name?"

"Matewda."

"Matilda? Well, that's a nice name. I had an Aunt Matilda once. She had a funny voice. Sounded like a frog."

He croaked for Sadie and she giggled again. It was clear he loved children. There was no faking there. He had that fatherly thing about him. I knew then he and Carolyn had a child. Or had

had one. Or wanted one desperately. You see this kind of fawning all the time with people like that. Mostly with people who want dogs. It's not as socially acceptable to tell a stranger on the street how much you want a child while you're cooing over theirs. They just might think you're planning some kind of *Raising Arizona* or *Kathryn Denai* hijinks and will generally cut the conversation short after you've explained how your body is attacking your husband's sperm.

Sadie liked Joe. Her giggle was proof she felt comfortable with him. Safe. I, on the other hand, felt like I'd just been sucker punched in the gut. But maybe that feeling wasn't jealousy at all. Maybe it was good old fashion fear because I'd realized we shouldn't have given them our real names. I guess it was a testament to their hospitality, I'd almost forgotten I was a wanted woman.

"Does Matilda like chocolate?"

Now he was just pandering.

"No, she likes strawberry, but I like chocolate."

"Not before dinner, munchkin," I said. Someone had to pretend to be responsible there.

"Sorry," he said more to her than me, like it was their private little deal.

"Let's get you two set up in the guestroom," Carolyn said as she headed for the hallway. I think she was sucker punched by the same nasty green fiend that got me.

"Great. Come on, honey. Let's leave Joe to his business."

"Can I help?" Sadie asked Joe.

"Sure," he said through a sudden grin.

"But I thought you wanted to take a shower?" I said, trying to keep her focused.

"I do."

"Well, let's do that then. You can help after dinner."

"Kay."

It was as if I'd peed on Matilda and set her on fire. Sadie's face hung down to her feet as she dismounted the chair.

"Bye bye, Joe. I'm glad to meet you."

"I'm glad to meet you too, Sadie. See you soon."

"Thank you again, Joe. I'm Kate. We weren't technically introduced." I kept my distance from him. Didn't want to give the wrong impression. He took a step toward me and extended his hand to shake, but I just waved awkwardly and fumbled back toward the door.

"Nice to have you both here, Kate."

"Thanks." I grabbed Sadie's hand and stumbled out of the room, just missing the doorway with my face. All grace.

We found Carolyn straightening the living room again. She was right about the fire. She couldn't have started it more than a minute before we came out and already the room was toasty. Felt very much like a real home.

I collected my bag from beside the couch and we followed Carolyn up the creaky stairs. The guest room was similar in décor to the rest of the house. Carolyn would have made Rachel Ashwell jealous.

An ancient armoire sat in the corner, its door open revealing an antique lead mirror hanging on the inside. Two thick mahogany nightstands from the Middle Ages flanked both sides of the queen bed. A quilt was stretched across the foot of it. I wondered if her mother or her grandmother had hand stitched it. Or if she had. It certainly wasn't bought online from Quilts-R-Us. This was authentic, like everything else in her house, except her happiness. Mountains of pillows were stacked on top of the bed leaning against the wrought iron headboard. There were a few vintage needlepoint pillows in front and one caught my attention. Sitting there innocently in the center of it all, the words reached out and bitch slapped me, "You Have A Good Life, Use It Well." The pillow was beige and the words were stitched in red with a mini-rose trim boxing them in. I felt pretty boxed in myself right then.

Was Someone trying to tell me Something?

Carolyn saw me gawking at it. I didn't know if my expression made her feel self-conscious about her capacity for decorating, or if she just always explained her pillows to strangers, but she was determined to tell me the story behind it.

"This is my favorite pillow," she said, fetching it off the bed and bringing it even closer. Now I could see every little red stitch of *good life, use well.*

"I found it at a yard sale in Salt Lake when I was visiting my sister. I just thought it had a great message, you know?"

I didn't respond.

"Are you all right, Kate?"

"Whussa matter, Katie?"

Carolyn glanced down at Sadie, then back to me with a quizzical look.

"Oh, I'm fine. Sorry. She's going through that phase. You

know, who's Mom? It's all Katie this, Katie that. Right, munch-kin?" I flicked Sadie's little bunny slope nose and she giggled.

"Right."

"Chelsea went through that. She was a little younger than Sadie, about three. She couldn't quite say my name. It came out more like Karen."

The room got still. Sadie and I both waited for Carolyn to say more, but she was lost in her memories. She squeezed the pillow to her chest and held it there for a few uncomfortable seconds. Tears welled in her eyes and I wanted to leave her so she could feel what she needed to in private, but I figured the sound of me running away might wrench her from the moment she'd slipped into.

"Cowlin's sad," Sadie whispered, but not quietly enough. It yanked Carolyn back to her present reality.

"Gosh, I'm sorry." She wiped her eyes and threw the pillow on the bed. It landed face down, showing a small purple heart stitched in the middle. An odd color. The Purple Heart of Valor for using your good life well.

"So, the towels, bathroom is...there are toilets, towels in the toilet cabinets. If you use soap it's the cabinet over the shower sink."

Wow. The Disconnect. I'd experienced that phenomenon so many times I'd lost count, but I'd never seen it happen to some-one else so up close and personal. For me it usually happened talking to a cute guy or after I'd had too much sugar. The scien-tific evidence that my tongue was in any way attached to my brain disappeared and I was left with a mishmash of unfinished, incoherent twaddle. She had it bad. I felt a growing kinship with Carolyn, poor thing.

"Great. That's, we'll be fine. I'm sure you're exhausted after driving all day. I don't want to keep you from resting if you need to," I said.

"Good. Yeah. Good. I'll just, I'll be down in the fire if you need anything."

"Thanks again." I wanted to reach out to her. To hold her and let her weep if she needed to. I wanted to do something. But I did nothing.

"Thank you, Cowlin." Thank God for Sadie. She raced over to Carolyn as she was almost through the door and yanked on her hand. "Thank you."

"You're welcome, Sadie."

They stood and looked at each other for an unnervingly long time, for me at least. *They* seemed very much settled in it. Never a quitter, Sadie tried to get Carolyn to pick her up. She didn't, but she did squat down to Sadie's level after she came back from wherever her babbling had kept her. She still shied away from any physical contact though. Of course Sadie remedied that.

"I like you." She puckered up and kissed Carolyn's pale cheek. It took her off guard and before she gained use of her body again Sadie wrapped her tiny arms around her neck. She struggled against reciprocating, but gave in when she realized Sadie wasn't planning to let go any time soon.

"Thank you, Sadie," she whispered. From across the room I could hear the emotions trembling through her voice. "I like you too." Carolyn yanked away from Sadie just as the tears came. She didn't want to share any more of her grief with strangers. I had to respect that. It was hard enough sharing it with yourself.

"Have a good shower," she choked out then dashed down the hall to what I assumed was the master bedroom. The door didn't slam like I expected it to. Just clicked shut with a distinct authority. Like it had decreed it wouldn't be opened again. At least not while Kate and Sadie were staying here.

"I didn't mean to make her sadder," Sadie said, turning to me. Her face had drooped to her knees.

"No, of course not. You tried to help her. It was..." Everything I couldn't bring myself to do? "...so good." I picked her up and set her down on the bed. "Can we take this off now?" She nodded and helped me take her backpack off. I put it on the chair in the corner and went back to the bed, squatting in front of her so we were on the same level.

"Sadie, you have...a beautiful heart. I don't want you to feel bad because she cried. Honey, you didn't do that. She cried because, well, because of other things we don't know about."

"I know."

"Oh. Okay." And here I was thinking I was giving the parental equivalent of an Oscar winning performance.

"But I think I make her sad."

Whoever said children and animals don't intuitively understand things was a moron. They are more in tune with raw emotions than any adult I've ever known. It's because they don't have all the years of shit and disappointment and pain to pad and dull and numb their senses.

"No, no you don't. Whatever she's sad about makes her sad."

Quite a mouthful of profundity. "Let's just take a shower. We'll both feel better after we're clean and cozy in our PJs."

Of course neither of us had PJs exactly. I'd be making do with a ratty old pair of shorts I'd had almost since birth and my favorite nearly see-through tank top. Sadie just wore the same clothes. She hadn't brought anything else. Just a couple changes of underwear. It made me realize we'd definitely need to do some shopping as soon as we landed in Portland.

There were too many things to think about. Clothes, food, school, Chloe, transportation, cops, jail, oh God. If I thought about it all I might make myself sick, so I put it out of my mind and concentrated on the task in front of me.

"I'm hungry but I don't want the pretzels."

"I know. We'll eat right after we take a shower. Joe's cooking dinner for us right now."

"I like Joe. He's good." She said it with the authority of an eighty-year-old shaman. Like she *knew* something.

"Yes, he seems like a lovely person. Now let's go get cleaned up."

We were in for a pleasant surprise when we walked into the bathroom. In keeping with the rest of the house everything had personality, but the shining glory was the claw-foot tub sitting grandly next to the picture window. It was enormous. I'd seen some tubs in my day but this one dwarfed them all. It must have been eight feet long and three feet deep. A bucket of bath oils and accessories sitting in the corner made the whole picture too enticing to pass up.

"How 'bout we take a bubble bath?"

Sadie's face lit up like a crack addict who's found a forgotten stash. "I love bubboo baths! Row row row your boat gently down the stream...sing along with me, Katie!"

It's amazing what a tub of hot water can do for the human spirit. Sailing in lavender-scented bubble clouds, I forgot for that blissful half hour all the assorted goodies I was wanted for, content to bask in Sadie's fizzy laughter and the stillness of the night for as long as time would allow.

ELEVEN

The aroma of Joe's homemade tomato sauce enveloped me when I opened the bedroom door to go back to the kitchen. We ventured down scrubbed and shiny, bellies on empty.

"I hope you're hungry because I made a lot," Joe said, turning to greet us, tongs in hand.

"I'm super hungry!" Sadie said. "I'm going to eat all of it."

"Excellent."

Joe wore his Boston Red Sox cap backwards and an apron that shouted "CHEF!" in big bold red print. "We're having spaghetti and meatballs. I figured that would be fairly safe," he said.

Carolyn sat at the table folding cloth napkins. She glanced at us when we arrived then went back to her work.

"Sgetti! I love sgetti and meatbows!"

"Excellent again!" Joe said. He dumped the pasta into a large bowl and put it on the table next to a huge vat of sauce.

"Can I help with anything?" I asked, more to seem gracious than to actually be helpful. I was less than adept in the kitchen.

"Actually, yes."

Damn. I wasn't giving off a strong enough useless vibe. They both said it at the same time.

"Ladies first," Carolyn said. "Would you mind setting the placemats and silverware around? We'll use these napkins."

"Sure."

The placemats were stacked on the table with the silverware, so I took the folded cloth napkins from her and set about my task. This I could handle. Carolyn went to the fridge and busied herself pouring water while Joe put the finishing touches on a salad by the sink.

"Can I help?" Sadie asked, standing in the middle of the big room with nothing to do.

"You sure can. Come on over," Joe chimed in before I could answer. I was going to have her help me set the table, but he got her first.

It's not a competition, Kate.

"Be careful, it might be heavy."

"I'm strong."

"All right. Arms out," he said.

Sadie did as she was told and Joe placed the salad bowl between her little sticks. She held it tight till she arrived at the table then I had to help her heft it up.

"Teamwork," he said. "I like it."

We were a little like a team, or a family. The four of us working together reminded me of what an actual family might be like. Without the stranger part. I enjoyed the bustle, everyone having a task. Sadie did too. I could tell she felt useful.

And then came grace. The closest my family had ever come to it, at least when my mother was still alive, was thanking her for not burning the chicken again. After she died, my father found God. And I lost everything.

He'd joined the Church of Christ one Tuesday after Chloe ran away. I came home from school that day and found his note on the dining room table. "Gone to study the Word of God. Be back later." He never really came back.

In my limited time being human, I've realized people turn to God for many different reasons. They need something to get them through a bad break-up. They need something to explain their existence on the planet. They need something to believe in other than sports or sex. The common denominator is need. We all need. My father needed to forget. He went to God to forget about his former life and start a new one.

The more comfortable he became with the members of his church "family", the more he invited them over to our house to study. Soon he was hosting three times a week or more.

Martin Flemming was a member of my father's group. Not to paint a reckless picture of Christians, I found the rest of the congregants to be loving, supportive people. The difference between them and Martin was his burning desire to include everyone in Greg's household in the teachings of Christ. He claimed to lead a Bible class for kids my age every weekend at his house and asked my father if he'd like to bring me by. My father welcomed whatever time away he could get. His favorite daughter had run away and the one left only reminded him on a daily basis of the love he'd lost. He did his best to lose me too.

My lessons began a couple months after I turned eleven. A couple months after the night my mother's ghost apologized to me as she rocked in our chair. Maybe she hadn't apologized for dying after all. Maybe she knew then what would happen but couldn't do anything about it.

Martin was smart enough not to pull his dick out in front of me on our first day. That would have been bad form. No, he gained my trust first. He'd already gained my father's, although, I think at that point my father would have released me to a complete stranger if one had shown up at the door asking to borrow a child.

There were no other children at Martin's Bible session that first day, not even his own. His wife had taken his two daughters out shopping for the whole afternoon, he'd said.

"Greg! Glad you could bring her," Martin roared from the front door as he opened it to us. I should have known then, by his too-honest-to-be-honest tone, something was off. "Hello, Katie. Happy to have you. This is going to be fun. Come on in. That a girl. So she'll be ready 'bout four, Greg. I'll give you a buzz if we're going to be long."

We weren't long until a few months later, but my father didn't notice. By then I was walking home on a regular basis or Martin would drop me off on his way to the five o'clock service. I'd be welcomed home by an empty house. Greg would already be gone to church or his study group. The only time my father ever asked how I liked my Sunday excursions was after the very first one.

"Kathryn, did you enjoy your lesson?" He'd started calling me Kathryn shortly after my mother died, when he called me anything at all. No more Bits or Tits or Katie or anything giving the impression he actually cared about me.

"It was fine. Daddy, you can call me Bits if you want to. I know I told Mommy to tell you not to but—"

"Kathryn you're eleven years old, it's time I call you by your birth name." And that was the end of the discussion. He never asked about my Sundays with Martin again.

The first time you see an erect penis will always stay with you. Martin's was not my first. One night when I was six I got up to go to the bathroom and caught my father sneaking upstairs from the kitchen carrying the fresh strawberries and chocolate my mother had bought earlier that day. He'd turned on the hall light so his everything was in full shining view as I rounded the corner from the bathroom. I froze and so did he. Then he dropped the fruit and chocolate, whipped his hands over his crotch and told me, in the sweetest, tightest voice I'd ever heard, to go back to bed. To his credit, his hands didn't fully cover it.

And he had long fingers.

That night I went to bed feeling sorry for my father. I couldn't imagine having to lug that big stick around. I thought it must get in the way of *everything*. I'd also realize later that Mommy was to blame for it.

I was to blame for Martin's. That's what he told me the first time I saw it. Finished with the lesson that day, he'd invited me into his den to see his collection of butterflies. He knew about my passion and even though I was disgusted by the idea of an actual collection, with their beautiful wings pinned down to a corkboard, I was still fascinated to see all the different species he'd claimed to have. During the nine months I "studied" with Martin he'd made countless claims about myriad things and not one of them was true. When I opened the door to his den he was sitting on the couch rubbing his crotch. No butterflies around except for the ones careening in my stomach.

"Come in. Sit." His voice was raspy, thin. And he didn't stop. And I stood there watching him. I didn't try to leave. Maybe if I had, things would have been different for me.

"I want to talk to you about some very important things. Things maybe your daddy doesn't know how to explain to you."

I did not want that conversation with him. Did not want to watch him do what he would not stop doing. But I felt trapped. I didn't want him to go back to my father and tell him I was disrespectful. By then I was doing everything in my power to be a perfect daughter. A daughter any father would want. I got straight A's in school and had recently been promoted to first chair flute. I just said no to drugs and yes to Bible study. I didn't want anything to ruin my hard work. And, unfortunately, I wasn't clear about whose side my father would be on if things went bad.

"Close the door and come sit next to me, Katie." It was an order. I shut the door and sat down next to Martin and his penis. The room was musty, like it had been locked up for ages. Dim light filtered in through a set of old beige curtains barely illuminating his face. I stared straight ahead, keeping my focus on the walls. Felt like I was suffocating, like they were closing in around me, on top of me. That room became my cocoon. But, instead of a beautiful butterfly, I would emerge from my shell week after week as the same ugly worm, one giant leap closer to adulthood.

"I can't help it, Katie. You're so pretty it just makes my organ sing." He actually said that. "You should be proud. Not everybody can do this to me. It takes a special kind of lady."

Yeah, anyone without "teen" in her age yet.

The first few times he just made me watch him. After a while the fear leaked away and curiosity seeped in. I was fascinated by how much it grew. But the day he coerced me into touching it, fear surged back. I knew I shouldn't have been doing that with him and I worried about getting caught, although, I'd been going to him for four months by then and had never met or even seen anyone else in his family. It wasn't until the last day I saw him that I found out there was no family. It had all been a lie.

"Amen."

"You're s'posed to say Amen, Mommy." Sadie's voice sounded far away, but it pulled me back to dinner.

"You all right, Kate? You're white as a sheet," Joe said.

I reached out for my water glass and nearly tipped it over with my quaky hand. No more trips down Memory Lane for me. At least not at dinner.

"I'm fine. I think I might be getting a little sick. There's, I have...scratch in my throat."

"Like me."

"Yes, honey. Like you. But you're feeling better, right?"

"Yes." She sniffled. "A little."

"Can we get you anything? Do you want some medicine?" This from Joe. Men always want to fix things. It's cute.

"No thank you. That's really nice. I'm sure I'll be fine." Truth was I did feel like I was getting sick. My limbs were heavy and achy and even after the hundred-degree bath we took I still got chilled.

"Bless you!"

This from everyone. I sneezed again and nearly spit my water all over the s'getti and meatbows.

"Thank you. Sorry. I'm just going to, where's your bathroom?"

"Down the hall to the left. The light is, there's a, well why don't I just show you," Carolyn said.

"Oh you don't need to. I can—"

"No no. It's no trouble."

Did she think I wasn't up to the task of a light switch? Hard to say, but I was in no mood to argue so I let her be my escort down the hall. She walked ahead of me into the dark bathroom and I could just make out her form reaching in the air for something. When she found the pull string the light flicked on.

"Thanks."

"Kate, I wanted to apologize for what happened earlier. I'm not usually like that. I just—"

"You know you really don't have to, we all have our—"

"I don't want you to think, well, I'm not crazy or anything, you know?"

"Of course not—"

"I'm—"

"You really don't need to—"

"We lost our daughter to leukemia last year. She was Sadie's age. It's been...difficult."

Wow. I figured she might drop that bomb sometime, but I didn't think she'd do it in the middle of her bathroom.

"I'm so sorry." What else do you say? *Hey, you want my kid?*

"Thank you. I wanted...sometimes it hits me harder than others. I felt I needed to explain that."

"Listen, you don't need to explain anything. We all have... things."

"Thank you. For understanding. Well..."

And then she hugged me. That was unexpected. I suppose I should have seen it coming since she took a step in my direction and extended her arms, but it still caught me off guard. I almost didn't know what to do. I couldn't help shake the feeling that I was hugging my mother. Even though Carolyn couldn't have been more than five years my senior she seemed older, more put together, her previous word salad notwithstanding. And the rosy scent of my mother hovered around her. Or maybe it didn't at all and I was just imagining it, needing it.

We separated and when it should have been awkward, that moment after pulling apart where you feel like you should make eye contact but don't really know what to say, it was.

"Well, I'll let you..."

"Right, thanks."

She left and took the roses with her. I splashed warm water over my face and inspected my worry line, the deep fissure cracking through the space between my eyebrows. It had grown deeper since grace. I pressed it with my finger to smooth it out, knowing that wasn't what I needed to do to get rid of it.

I sat down to pee and midstream I had a panic attack worrying that Sadie, alone, wouldn't remember our story.

"Shit!" I tried to wipe before I stopped and got an unpleasant hand wash. "Shit!" The bathroom wasn't far away from the kitchen; they probably heard me in there yelling at my shit, just like the kids on Halloween.

I tried to appear calm and unhurried when I got back to the kitchen, but I don't think I succeeded.

"Everything all right, Kate? You seem out of breath." That Joe was an astute sonofabitch.

"Fine. Good. Yeah. What were you all just talking about?"

That was good. Subtle. I sat. And waited. Why were they staring at me? Oh God. Did I just say something very bad? I had a nasty habit of unconsciously using expletives at inappropriate times. This was probably one of them. Damn it, I really did need to curb that swearing thing.

"Uh, well, Sadie was just explaining why you were driving instead of flying to your mother's funeral," Joe said.

"Oh? And-what-did-she-say?" Excellent progress, Kate.

"It's 'cause I don't like flying!"

Her zeal caught everyone off guard I think. We all had a little chuckle and adored the munchkin for a moment.

"Well, that's it, isn't it. The minute we taxi out on the runway she goes into hysterics. It's ugly. I mean ugly. That little dip after takeoff, you know where your stomach drops into the seat just after the wheels leave the ground, that's the part that really gets her going. It's like a, like a, baby coyote ululating over its dead mother. I mean I, you know, I personally, I like it. Not the screaming. The feeling, you know, of your stomach dropping like you're on a roller coaster, and that moment where anything can happen, but she just screams bloody murder. So, yeah, that's pretty much why we didn't fly." Very subtle. Good work, Kate.

"You said a word, ululating. I've never heard it. What does it mean?" Carolyn asked.

"Oh, it's just a sort of, wailing. You know, when you, or someone, anyone really can, it's crying. Or celebrating. It's one of those words that can mean both. You know, screaming or wailing in agony or pleasure. It's a strange word, really. I don't think I'll use it anymore. Wow that spaghetti looks good."

I took a big, sloppy mouthful and tried to tone my shit down and ignore the sadness oozing from Carolyn and Joe. He took her hand under the table and they both stared at their plates. The stillness of the room reminded me of my old house after Chloe left. The only sound I heard was the clicking of my jaw as I chewed. Sometimes it did that when I was nervous. Or tired. Or breathing.

I made it halfway through that mouthful before I realized I was masticating little bits of dead cow. Joe had prepared a lovely meat sauce. I didn't really have a choice but to continue eating it. I couldn't spit it out. That would be bad form even for me. It had been seventeen years since I'd consumed any kind of meat and I felt queasy. If I could just get what I had in my mouth down I'd come up with a great excuse for not eating the rest. I couldn't tell him the truth; it might hurt his feelings.

Over the snapping of my jaw and sudden clinking of Sadie's fork came a scratching sound at the back kitchen door. It was subtle, but unanswered it grew into an almost hysterical clawing. There were giant mythological beasts at the door frothing at the mouth to come in and eat me whole.

"All right, all right. Settle down fellas."

Or maybe they were just two giant slobbering golden retrievers with wiggly butts. Joe opened the door. They charged in...

"Doggies!"

...and beelined to Sadie, overwhelming her with kisses. One on each side. She sat there and took it, squealing with delight. I'm not sure how she was able to breathe through all the slobber.

"Butch! Sundance! No!"

"I don't think she minds," I said to Carolyn, giggling along with Sadie. My mouth was empty when I spoke. Thank God for distractions. Except when the distractions want to devour me too. They came at me together and tried to climb up on top of me with their collective hundred and sixty pounds of waggly love. I was helpless to resist. The distant sound of Sadie still squealing penetrated the layer of thick, cold fur and wet tongues on top of me. What was most surprising about the whole thing was that I too was squawking with glee at this undivided canine attention.

"Boys off! Joe, help me," Carolyn said, trying to pry them off me.

He grabbed a can from the counter and shook it once. "All right you two, enough!" A loud crunching sound came from the can, like there were marbles or pennies in it. They hopped down off me and sat at attention in front of Joe. I could breath again but part of me wished he'd let them stay a little longer. The interest was flattering.

"I'm so sorry, Kate. They didn't scratch you did they?" Carolyn asked.

"We're fine. Good, actually. They're beautiful boys."

"They don't usually react like that to people. They're kind of shy actually," Joe said, pouring food in their bowls. They sat quiet and still, panting and waiting for their dinner.

"I like the doggies! I want one. Please." She directed this straight to me, like I was able to do something about it. Like the "please" would make it impossible to say no.

"I know honey. Someday."

"How 'bout tonight you have two?" Joe said.

"Yes please."

"We can bring their beds into your room and they'll sleep with you. If it's all right with Mom."

It took me a few seconds to realize he was talking to me.

"Yes please please please!" Sadie said.

"Oh, well, I suppose." I couldn't wait to have a slumber party with the dogs.

"Yay! Doggies in the bedroom!"

"So, are you both fans of the movie?" I asked.

"More like she's obsessed with Robert and Paul," Joe said, teasing his wife.

"Yes, I may have a bit of a thing for Redford and Newman, but tell Kate what you named your truck."

"Oh, come on."

"Tell her."

"No."

"Tell. Her."

Joe sighed and rolled his eyes, not wanting to divulge. "Angelina." His voice was so low and deep I could barely make out what he'd said.

"And our boat?"

He smiled.

"And our cat?"

Joe pinched Carolyn's butt and she squeaked. This was definitely not pretend. They were actually enjoying each other.

"Do you hang a vial of motor oil on your rear view mirror?"

They didn't get it and both cocked their heads sideways like dogs when you talk to them.

"You know, the vial of Billy Bob's blood she used to—"

"Oh no, no. See he's into her post Billy Bob, post tonsil hockey with her brother."

"Carolyn Murphy!"

"What? It's true. You're into the humanitarian, Goodwill Ambassador, adopts half the world's orphaned children Angelina."

"Yes. Yes I am. Not that a little leather now and then is a total turn off," he said and winked at her.

"Joe!" She swatted him on the chest and he hugged her.

"I meant for you, my love." He feathered her lips with little kisses. They were cute together, giddy like teenagers, in their own little snow globe and someone or something had just turned it right side up again.

Sadie stood behind Butch and Sundance watching them eat. She giggled and nestled her hands up under her shirt when Butch stopped eating momentarily to give her a sloppy kiss on the cheek. She stayed there with her hands buried letting him plaster her face with kisses and stray food.

Joe and Carolyn gazed at her. There was something familiar about it; I saw it in the way they glanced at each other then back at Sadie.

"Joe," Carolyn said like a question.

"I know, babe."

The sadness surrounding Carolyn like a thick fog, lifted. Her eyes shined with new life and it had everything to do with Sadie. A twinge of jealousy struck me. I felt an overwhelming sense of proprietary right to that little girl, like I was the only one she could touch that way.

I also felt invisible. So I caught my plate, piled high with spaghetti and meaty sauce, on the edge and tipped it over onto the floor. I watched it crash and splatter and looked up to see everyone staring at me. Two birds, one plate.

"Oh God, I'm so sorry. I'm such a klutz!"

"No, no. It's fine," Carolyn said, knocked clear of her sudden euphoria. She rushed to the counter to retrieve a roll of paper towels as I bent down to scoop up the mess, but Butch and Sundance beat us both to it. They swooped in and sucked up like two furry Bissell cleaners.

"Boys, no! Joe, get them—"

"They'll be all right. Let's just see what they do."

"What if they—"

"Let's just see."

I was worried they'd cut their floppy tongues on the broken shards of the plate too, but somehow they managed to navigate the mess and emerge fat, happy and unscathed. They left the pieces clean and ready to be swept into the trash. Good doggies.

"Who needs a mop when you've got The Boys, eh?"

Carolyn scowled at Joe and pitched the paper towels into the sink. Then she rushed over to the dogs and checked both of their mouths while they finished their own food.

"Good boys. They cleanded the mess."

"Yes, *they* are good boys," Carolyn said. And just like that the fog descended again.

"Kate, do you need anything?"

Did she mean in general? Did she want a list?

"I'm going to bed now, so—"

"Oh, no, we're fine. Thank you. For everything."

She glared at Joe as she headed for the door.

"Come on. They're fine. It was just, I wanted to wait and see if—"

"You always *want to wait and see if*...It didn't really work out last time did it?"

I saw it in Joe's eyes; she'd landed a solid uppercut from across the room.

"That's not fair."

And she was gone. Sadie looked at me, wondering what to do. How should I know? I bent down to clean up the mess.

"Kate, no. I'll get it. Please leave it," Joe said.

"Night Cowlin. Thank you," Sadie tried. No response.

"It's been a long day. We're going to get some sleep too," I said.

"Give me a minute and I'll get The Boys' beds ready."

"Right. Thanks." I unplugged my phone and took it with me. Fully charged, it would be good for about ten minutes if I needed it in the next day or two.

"Come on, honey. Time for bed."

Sadie took my hand and I led her out of the kitchen. Halfway down the hall her little fingers wriggled out of my grip and she raced back in to Joe. I followed her and stayed by the door, peeking in.

"Thank you, Joe," she whispered, hugging him.

"You're welcome, Chelsea."

Oh boy.

"Who's Chowsea?"

He let out a long, low sigh like he was leaking.

"I'm sorry. I didn't mean to...she was my daughter."

"Can I meet her?"

"She went away."

"Will she be back soon?"

"No. She's not coming back."

"Why?"

"Well, because, she...went to Heaven."

"Oh no. My mommy went there too."

"You mean your grandma?" Joe asked.

"Yes, her grandma. I didn't go anywhere, honey. And I'm not going to. She's tired."

"I miss her."

"I know. Come here," I said, reaching out for her.

For the first time since we'd arrived, Joe eyed me suspiciously when he handed Sadie over. If I'd stood there and told him I had just kidnapped her that day he might have been more inclined to trust me. I couldn't have seemed more dubious.

I heard Joe come into the room with the dogs' beds while we brushed our teeth in the bathroom. The door was closed, so I didn't have to face him again.

"Good night," he called.

"Night," we both returned through foamy, toothpaste mouths.

When the coast was clear, I helped Sadie climb into bed with her backpack. She kept it next to her on the pillow. The minute she was tucked in, both dogs joined her. They snuggled up close, one fuzzy head on each little thigh. It was, I imagined, just as she'd hoped it would be.

I heard voices coming from behind the door down the hall and fought the urge to go eavesdrop. For about ten seconds.

"Where you going, Katie?"

"Shhhh. You have to be very quiet. I'm just, I'll be right back."

"I'm not sleepy. Will you read my book to me?" She pulled her bag from the pillow and unzipped it. I'd been avoiding the book, partly because it was crammed in with her mother and we'd have to dust it off before I could read it, but mostly because I was nervous about reading to her. What if I wasn't good at it or I didn't do it like her mother used to? I wanted to make her happy, which was definitely a foreign and therefore scary thing for me. Best to avoid it altogether.

"I don't know, sweety. I'm pretty tired."

"But I want to know what happens to Clyde."

Damn those sad eyes. Got me every time. "We'll see. I'll be right back. You stay in bed and rest."

I tiptoed down the hall toward the room at the end. Their heated whispering floated underneath the door and out into the darkness. Fear of a squeaky floor kept my movements measured, but I felt conspicuous standing in the middle of the hall so I slipped into the room just before theirs. A yellow nightlight lit the wall next to a small pink canopy bed, casting over that section of the room either a sunny or a jaundiced aura, depending on how full or empty your glass is. Upon closer inspection I saw the light was that odd little creature, SpongeBob SquarePants. I nestled up against the wall beside the bed wondering what the hell I was doing.

"Please Joe, just drop it." Carolyn's voice sliced through the still air, startling me, as she pulled their bedroom door open. I didn't have time to get back to the guest bedroom without her seeing me, so I scanned for a place to hide. The rainbow and butterfly called to me from the closet door. I took hold of the crystal knob and twisted slowly, slipping behind it right as Carolyn stepped into the room. I left it ajar just enough to see her.

She strode in with purpose, then stopped in the middle of the room, uncertain, like she was suddenly lost in her own house. Joe stood at the doorway watching her back in the dark. He didn't say anything, just waited, watching her breathe. His face, what I could see of it in shadow, was calm, concerned.

Envy for Carolyn and her life slithered inside me. I'd never had a man care enough to stand at a door and wait for me to do whatever it was I needed to do. But there he was, all patience. He didn't step any closer, trying to comfort her in his arms, or say anything to try to fix things. He was just there, like a safety net, waiting for her to fall into him on her own. I'd never wanted a safety net more in my life.

"I'm sorry. I shouldn't have said that. It's not your fault. I know it's not." She said this to the bed. Both stayed where they were.

"I don't know how to make this better. I—God, I just didn't

think it was that serious. She wasn't showing any of the normal symptoms. We wouldn't have waited to take her if she had."

"Please drop it, Joe. There's nothing—"

"But you still hold on."

"How do you let go?" She sat down on the bed and the yellow light from SpongeBob washed over her face, making her look even sicker than she seemed to feel. Her gaze inspired him to come sit beside her. He picked her hand off her lap and cradled it between both of his.

"One breath at a time," he said.

"I wanted this to be a surprise. I wanted to be telling you something different."

"What is it? Tell me."

"I didn't go to Salt Lake just to visit Sam."

"Okay. Whatever it is, we'll get through it."

"My body is attacking you."

"Right now? I wondered what that little tingle was."

"It's not a joke, Joe."

"I'm sorry. I don't, I'm not following you."

"My body, it's, here." She pulled a folded piece of paper from her pocket and gave it to him. He took it but didn't look at it.

"Just tell me."

"We're wasting our time. I can't get pregnant."

"Oh. Well, is it, how do you know?"

"Sam, when she and Jeff couldn't get pregnant she went to this fertility expert. He moved his practice to Salt Lake a few months ago. He's one of the best in the country. I went to get some tests done."

"What are our chances?"

"Ten, maybe fifteen percent."

"So we've still got a shot?"

"In Hell."

"Well, it's still a chance. And it's never a waste of time." He winked and gave her a sly little sexy grin.

"I can't. I can't do this anymore."

"Do what?"

"Hope."

She pulled herself off the bed. Though she was thin, she seemed to weigh five hundred pounds as she slumped away from him. Her anima fell off in big, globby chunks as she left the room.

"Carolyn..."

Joe sat on the bed a few seconds longer. His transformation was fascinating. Pain carved itself around his eyes in wrinkles and darkness and the energy he'd had moments before was silenced with a breath.

"I'm going to go downstairs. Listen to the scanner. I won't be long," Joe said to the empty room as he left.

I heard him say good night to Sadie on his way down the hall. For a minute I was petrified he might ask her where I was, but he was too preoccupied to notice my absence. He shuffled his way down the stairs and I crept back to the guestroom as soon as I heard the click of their bedroom door.

Sadie was wide awake and using the dog's belly as a shelf to rest the book on as she read.

"You can read?" I said.

"A little. Will you do it now?"

188 | KELLY BYRNE

There were no more excuses.

"Just for a few minutes. We need to get some sleep."

Her face lit up when I climbed on the bed next to her and took the book. My neck was tight and my fingers tingled with the anticipation of sucking.

"Clyde the Clou—hughn hughn." I spent the next minute clearing my throat.

"You all right, Katie?"

"I'm fine." Was I? "Clyde the Cloud's Amazing Adventures. Where did you leave off?"

"Can you do from the beginning?"

"The beginning?"

"Yes please. Then it will be special with us."

I complied, hoping our special beginning would have a happy ending. Page one: a watercolor picture of Seattle. Promising. The Space Needle poked up through a cloud into the sky. The cloud had eyes and a nose and a tongue that lay limp, falling out of its mouth. A dead cloud. Promising was rapidly crumbling. There were two larger clouds off in the distance. They were chatting up a few other adult clouds. Cumulus one and all.

"Clyde the cloud was desperate for his parents to notice him. He would play lots of silly tricks to get their attention. Things he shouldn't have done that could have—oh, I get it, he's impaling himself on the top of the needle to get his parents to—"

"He's not really stuck. He's just pretending."

"Seems like a lot to go through to get their attention."

Sadie got still and stared at the book. Our discussion period was over. I read on to learn how Clyde, at the end of his little rope from neglect, decides to run away to the mystical land of Los Angeles. He'd heard some crazy stories from his friend Frankie whose cousin's brother's father told him it was the most beautiful place on earth because clouds were banned there. So he ran away to see if there was any truth to the rumors. And to see if his parents would even notice he was gone. But as soon as he crosses the state line into Oregon trouble greets him at every turn. Was this my life story or what?

"The storm was stirring up a mighty mess out in the ocean and on shore things weren't much better. West Wind had a ball whipping and spinning and just as Clyde got caught in his horrible breath being pulled out to sea, someone grabbed his tail and pulled him back to shore. Wow, lucky for him, huh?"

"I have to go pee."

Or not.

"All right. Do you need help?"

"No, silly. I can do it myself." She jumped down off the bed and scurried into the bathroom without closing the door. Was it wrong for me to wish she needed my help? She'd only been with me two days and already I wanted her to need me for everything. A little shocking.

"Look at the mooner!" she said, walking back to bed. She pointed to the moon dangling low in the sky, centered between the two sides of the window frame.

"Yep, that's the mooner." It was perfectly white. Not even a suggestion of blue. That made me a little sad.

"It's waning," she said, climbing back up on the bed.

"Is it? I don't hear anything."

"You don't hear it wane. It just does it."

"Honey, rain usually makes some kind of pitter patter sound on the roof. Especially if it's coming down hard." I felt superior for my vast experience and knowledge of rain and its effects on rooftops.

"Not waining like with water. It's shwinking."

Superiority ended abruptly. She pulled the covers up over her belly and took hold of one side of the book.

"How do you know about waning?"

"My mommy taught me about astromony."

Wow. When I was five I knew about hula-hoops and stuffed animals. Not the phases of the moon.

"The kisses are shrinking too."

"Honey, what are the kisses?" And why can't I see them?

"They're from God."

Right. When would I learn?

"Mommy said God gave them to us so when we feel upset or sad we look at the kisses and know He loves us."

Ah. That's why you have to be "down" to see them. I wanted to ask her what I was supposed to do if I was suicidal during a new moon, but I didn't have it in me.

"Do you love God?" she asked.

"Let's read some more. Where were we? Right, Clyde's on the verge of being blown out to sea. Wow, that's scary, huh? So they grabbed his tail and he was dragged all the way up through the swirling angry clouds of the storm until it was nothing but sunshine and fresh air. Clyde was higher than he'd ever been, up above everything. He could see for miles in every direction."

"I love God and I want to be Clyde's friend, Clancy." She snuggled up closer into me, almost lying on my lap. Her head rested on my belly, dropping and rising with each breath I took. I held the book with my right hand and used my left to caress her hair. It was silky and fine, like rabbit fur.

"I like it."

"What?"

"When you pet me. I like it."

That was petting? Huge relief. I'd gone in a whole other direction in my head when she'd mentioned it before and I was thrilled to know how innocent it really was. I was happy to do one thing right.

"What's that? It's bumping my head."

"It's a charm bracelet."

"It's cold. Can I see it?" She took hold of my wrist and brought it down in front of her. Brushed her tiny finger over the ceramic. "Is it special?"

I pondered the butterfly on my wrist. "Very."

"It's pretty. I like butterflies. They're my favorites. And armadillies 'cause they look funny. And doggies."

Butterflies and armadillos and dogs. All beautiful creatures to Sadie. She placed my hand back on her head and I continued to pet her.

"'Oooops,' said Clancy. She'd tripped on an air pocket and landed right in the middle of Clyde as she pulled him skyward. 'Sorry, I'm a little—'"

"Katie, I said I want to be Clancy."

"Oh, you want to read her?"

"Yes. Will you be Clyde?"

"I thought I was being Clyde."

"You have to be like a little kid."

This was what I was afraid of. Role playing. I was no good at playing myself, how could I play someone else? A child no less. I'd had such limited experience to draw on. I would have tackled being a tree with more expertise.

"Let's just read and see how we do."

"'Oooops!'"

"What's the matter?"

"I'm being Clancy. 'Oooops'..." She stopped and waited. The air in the room was cool and heavy with the snoring from The Boys. I didn't know why she'd stopped but I didn't want to cut her off so I waited for her to continue.

"Now you read the other parts till she says something else." Her voice was patient. Edifying.

"Oh. I'm sorry."

"You didn't know. I'll teach you." She reached up and patted me on the cheek with her clammy little palm. It was very sweet, but I felt totally incompetent. I was the adult. I was the one who was supposed to teach her things. But somehow it wasn't working out that way.

"She'd tripped on an air pocket and landed right in the middle of Clyde as she pulled him skyward."

"Good," she said, then looked up at me and smiled. Seriously, though, who was the adult here?

"'I'm Clancy, but pe, peep...'"

"People."

"'...people call me Cluh...'"

"Clumsy."

At that rate we wouldn't make it off the page before sunrise. Sadie sighed and buried her head under the pillow on my lap. I waited a few seconds to dive under after her. I hadn't yet spent enough time with her to discern the meaning behind all of her actions, so I didn't know if she was just taking a break or if something else was happening there. Right before I pulled the pillow off, she came up for air.

"Can I please do it by myself?" Her voice was sweet, but tight and irritated now.

"I'm sorry. I was just trying to help."

"Please let me do it on my own."

She was a sixty-two year old Indian Chief named Red Hair Knows-A-Lot reincarnated as a five-year-old Tater Tot.

"Got it. Sorry."

"Are you having fun?"

"Yes, I am." My answer was simple and true. She smiled and knelt beside me. Suddenly, she was serious and I wondered if something had just now clicked about her mother or Chris. She stared at me with intimidating intensity, tiptoeing around inside again.

"I love you, Katie." She wrapped her whole body around my head. I could feel her little heart racing. "And I always will no matter what." She whispered into my cheek. Her breath was moist and warm and smelled like a candy cane.

Nobody was more surprised than I to discover I felt the same way. I wanted to tell her but something stopped me, caught it in my throat and wouldn't let it pass. "If we're going to find out what happens to Clyde, we better get on it. It's getting late," I said instead, patting her back.

She scooted down next to me and took the left side of the book in her hand. I held the right side in mine. A team effort. If she was disappointed that I didn't return her sentiment she didn't show it.

We read for another ten minutes. I realized she was asleep when she didn't read her next line. I was a little disappointed we hadn't finished the book. I wanted to find out if Clyde would make it to sunny Lalaland and find everything he thought he was missing. I closed the book and put it on top of my bag on the floor. I would wait for Sadie.

Her eyelids fluttered in the midst of a dream and I was struck by how much she looked like an angel. Her skin glowed as if something else lived inside her. Something that had nothing to do with blood or bones. For the second time in my life, I found myself in the presence of God.

I watched her sleep for a few more minutes hoping her innocence would materialize in me through osmosis. If I could have I would have lived in that little snow globe for another week just to get a nibble of normal. I loved the flavor, like a big hunk of Belgian dark chocolate.

I turned off the light and snuggled in next to her in the darkness. Everything felt right, good. Thing about right and good, it just takes one thin, scratchy voice in the middle of the night to wake you and screw it all up.

TWELVE

"Scanner!" I bolted awake at 5:19 a.m. suddenly processing what Joe had told Carolyn earlier. The sky was inky without any indication it would ever be otherwise and Sadie was still swaddled in deep sleep next to me. The boys had ultimately found their beds on the floor somewhere after we'd drifted off and they were both sprawled out on their backs, chasing bunnies in their dreams.

The dispatcher's voice, thinned by wires and speakers and walls, had come from downstairs. I knew it hadn't been a dream. I'd heard it. Or my subconscious had. It was sharp, like a machete, cutting through my sleep. They were looking for us. They'd found the jeep and they were heading north. That's what my gut told me.

When my feet hit the floor I had to stuff a fist in my mouth to keep from screaming. It felt like dry ice. I was afraid when I took a step I'd leave part of my sole stuck to their hard wood forever.

I crept down the stairs two at a time. The closer I got to the hallway leading to the kitchen the louder the scanner became. Light, snowy voices seeped through a door set ajar across from the kitchen. I peeked in and saw a staircase leading down to the basement. A bright white light with no cover illuminated the concrete walls and the clean scent of sawdust floated on the cold air. I thought of my father. That was his scent. His cologne.

When he wasn't designing things, he was building them. Just like Jesus, my father the carpenter.

The scanner and Joe were at the bottom of those steps. This was the stairway to Hell, but I had to find out what he'd heard.

I began the descent with my heart tap dancing in my mouth again. The last few days had aged it about ten years. I blew on my hands to keep them from going numb when they weren't helping me steady myself on the railing. The steps were old and creaky and covered in a thin layer of sawdust. It was soft under my feet like a thin coating of powdered sugar.

Shards of cedar and pine were scattered around on the concrete floor at the bottom. I stepped down onto it and nearly screamed. If the hardwood upstairs had been dry ice, this was the surface of Uranus, about -500 Fahrenheit.

I scurried around a corner and hid behind a hunk of freshly sanded wood. The smell was intoxicating. Upon closer inspection I saw it was a dresser and when I peeked around it, I found Joe. Fearing he'd seen me, I popped back down, but when I heard his soft, gurgly snoring I knew I was safe. For now.

I poked my head around the side again and saw him splayed diagonally across a red futon, mouth wide open like an algae sucker, with a sanding block strapped to his right hand. He hadn't heard anything. I was beginning to wonder if I had. The only call from the scanner on my trip down to the basement was for domestic disturbance somewhere a little north of Caldwell. Maybe it was just a dream.

I wanted to turn the scanner off, but I was afraid the absence of noise would wake him. Sometimes stillness comes like thunder. I left it and on my way back up the stairs panic thrashed the dream theory.

"Be advised we are approaching the 11-24 on I-84. Vehicle appears to be gutted by fire. Over." I stopped, listened with an acuteness I don't recall ever having before. It was like every syllable was sent through a bullhorn straight into my head.

"Copy that. Backup needed? Over."

"Negative. Send a wrecker. We're checking plates if they're recoverable. Over."

"Copy that. Over."

I don't remember how I got back to the room; everything was a frozen blur. I even dressed in fast forward.

"Sadie, honey, wake up. We have to go. Now."

"Mmmm. He didn't get, Clyde, Los Angeles, he didn't..."

"Shhh. We have to whisper. No, honey, you have to get up. We're leaving."

She was like warm taffy over pull-sticks when I picked her up and tried to dress her. She slumped on my chest. My pillows broke her fall.

"Clyde didn't make it," she slurred. "He got blowded to the sea."

"No Boys, lie down. Leave her alone." The dogs had woken and were trying to sabotage my efforts by assaulting her with morning kisses.

"Clyde got blowded away," she said wiping her cheek.

"In the book?" I asked putting her jacket on trying not to jingle the little bells.

"My dream."

"Oh. Well I'm sure he'll make it. No Sundance. Or Butch. Whichever one you are. No kisses. Lie down."

"I donwanhim to be gone." Her tiny voice was still thick with sleep and phlegm, but when I felt her forehead, she was cool to the touch and she'd only coughed a couple times all night. She was definitely getting better. I liked to think I had something to do with that.

"He'll be fine, honey. You'll see."

Weren't all children's books supposed to have Hollywood endings? The frog turns into the cute guy, the princess gets the cute guy after the requisite hijinks and they all live happily ever after. Right? That was just The Way of Things, wasn't it?

"You have to be very quiet. Everyone's still asleep and we don't want to wake them."

"But why do we have to go?"

"Well, because, it's just time to go."

"I like it here."

"I know, I do too. But sometimes you know, you just, we...sometimes you have to do things that...I know. I do too."

I stuffed Trindle's candle, the Blue Moos picture and my own desires in my bag, picked up the munchkin and her mother and carried us all out of the room. I closed the door so The Boys wouldn't follow me down the stairs.

I stopped at the landing. These people helped me, fed me, and gave me a warm bed and this was how I repaid them? Forget frozen soles, I was leaving a big hunk of another soul there. Infinitely more painful. So much for using my good life well.

I scrabbled for purchase down the stairs and decided whatever the outcome of this, I'd give something back to them. Return their unfettered generosity. Somehow.

I grabbed the keys from the small ceramic dish by the couch and stole out the front door, eyes forward scanning the path before me. Frost clung to the grass and crunched under my feet with each step I took to Carolyn's Volvo. I sheltered Sadie with an arm and herded her along to the car. I was willing to do whatever was necessary to keep her safe and by my side. That notion gave my conscience a *Get Out of Jail Free* card. Like this was almost okay. Almost.

I strapped Sadie in and put my bag in the back seat. She snuggled up with her backpack on her lap for a blanket.

"It's cold. Why are we taking Cowlin's car?"

"She's letting us borrow it." Sadie peered up at me and even in the dark I could tell she was seeing straight through my bullshit as usual. "We're going to give it back. We just have to borrow it for now. For a while."

"I have to go," she said.

"Yep. We're going."

Did she hear the scanner too? Was there nothing I could know she didn't already?

"No, I have to go potty."

Oh, that. Right. Kids. I couldn't, with good conscience, make her squat in the bushes, though I would have much preferred that to actually going back into the house. In the end, common decency prevailed and I carried her quickly back through the door to the downstairs bathroom, all the while keeping a lookout for activity from above and below. No sign of Carolyn or Joe. Yet.

"Can I say goodbye to Joe and Cowlin?" she whispered as I carried her back to the door. One set of quiet feet much better than two.

"No, honey. They're sleeping. We don't want to disturb them."

"But I want to say goodbye," she said a little louder than I would have liked and slumped her head down hard on my shoulder. Sadie's form of a fit. God love her.

Back in the car I got her settled in, but when I tried to start it, the thing bucked and jumped and argued with me. It would just be super if one more thing could hamper our leaving. Maybe Bigfoot could mosey out of the woods, scare the pants off Sadie, and rip the engine apart. That would be a fun challenge.

I looked down and saw the shifter. Come on. "Stick? Who the fuck drives stick anymore?"

Tackling Bigfoot might have been less daunting. I'd never driven a car with a manual transmission and I really didn't want my first lesson to be on one I was stealing (on a hill no less) in the middle of the night, but hey, we can't have everything our way all the time. I just wish I could have things my way one time. Hell, I'd settle for three minutes of half of one thing going my way.

I decided to take a little performance pressure off and put it in neutral. They had a pretty long driveway that sloped down to the road. I'd start it there.

As we backed down, I gave her a name. I'd been on a first name basis with all of my other vehicles since I was eighteen and hadn't had any problems, excepting the last twenty-four hours. I thought maybe she'd be more apt to cooperate if we were friends, so I dubbed her Betty, the Silver Angel. She'd saved us once; I hoped she'd continue in that spirit.

As soon as we hit the road I remembered something Adam used to do with his 4Runner. He'd park it in neutral and pull the parking brake instead of leaving it in gear so he didn't have to remember to push the clutch in when he started it. I kept it in neutral and turned the key. She didn't buck, but she didn't start either. She wanted to argue a little more with me, as if she knew I was trying to steal her away from her rightful owners.

So much for Silver Angel. Silver Asshole more like.

"Listen, you little fucker, I'm so not in the mood for you right now. You will start and you will start now."

"Listen you little fick—"

"No, Sadie. You don't, don't say that. Don't repeat anything I say for the next ten minutes at least."

"Kay."

Betty tried to resist one last time, but I intimidated her sparkplugs enough to fire up. She whined to life. Then shit got tricky. "What did Adam do? You drove with him like eleventy billion times. Why didn't you just let him teach you when he wanted to? Just focus. Clutch in, first gear."

"Are you talking to me?"

"No, honey, I'm talking to myself."

"My mommy says that's crazy."

"It's only crazy when you answer yourself."

"Oh."

"You didn't let him teach you because you were too busy with *his* stick."

"Now are you talking to me?"

"Why don't you try to sleep? It's still night. I'll wake you when we get there." Or somewhere.

Sadie closed her eyes and rested her head on her bag. I put the car in gear and eased off the clutch. I didn't know about clutches but this one seemed like a particular kind of bitch. No wiggle room with it. The more I let up on it the harder my other foot pressed on the gas. I was really excited for something to happen. Anything at all. The only thing I was accomplishing was waking everyone up with the screaming engine. I let the clutch completely out and the car sputtered and choked and died.

"Fuck! What the—"

I looked at the stick and saw it was in third gear. I was just waiting for Joe to come barreling out of the house in his bathrobe and slippers and shotgun. I tried again. This time in first. The bucking bronco knocked me off again. Sadie sat up and giggled.

"That was fun. Can we do it again?"

"I'm sure we will."

In fits and starts I was doing my level best to add grand theft auto and a stripped transmission to my growing litany of no no's. How mortifying. I couldn't even steal a car right. I gave it another shot. And it shot right back at me.

"Wee!"

I was thrilled to know one of us was having a good time. Had they been slightly different circumstances I might have been able to see the fun in it too, but I was too busy wondering when the blue and red lights were going to erupt in my rear view mirror.

I couldn't keep it up, at least not there, right out in front of their house. "Sadie, I need you to take the wheel and make sure we keep going straight. Can you do that?"

"Yes."

I put it in neutral and got out. Sadie unbuckled, scooted over into the driver's seat and took the wheel with both hands. She was overjoyed to have a task. Of course, she couldn't see past the odometer. Even if she'd been able to see above the dash, the lights were off so we were driving in a cave.

I pushed the trunk and slipped on the cold, slick pavement. The only thing that moved was me. I was truly a disgrace to the whole ignoble profession. Without gloves, or any proper protection at all, my fingers seized up in the frigid air and became useless. I tucked them in my jacket and tried simple brute force. Heaving my chest up against the car's rear end it slowly began crunching along the frosty pavement.

I allowed myself a brief moment of pride. Finally, I'd managed to accomplish something. Pride vanished when I noticed the car moving a little too quickly all of a sudden. I couldn't see ahead of us on the road, but I gathered, by its speed, there was a bit of a hill.

"Shit. Sadie hit the brake. The brake! It's the one in the middle. The big pedal on the floor in the middle." I tried not to shout, but I thought I heard Sadie squealing and I was afraid she might freak out and take the car into the ditch or the woods. She didn't have a seatbelt on and there was an airbag packed in the steering wheel that, upon impact, could pop her head open like a squeezed grape.

The road was a skating rink and after a minute of slipping in place Bambi style, I got smart to it and used it like one. I skated as quickly as my sticks would take me toward the runaway car, then Sadie found the brakes. The car skidded and stopped. And so did I, impaled on the trunk. It knocked the wind out of me, but at least Betty was still and Sadie was in one piece. We'd fled to the bottom of the hill and stopped on a flat behind a thicket of trees that would at least buffer the sound of my continued incompetence.

I scraped myself off the back of the car and wheezed to the front door to find Sadie stuck, nearly parallel to the floor, with her tiny foot holding steady on the brake. Lovely. My five-year-old accomplice.

"I'm sorry, Katie. I couldn't find the brake. I didn't know where it was and I tried the one pedal and it didn't do anything and I tried another one and it didn't either and I got scared and I thought I was going to go off into the trees and—"

"Shhhh. You did a great job. You did it perfectly." You'll be graduating to grand-theft-something-else in no time.

"I did?"

"Yes. You did."

Of course it could have been a little sooner, but I didn't want to ruin the moment.

"Now keep your foot right there for a second." I pulled the parking brake then asked her to slide over. She needed a hug first. I was ripe for one too.

After a few more embarrassing (even in front of myself) mishaps with that damn feisty clutch I managed to get the car to move a few feet before it stalled. Progress is progress. I've found the little things in life sometimes offer the greatest rewards. Although, I sure would have loved to hit ten miles an hour before the sun rose. On my fifty-third try I thought I finally had it licked. I shifted into second and didn't look back. I was afraid if I did it might confuse the direction in which I really wanted to go.

I had no idea where we were or where we were headed. Well, I had an idea where I was headed. It had very little to do with the road. Nearly six o'clock and the sky still showed no intention of lightening. Without glasses my vision was less than ideal in the dark. Ideal being: able to see anything at all other than dim, blurry shapes. Note to self: next time, look before you sit.

The road was shrouded in pitchy darkness, no streetlights out there in the country to guide the blind. I saw a red caution light flashing in the distance. Shit. Downshifting. First gear all over again. It took about two minutes to reach the light and in that time I'd come no closer to a solution for my current situation. I stopped at the crossroads and waited for inspiration to strike. Sadie was slumped over, her head resting on the bag next to me. That whole hill episode really took it out of her.

The engine had settled into a smoother rhythm after our rocky start. Its quiet hum was reassuring in a way, but only because I had it in neutral. I sat watching the light blink; the air was so still I could hear it clicking each time it lit up.

I had a choice. Left, right, or straight. I'd never felt so burdened and so free all in the same moment. I didn't enjoy making these kinds of decisions. Ones with such uncertain outcomes I'd be responsible for.

The problem with life is there are too many options. Given the opportunity I usually chose the wrong one. I just wanted someone else to figure it out for me for once. So I closed my eyes and let Betty, the Silver Angel, decide where she wanted to go. Whichever way she pulled was to be our chosen path. I put pressure on the gas and let the clutch out in small increments that didn't piss her off too much. It was a relief giving it up to a mechanical object. No messy thoughts or feelings to get in the way. I would trust in her decision and commit to it fully, without question.

Keeping my eyes closed I put more pressure on the pedal and lifted off the clutch. We jerked and sped up. I felt us veer right a bit and opened my eyes just in time. My foot scrambled for the brake forgetting the clutch and we bucked to a dead and final stop just before taking a header into a ditch on the other side of the road.

"Shit." Maybe I'd reconsider my new decision making process.

"Shit."

"Sadie, I told you not to—"

"It's been ten minutes."

And so it had been.

"What happened?"

"Everything's good. You can go back to sleep."

"Where we going?"

"To Portland. My sister's, remember?"

"Awe we going back to visit Joe and Cowlin and The Boys soon?"

"Sure, someday." I didn't have the energy to tell her the truth.

That she'd most likely never see any of them again, except maybe in court. Too many questions to answer.

"Someday soon?"

See?

"Someday fairly soon. Now why don't you get some more sleep. I'll wake you when we're there."

She snuggled back up against her mother and I snuggled up with my jealousy. Why did she want to go back there so badly? What did they have that I didn't? Did she like Carolyn more than me? Maybe I'd get her a dog. The scales would be balanced then and I wouldn't have to hear about Carolyn and Joe and how god-damn special they were.

Sadie was obviously drawn to people burdened with great sadness, suffering the sort of misery that lives in your bones until you decide to kill it or the other way around. I'd yet to choose which would be my destiny.

I turned right and drove about ten miles without seeing one sign of human existence. Ready to about face, declaring to never let a car make a decision for me again, I saw a speck of light off in the distance. I sped up.

It was one of those quaint rural pit stops with a wooden sign above the door that read, "Burt's Busy Bee." Two ancient cars were parked next to a decrepit garage that leaned left. The front license plate was dangling off one of the cars because the whole bumper had been creamed and the other's windshield had been smashed in.

Betty's belly was nearly full. I just needed to find out where I was and how to get to where I wanted to be.

I parked her in front of the hanging license plate then pulled a screwdriver out of the glove box (I knew Carolyn would be the responsible type to have tools) and put it in my pocket.

The sky had finally acquiesced to the sun and began to lighten. It made things seem a little less impossible in a way. Although, it would be more difficult to hide in daylight.

The tinkle bell jingled when I opened the door to the store. Aside from the smothering heat of the place, my only company was a mug of coffee on the counter next to the cash register. A thin veil of steam danced in spirals up through the air above it. It was the only thing that moved in the whole store. Wait a minute. Cash register. Dark Side. How easy it is to keep tiptoeing over. I'd just burned my bridge back to good with the whole car debacle and the register was old, like everything else in there. Circa 1930's probably. How easy it would be to—

"Hang on, Slingshot, we got a breaker. Breaker, you legit, come back?"

The man's voice was scratchy, but full and deep, emanating from the CB radio by the window behind the counter. It startled me and I retracted my hand from the cash register.

"Legit, Amigo. I'm shakin' the trees down here on I-84 south just past Bliss, and we got a bear in the bushes at marker one-two-five, so brush your teeth and comb your hair ladies. It's all double nickel here. Copy? Over."

"That's a big 10-4, Amigo. Much obliged. You copy that, Slingshot? Come back."

"That's affirmative. Backin' down. Over."

"Breaker, breaker! Whole fleet of advertising Boy Scouts just blew my doors off at marker one-five-nine headin' up to you boys in Fruitland. Smokies out in full force. Over."

The radio went dead again. Fruitland? Advertising Boy Scouts? Smokies? Like Smoky and The Bandit? Like fuck they found us already?

There was still no sign of anyone in the store, no one to help me figure out how to get the hell out of there, no one to catch me being bad. With the hard push of a button I could grab a little extra something for our trip and be gone.

But I'd made enough wrong decisions lately so I just got the hell out of there. On my way to the door, I noticed a rack of maps in the corner. I grabbed several that looked like they might be useful, dropped a couple bucks on the counter and left.

I stuffed the maps in my pocket and strode over to the dangling license plate. The morning air was still, no sound from any direction. I checked the road, just to make sure I didn't have company coming. The windows above the store were covered in blinds; no one peeked out at me. Seemed like Sadie and I were the only people alive at that moment. It was all lovely and peaceful until I thought about the fleet of Smokies charging up there to shoot me and take her away.

The screwdriver was warm in my hand when I pulled it out of my jacket, but it didn't stay that way for long. It was still frigid outside, though lighter now. It wasn't easy to extract the rusty license plate, it had probably weathered a couple decades in its current position, but when it finally dropped off into my hand I felt a bit of pride at having done one more thing right. Right being relative of course. Sometimes right is what is necessary.

I kept telling myself that as I drove away in a stolen car with a stolen license plate. I wanted to take the rear plate as well, but there was no rear end on the car so one plate would have to suffice. If I was going to have trouble it would probably come from behind, so I stopped a few miles up the road and changed out the new with the old. I was proud of myself for thinking of it, for thinking like a criminal.

I'd gotten lucky with the maps. We were headed west on route twenty in less than a half hour. It was the slower route to Portland, but I wanted to stay well clear of I-84. Way too many "Smokies" and with my virgin stick skills still blossoming I couldn't take a chance of stalling Betty in the middle of the freeway. It probably wasn't even possible to do that, but I was sure I'd find a way and we had no room for mishaps. An impossibly silly statement coming from me.

THIRTEEN

"Matewda!"

I almost drove off the road when Sadie screamed. She'd been lost in sleep for hours and we'd had no trouble. The route we'd taken ran through the belly of Oregon and it was rural enough to feel safe. Or the closest I could come to safe under the circumstances.

We were at the junction where route twenty turned into route twenty-two about an hour outside Salem when she woke realizing she didn't have her doll. I was dizzy from the shock of her sudden voice in the quiet car. I'd been swirling around in the vortex of my mind just before she woke, wondering what we'd find in Portland and what our future would be.

"Matewda, Katie. Where's Matewda?" She was red-faced and panicky and I could feel her desperation growing stronger with every shallow breath she took. I hadn't paid close enough attention when we left to make sure I took the doll along with everything else. The living doll was my first and only concern.

"Did you bring Matewda?" She felt around on the floor in the front, even though we were well into daylight and she could clearly see there was nothing down there.

"I don't think..."

"Maybe she's in back." Sadie unbuckled and flipped over the seat before I could stop her. The girl had skills. If the whole spy thing didn't work out maybe she could look into the require-ments for Ninjas.

"Honey, I don't think—"

"Maybe she's back here. Maybe you don't 'member putting her back here. I have to have her. I can't lose her!"

She was a category five in the back of the car. Whipping things around to check on the back seat, under both front seats, in any nook or cranny holding an ounce of air. Up front, I pulled a few broken pretzels out of the back of my hair. She had hurled the squished bag onto the dashboard and a couple pieces got stuck on me along the way, like salty ornaments on a red Christ-mas tree. She was desperate for that little yarn-haired thing and though I understood it was important, I didn't think it was cause for all that.

She stopped, defeated. A tight squeak escaped from her throat. It was a sound you make when you're using everything you've got to hold yourself together. First come the involuntary noises and nervous ticks, then the tears. They came like a deluge and carried with them a severe and comprehensive anguish that overtook her like it had the day before when she'd learned of her mother's true fate.

I pulled over.

"Honey," I said, climbing into the back seat with her, "we'll get, I'll get you another doll just like Matilda."

I knew it was the wrong thing to say as soon as it came out, but there it was. Her little face crumpled up like a dried apple. There was something else happening here other than the loss of a doll. I was sure any moron could have figured that out by the look of her, but I knew it was something to do with her mother. A pact they'd made. I remembered wailing like that after I'd broken mine.

"Shhhh. Breathe, honey, breathe." I pulled her into me and held her as she took big gulps, trying to stay afloat. It broke my heart to see her like that. I'd developed such a strong sense of protection for her I didn't want to see her in pain ever again. I knew that was irrational, but it was what I wanted. Just like a mother.

The sun crashed in through the rear window and I felt a little heavy headed from the heat. I took my jacket off and when I put it on the back of the seat I saw a car approaching us in the distance. My stomach whipped itself into knots every time I saw a car and only settled when the vehicle in question was close enough to see there was no rack of red and blue lights on the roof. This one looked like it had a rack.

I decided it would be better to be moving than to be at a stand still. Being the eternal boy scouts, they were likely to stop and find out what the trouble was if we were pulled over.

"We've got to get going. Do you want to come up front with me?" She looked up but didn't say anything. I wanted time to talk, but if we were going to get, we needed to get then.

"You can stay back here if you want. Maybe you'll lie down and get some sleep. Don't worry. We'll fix this. We'll figure something out." My hand was on the latch ready to pull and the car was only about a mile away, shooting down a hill at a precipitous pace. Somewhat disconcerting. The pterodactyls in my gut were at each other again.

"She gave me Matewda for my birthday," Sadie choked out.

Oh boy. Here we go. We had maybe thirty seconds before the car was on top of us.

"Okay, well, we'll—" I turned the handle to open the door.

"A little before she went away. Before she went to Heaven."

I took my hand off the door and put it around Sadie's back. The ski rack was a blur of black as the car whipped past, rocking us in its wake. My lips parted involuntarily and released the breath I was holding in a protracted hiss like a leak in an air mattress.

"I promised her I would, I would keep Matewda safe and take care of her 'cause she's ode and my greatgrammy Junie made her."

I knew it had been about a promise. I'd made a similar one to my mother just before she died. Only mine was about people. And like Sadie, I too failed to keep it.

"Can we go back and get her?"

"Not right now, honey. We have to keep going."

Her face took on a near purple hue and I realized it was because she'd stopped breathing. Her first temper tantrum. It was pretty adorable because she wasn't rotten, just sad, and I could relate to that.

I wanted to say something to make it better without having to lie again. I was tired of the lies. It was hard to keep up with them. I couldn't remember what was real and what was my fantasy.

"Listen, I promise we will get Matilda back somehow."

"She's my angel! That's what Mommy said when she gave her to me. She's my angel and I have to take care of her so she can watch over me. It's a traditional. And I ruineded it."

"You didn't ruin anything." I did. Now we really had to go back and get the damn doll. How did everything somehow always end up being my fault?

"What do you mean it's traditional?"

"My greatgrammy Junie made it for her little girl for her fifth birthday and that's what they did ever since then. They give it to the little girl on her fifth birthday."

"When was your birthday?"

"September twenty-two."

"Wow, that's my birthday too." She wasn't as excited about it as I was. Just looked up at me with her wet, snotty face and nodded like she knew it already. Of course she did.

"We'll get her back. All right?" I could see I wasn't convincing anyone. We returned to the front and started up again. I looked over at her sitting there on the seat with her backpack scrunched up under her arms. She could feel my gaze and returned it. There was such a gentle wisdom in her eyes; I didn't know where it came from in one so young. And I didn't think I'd ever catch up with her. Maybe I was going in the wrong direction. Maybe going forward meant going back first.

The stretch of road ahead of us was interminable. I could see for miles. Farmland, vast fields of crops on one side, shrouded woods on the other. The yellow divider lines were hypnotizing, wriggling the past through me like worms through the earth.

My mother woke me early one morning two weeks after we'd planted the Crepe Myrtle. She tiptoed into my room and tickled my nose with her pinky, knowing full well that always drove me nuts. I'd come out of my dreams sneezing and there was really no worse way to wake in my opinion. I think she loved watching me get riled up about it.

She took my sleepy, angry face in her hands and kissed my cheeks. The brightness of morning assaulted me when I opened my eyes. As did her beauty. I'd never seen her glow like that. The sun exploded through my windows and crashed against her body, splashing off her corners. It created an aura around her, like an angel. Like the one I'd see years later surrounding Sadie late at night in a motel room in Bliss.

"I've got a surprise, Bits, come on." She whispered into my face and pulled me from my cocoon of sheets. I couldn't imagine what would get her this excited so early in the morning. She could be a late sleeper sometimes. I'd come to understand years later, it wasn't sleep that kept her in bed. It was something malignant and crippling she'd never conquer. Though the doctors disregarded it, I know in my bones my mother's depression opened the door to the illness that took her life.

The cool grass tickled my bare toes. I stood outside next to her, gripping Shortcake's bonnet between three fingers, peering down at the tiny green tree shoot. I didn't see what was so thrilling about something that looked like another short piece of grass. She bent down to inspect it and suggested I do the same. I squatted next to her and inhaled the roses perennially blossoming on her skin. At least there was something I could enjoy about this.

"See, baby, new life. Isn't it amazing?"

I was expecting, or at least hoping for, something a bit more amazing. Like dinosaurs suddenly popping from the woods behind our house or a unicorn floating down out of the sky to take me for a ride. A little wound up leaf just wasn't doing it for me at the demanding age of five.

"It's gwass."

"No honey, it's our tree. It's Myrtle."

"Myrtle's a turtle."

"She can be a tree too. Now, we have to be very careful and take good care of her so she'll grow and blossom. Remember what I told you about her magic?"

All I remembered was she wasn't going to spit bunnies out her trunk. That was all I needed to know.

"With any luck she'll blossom next summer around this time and you'll get to see how wonderful she can be."

We didn't have much luck because she didn't blossom the next year. Or the year after that, or the year after that. I'd given up hope she ever would. But my mother refused to. I think it was part of what kept her alive. A month after Myrtle blossomed, Joanna died.

Five years after that first sign of life I had another early morning wake-up call, but this time she didn't wait for me to get up. She'd committed a wake-and-run and was already outside when I came down. The late August sun had warmed the grass by the time I reached the back yard. I slugged through it with bare feet and an attitude until I saw her glowing under the brilliant pink blossoms of her beloved Myrtle.

That vision stole my breath and my ability to move. In almost ten years I'd seen my mother smile many times. But never the way she did that morning. With that glimmer of ecstasy. She'd been right all along. Myrtle *was* magic. She'd brought my mother to life.

I watched her from a distance, mesmerized. She was magnificent with her arms outstretched, her long ginger hair flowing like liquid down her back. Her eyes were closed so she didn't catch me spying. I didn't want to disturb her. She was having a spiritual moment. Turned out that way for both of us.

She raised her face to the sky. I thought she was enjoying the sun dappling her skin through the delicate crepe paper flowers attached to the branches above her. The tree was suddenly resplendent with them, like they'd sprung to life overnight. But it wasn't the sun. She'd found her bliss in the fragile drops of rain, "angel's tears", being released from the blossoms.

When she floated back to Earth she called for me to join her, unable to keep herself from smiling. She hunched down to my level so we could huddle close together and wrapped her long, thin arm around my small shoulders, pulling me into her.

"Isn't it just..." She didn't finish, but I knew what she was thinking. And it was. Frankly, at almost ten, I couldn't have cared less about a tree, the magic of it was what it did to her. Screw bunnies. This was way better.

"Angel's tears," she said.

"What?"

"They're angel's tears."

"What are?"

"Don't you feel them?"

"I feel sprinkles."

"Exactly."

"Angels cry?"

"When they're happy." It was the first time I'd ever heard her mention anything about angels in my life. What was it about this tree? "Your grandmother used to say that if even just one fell on your face, you would never know grief because the tears of the angels protect you when you need it most."

"That's a load isn't?" I was nine.

"Well, whether it's a load or not is up to you I guess."

"I don't get it."

"You have the choice to believe whatever you want to. You always have a choice."

"So if I chose to believe it's a load, that's okay?"

"Sure. And if you chose to believe it's true with every fiber of your being that's all right too."

"Do you?"

She didn't answer me. Just smiled and kissed my forehead.

"Mommy, who's God?"

"Wow, where did that come from?"

"You're talking about angels and I know angels are supposed to be God's elves or something so I just wanted to know who He is."

"Well, it's, He's, I mean He's not like Santa with the, I mean, He is a little like Santa in a way, I guess. I'm not making any sense am I?"

"No." I was nine.

"God is, He's—"

"What does He look like?"

"No one really knows."

"Nobody's ever seen Him?"

"Well, no."

"Then how do you know He exists?" She smiled again, this time with a great deal of pride attached to the corners of her lips and the lines around her eyes, like I'd just saved someone's life.

"Look up. What do you see?"

I looked too far up and was blinded by the sun through the branches. I flinched and closed my eyes. The only thing I saw then was the orange ghost in my head. But when I was able to open my eyes again I began to see the world in a different way.

"Look around. Everything you see, it's all from God. Every time you see a butterfly, or smell a rose, or look at yourself in the mirror. It's all God."

"Why don't we go to church or say grace like Trindle's parents do?"

"I don't think you need to go to church or say grace to know God."

"Well what do you have to do?"

"You just have to listen when He speaks to you."

"Is He going to wake me up 'cause you know I don't like that."

"He might. But not in the way you think."

"Well how? And when?"

"Be patient. You'll find Him in your own time."

"Now I have to go looking for Him?"

"You don't have to do anything, honey. You are so good. Just use your life well. He'll be with you."

It was one of the last conversations I had with my mother.

She began the next day with an extended episode of the most hideous and violent vomiting I'd ever heard, launching her shocking and inexorable flight to death.

I never asked her why she loved that tree the most out of all the ones she had to choose from in the world. I knew it couldn't be just because it was a special raining tree. There was a real, scientific reason for that. The roots lapped up too much water from the ground and when it was overfull it had to expel the excess, so it fell out through the flowers. Besides, if you wanted to get rained on, you just needed to step outside during the nine months of fall in Seattle.

A month later, two days before my tenth birthday, she told me why. Through tubes and shallow whispers she said, "Katie, things will change, but I want you to do something for me. Okay?" I nodded and waited while she took a slow, quiet breath. "Hold on to your wonder." Another breath and the quiet beginnings of a smile. "Please."

It was the first time she'd called me by my name in five years. And it would be the last.

The raining tree was a piece of her childhood wonder puzzle that had been lost through disappointments, miscarriages, and synapses not touching. But instead of throwing the whole picture away she kept searching until she found it again. She'd had faith it would blossom, that she'd be able to pass the piece on to me, and she was right.

The day she died we were all by her side but she wanted to talk with each of us separately. My father went first. Then Chloe, then me. They'd taken the tubes out, a resignation to the inevitable, but she still struggled to speak. "Love you. Please take care of them." It was everything she needed to say.

I took her bloated hand in mine. It felt more like a waxy water balloon. I didn't understand why she'd swelled up and turned the color of a banana. I didn't understand pancreatitis or sepsis or any of this.

She was leaving me way too soon. That, I understood. We wept together for everything we'd shared and everything we'd never get to. And I promised her I'd take care of our family.

Then I failed.

The first year I learned to cook and do laundry. I cleaned the house and mowed the lawn when my father couldn't pick himself up out of his chair. Chloe kept running away with the neighbor kid, Todd Thacker. She'd be gone for days and Gregory would be a basket case till she returned. She usually came back dirty and strung out on something. My mother had been the disciplinarian because she'd been a wild child in her youth and wouldn't put up with it from her kids, but my father didn't know how to handle Chloe. He'd ground her, but she'd just run away in the middle of the night again. It went on like that until she got pregnant and decided not to come back.

After Chloe left, my father retreated further into his shell. Before the days of Bible Study, he'd come home from work and pop his meal (that I'd prepared) in the nuker, then wander off to his study and close the door. A few hours later I'd hear the soft click of the doorknob turning and I'd listen for his slow footsteps touching down on the wood floor. It was my cue. I'd time my trip to the bathroom to coincide with his journey to his bedroom.

Since they were on the same path we'd usually collide in the middle. If he was feeling generous he'd thank me for the meal and ask what I was up to, listening with a thin glaze over his face like he'd already flown off to some other place. Sometimes he barely even noticed I was in front of him. It was frightening how he'd given up.

After Martin, I gave up on my promise. I'd failed her; my family had fallen apart. I'd fallen apart. So I tried to concentrate on myself. Getting back to the good, I thought maybe things would change. But my father didn't notice my straight A's or my excellence in flute or my distinct lack of boyfriends. So I grew to care very little about butterflies or smelling roses and I certainly couldn't look at myself in the mirror anymore. Myrtle never blossomed again. My father chopped her down when he burned all of their pictures. It was a violent end to a life that had begun auspiciously. I'd lost my mother's puzzle piece. And God had disappeared.

"I want to leave her with Cowlin and Joe."

The sweetness of Sadie's unexpected voice brought me back to the road. Somehow, in the middle of my mother living and dying, I'd managed to find the correct onramp for I-5 north. We were getting ever closer to Chloe, to the unknown. It frightened me that I could wholly check out like that when we were fugitives on the run, so I made a marked effort to remain in the present, at least while I was in the car.

"Maybe she might help," Sadie said.

224 | KELLY BYRNE

I wiped my moist cheeks with the sleeve of my jacket and re-adjusted myself in the seat. I'd been slouching a little.

"I'm sorry, honey, what did you say?"

"We don't have to get Matewda."

"Why not?" Ah, the fickle delights of childhood.

"Because maybe, maybe they would need her more than me. Maybe she might help them."

"But what about your promise and Grandma Junie and—"

And then I understood what she was saying. Damn, I was slow on the uptake. None of that mattered to her because she was seeing Matilda as angel now, not as gift, or promise, or tradition. She wasn't thinking about passing her on to her child because she couldn't go that far ahead. She was in the now, as children are, and thought her doll might help to heal Carolyn and Joe's pain somehow.

I longed for such otherworldly selflessness. God was tapping on my shoulder again, seeping in like rain through a desiccated desert floor, and Sadie was His elf.

"I think that's a beautiful idea." She smiled, happy to know she had my approval. I caressed her head, dropped my hand down to hers and cradled it. She squeezed mine and held on.

I drove on feeling things would be good, no matter what happened. My positive musings came to a crashing halt a half hour later when I saw the flashing lights merging onto the freeway next to me. Two motorcycle cops. No sirens.

"Sadie wake up! Honey wake—you need to unbuckle and get down!"

Her motor skills didn't cooperate in time, so I reached in back for the blanket crumpled up behind her seat and spread it over her the best I could while downshifting in the slowing traffic.

"Sadie you have to stay under there. I unbuckled your belt so I want you to scoot down onto the floor and stay there. Make a little fort with the blanket and don't come out till I tell you."

"Why?"

"Just, please, do it now."

"I'm scared."

"Don't be scared, honey. Everything's fine. Just pretend it's your fort and you're making house down there."

Right. On a cold, dirty, car floor. Good mother, Kate.

The cops swerved back and forth across all the lanes in front of me, slowing traffic. Then they stopped. Traffic stopped. My heart stopped.

FOURTEEN

The tricky part about arson and kidnapping and auto theft is you begin to justify your actions by creating reasons and explanations for everything you've done. It settles your conscience into believing you're right. The bad part about arson, kidnapping, and auto theft is that whole justification thing only holds up in your own mind, not in court, or in the face of the officer who is staring you down from his motorcycle and mustache ten feet away.

My head was tight, suddenly crammed full of excuses, explanations. Lies. I bent down to peek under the blanket. Sadie was curled up in a little ball, resting her head on her mother.

"Are you okay?"

"Why did we stop? Is the police coming to get us?"

"No. No. No." I wasn't lying as much as employing wishful thinking. Sending it out into the universe. I stretched my hand under the blanket for Sadie to take. She squeezed it. There we were, holding hands in my new stolen car, idling in front of Mr. Officer. Sitting ducks.

I'd turned up the radio when I saw the lights, but I didn't hear any information about the Amber Alert. That didn't mean there wasn't one to be heard.

"We're going to be fine. I just need you to be still and stay put till I tell you it's all right to come out."

"Kay."

Sadie's magnificence struck me. She was such a special child and my inadequacy as any kind of mother-figure/caregiver became all too clear again as I pulled the blanket over her tiny, ginger head. What was I doing? And more importantly, what was I doing?

My biggest fear at that moment was not getting caught and going to jail. It was losing Sadie. If I'm honest though, going to jail did come in a particularly close second.

"Katie?"

"Yes, honey."

"I'm hungry."

Are children like cows? How many stomachs do they have to fill? Seriously. I thought about offering her the pretzel pieces I'd pulled from my hair earlier, but decided against it, simply proving to myself I wasn't *that* inadequate as a mother-figure.

"Honey, I don't have anything for you right now, but if you can hold on, we'll get something soon." They feed people in jail, right?

"Kay." The smallness of her voice broke my heart.

I hauled myself upright and pulled my purse onto my lap, making it seem like that was the reason for my disappearing act. I smiled at Officer Mustache perched on his bike, a statue, but he didn't smile back. Part of me wanted to take it personally, but then thought better of it. Now was not the time to be petty. The other cop was on the far left side of the freeway but neither of them moved.

I wondered if this was standard police procedure for capturing a fugitive. Sit on your bike and shoot dirty looks at the perp until something happens. This one had it down. I imagined he'd graduated at the top of his Menacing Faces class. The mustache definitely helped.

I kept myself busy so I didn't seem too focused on what they were going to do next. Did they usually stop traffic to catch criminals? That was a question for my sister. Maybe they were waiting for backup. I flattered myself with the idea that it took all that to capture me and rummaged around in my purse looking for nothing in particular. Then I checked my lipstick even though I wasn't wearing any. I pulled the visor down and when I glanced up at the mirror, the vibrant green of my eyes shot back at me. They were more alive than they'd been in years. I almost didn't recognize myself. In fact, for a second they weren't mine at all. They were Sadie's. Like forest foliage in a midday sun. When I blinked they returned to being mine. Duller, but hinting at some kind of change.

When I looked back at Officer Happy I saw his eyes wander down to my license plate. Damnit! Why didn't I put the fake on the front? He pushed a button and talked into his nifty headset and I knew some proverbial shit was about to hit the fan.

"Sadie, honey, we're going to start moving and we might go really fast but I want you to stay down."

"Should I hold on?" Her voice was far away, muffled under the blanket, and all I wanted to do was bend down and give her a big hug.

"Yes, honey, hold on." What the hell was I about to do? I pushed the clutch in and shoved the stick into first gear. I had a clear path to the shoulder and there was an off ramp about a half-mile away. I'd wait till he was off his bike and approaching, then I'd gun it. That was the plan. Not a very good one.

He moved. My head pounded. He gripped the handlebars. I revved the engine. Then my leg disconnected from my brain and let the clutch up too quickly. We bucked and stalled just as he pulled his bike upright and stowed his kickstand.

A long procession of cops, all silent with spinning, flashing lights followed a hearse onto the freeway to my right. Officer Mustache and the other highway patrolman waited for the end then took up the rear. He didn't look back.

And I couldn't look forward. I was stuck. The line of cars behind me became impatient and loud. Traffic had begun to move, but I stayed. Realizing their honking was doing them no good; they slowly snaked around us. The car was probably fine; I just couldn't remember how to work her.

I used to get straight A's in school. I was a good girl. Sort of. And I'd just been prepared to flee from the authorities for the second time in less than a week. Possibly engaging them in a high-speed chase, endangering myself and Sadie and anyone else in my path. When had *I* become a category five?

"Can I come out yet, Katie?"

"I'm sorry, honey. Come on out."

She threw the blanket off her head. Her hair was mussed and filled with static. A bunch of it stood up to greet me.

"Are you all right? Could you breathe all right?"

"Yep. It was toasty warm."

"Good." I wondered if optimism was a gene you were born

with, like the one for curling the tongue. Was the world split up into the Sadies and the Katies? The Sadies could curl no matter what happened to them because that's just the way they were born. But no matter how hard they tried the Katies' tongues would forever remain flat because they just didn't luck out in the gene pool. Was it as simple and random as that, or was there more choice involved?

"Let's get you buckled up again." I helped her climb back up onto the seat while the line of cars behind us kept reminding me of their displeasure. Her face was clammy from being under the blanket. I smoothed her hair down and ran my palm across her cheeks. Her skin was velvet. The luxury of youth.

"Thank you," she said, smiling up at me as I latched her seatbelt.

"For what?"

I couldn't possibly think of anything I'd done in the last, well, since I'd known her that she'd want to thank me for.

"For taking care of me."

Especially that.

"Do something for me?" I said. "Roll your tongue. Like this. See?"

She took a deep breath before she spoke, her voice was low and airy, like what I'd done was magical. "How did you do that?" Try as she did, and she did try, contorting her face for several minutes because she's a trooper, Sadie Beck could not curl her little pink tongue.

"Some people can, some can't. If you can't it just means you didn't get that gene."

She wasn't listening to me. She was trying to roll her tongue. Determined to make it happen, she kept herself busy the rest of the trip training her tongue to do something it wasn't born with the ability to do. She even tried rolling it with her fingers when all else failed. Part of me believed she'd succeed. Genes be damned. Maybe she was on to something there.

My most recent encounter with the Men in Blue really shook me. I couldn't keep running. Things would change when we got to Chloe's, but I didn't know if I should tell her the truth about my situation or not. That was the problem with our relationship. She was more likely to help me if I lied. She owed me though, so at least I had a little leverage.

I contemplated calling Chris when we arrived, so he would know Sadie was all right. We could talk about her future, and him calling off the search, but then I remembered how he looked at me. He seemed like the kind of person who would hold on to something he didn't want just because he knew someone else did.

When we were about fifteen minutes outside Portland I called my sister again. My phone only had one flashing bar left. Piece of—well, at least it had that. Glass half full. Glass half full. I'd try emulating Sadie's determination to hurdle her limitations.

Chloe didn't pick up and it went to her machine. As instructed I started leaving a message, wondering what the hell we were going to do if she didn't get back to me within the next few miles, then the phone crackled and beeped in my ear and I heard a pale voice on the other end. "Hello?"

"Chloe?"

"Well it's not Mrs. Santa." My lovely sister. "You're coming?"

"In about ten minutes. We're on the five north. How do I get to you?"

"We?"

"Yeah. I sort of have a surprise."

Silence. Silence. Silence.

"So you going to tell me?" She never did like surprises.

"Not yet, just get me there and you'll see."

"Aright, but I'm heading to work in an hour, so..."

"So?"

"So make it quick."

That's what I loved about my family, their unfettered excitement at the prospect of seeing me after years of absence. The anticipation was killing her, I could tell.

Now I had to decide what my story would be about Sadie. She could easily have been my daughter. I hadn't seen Chloe in the flesh since I left ten years ago for Larry's in Atlanta. We'd talked on the phone a few times in between her vacations in prison but those conversations usually consisted of her asking me for money and me telling her no. Not too much personal information had been exchanged between us for quite some time. Not since I was born, actually.

Maybe I should just tell her the truth. She'd find out eventually anyway. If you can't tell your family the truth about your life, who can you tell?

She unlocked the fourth deadbolt, cracked the door open and peeked through the chain lock at me. "Hey." Love gushed from her. She was helpless to contain it. She glanced down at Sadie then back up at me. "Christ," she said under her breath, then took a deep drag on a cigarette. She rolled her eyes and slid the chain free, opening the door. I took Sadie's hand and we ventured forth.

It was dark and cool inside, like a cave. The curtains were closed even though it was only three o'clock and still light outside. The air was thick and fusty.

She closed the door and I turned around to get a good look at her in the dim yellow light of the kitchen. The picture was shocking. She was fully three times the person she'd been ten years ago. Granted, ten years ago she was a skeleton addicted to any number of reality altering drugs. She wasn't eating as much as shooting up, snorting, and burning then, but this was overkill in the other direction. Three hundred pounds of lard did not settle well on a five foot six inch woman. She was a big bag of marbles, all loose and round. I think I still had bigger boobs, though. I saw her looking when we walked in.

"So who's this?" she said.

"Can't I even get a hug first?" Not that I wanted one really, but it would give me time to settle my nerves and get my story straight in my head. Besides, if I hugged her she'd become real to me. I still couldn't believe how much she'd changed. Physically anyway.

"Fine, but I got to go to work soon."

What that had to do with hugging her sister for the first time in ten years I didn't know. I let it go. Some things just aren't worth the fight.

I waited while she made a fuss about having to put her cigarette in the ashtray. She took a long drag on it before putting it down, trying to increase the distance between us. I almost told her to forget it. Then she blew smoke in my face, put her arms out and took me in them.

It was the best hug she'd ever given me. Not her usual bend at the waist, two pats on the back kind of nicety that should have been reserved for acquaintances and distant cousins. This was an honest embrace, the first of its kind from her. Both of our mushy parts mushed together, no distance between us at all. I suddenly had high hopes for our post hug conversation.

We separated and sat down at the kitchen table. Sadie stood next to me with her hand on my leg. She observed my older sibling with reserve. I had a feeling she'd already figured her out.

"Do you have anything she can eat? A sandwich or soup or something?" Chloe stared at me for a minute as if she didn't understand the question. Then she stood, whipped around to the counter and grabbed an opened pack of Ritz crackers. Without a word she handed it to Sadie then sat down to resume the silence.

"Thank you," Sadie said. Chloe didn't respond to her. She just stared at me like I had a foot growing from my head. She'd put her wispy bleached hair up in a ponytail and it made her seem younger, even with her chocolate roots showing through. Her features were bloated but I could still see a faint glimmer of her former self in there.

"Wowcome," Sadie said.

"What honey?" I asked, glad to be participating in any kind of conversation to break the heavy silence.

"You're s'posed to say wowcome when somebody says thank you."

"You're right. Thank you," I said.

"Wowcome."

"So?" This finally from Chloe. Her mocha eyes had aged beyond their thirty-four years, but there was still something there. Something alive. She hadn't lost it all yet, but I feared she was teetering on the edge. She'd been in prison more in the last ten years than she'd been out. One of her children had been born there.

"So. This is my daughter, Sadie."

Well? Come on. Four deadbolts? Huge trust issues. I didn't need to compound our problems.

"Bullshit."

"Booshit," Sadie said through a mouth full of cracker.

"No, honey. Do not repeat anything your Aunt Chloe says. Please, don't swear in front of her. She's very quick." Telling someone else not to swear sounded funny to me.

"No way she's yours."

"What do you mean?"

"You never said anything about her ever. Even when I was junked up I still talked about Jimmy."

I picked Sadie up and put her on my lap. She held tight to the crackers and leaned against me, crunching.

"How are your kids?"

"Don't change the subject."

"I'm not." Of course I was. "I was wondering how your children are, Chloe. Obviously you've cleaned up, congratulations on that, so I just assumed you'd be trying to get them back. No?"

"Jimmy ran away from his fosters last year. He stopped by long enough to tell me to go to Hell. Haven't heard from him since. Nobody has. Justin and Jenny are, you know, good as they can be. They went to a different foster last May, but I'm up for review in January so I'm hoping, you know..."

"You're going to get them back. Just keep doing what you're doing."

"What the hell does that mean?"

Wow. I didn't think we'd get here in less than five minutes. That was a record.

"It means exactly that. I'm proud of you for, you know, I don't know, getting your shit—yourself together."

"Well, hallelujah! My little sister's proud of me for not being a fuck up anymore."

Well, yeah.

"Please with the f-word. Listen, I'm sorry if I offended you somehow, I was just trying to say it's nice to see you off the stuff. I'm happy to see you, I want you to get your kids back."

I wanted to offer the idea of a diet too, but I thought that might be pushing my luck. My sister had obviously been afflicted with the same disease my mother and I had. Overindulgence. She chose drugs first and they almost killed her. Now she was using food. Similar path. This one just took a little longer to reach the end.

"Goddamn, she looks, it's like I'm looking at a picture of you when you were little. She's really...?"

"Yes, she is."

Sadie glanced up and gave me a big crumb-filled smile.

"So what's going on? Why are you here? I don't mean to sound, you know, whatever, I'm just, what do you need?"

"Well, we're sort of transitioning right now."

"Transitioning. Right. Who're you running from?" Damn. She was good.

"Well, her father for one." I knew she would understand. Her first ex, Todd, was still in jail, but she worried about what he'd do when he got out since we'd sent him there.

"Who else?" She lit another cigarette. I didn't want to push any more of her buttons by asking her not to smoke in front of Sadie so I left it alone.

"That's about it, really," I said.

"You're a terrible fucking liar."

"Please, with the language."

She took a drag and blew the smoke in my face. Sadie coughed and waved her hand around trying to dissipate it.

"That's sweet. Thanks," I said, taking Sadie into the living room. I set her down in a ratty old recliner to watch TV. She put her mother on her lap and settled in with the rest of her snack.

"Sorry about that. She can be...difficult."

"She just needs some love," Sadie said, shoving another Ritz in her mouth. It came out like she was saying the plants needed watering, but the profundity of those words spoken by a five-year-old was almost beyond my comprehension.

"Thank you, honey, I'll definitely keep that in mind. Stay in here while we talk, all right?"

She nodded and I turned on the television, trying to make it loud enough to drown out the sound of our voices in the next room.

"Cut the shit and tell me what's really going on," Chloe said when I sat down.

"Do you have anything to drink?"

"Kate, I don't have time for this. I got to go to work. What's going on?"

I couldn't look at her. Suddenly I felt like I couldn't possibly tell her what I'd done because then we'd be on the same level. She'd always been the one in trouble and I'd always been the good girl. Now I'd fallen into the pit with her. I had a feeling nothing would make her happier than to know I was running from the law.

"I'm telling you right now, you ain't staying here if you're in some kind of trouble. I can't afford it."

"What?"

"I finally got my shit straight. I get so much as a jaywalking ticket, my PO sends me back and I don't get my kids. Ever."

"But we don't have anywhere else to go."

"Sorry."

I stood up, but too quickly I think because the room spun. My hand caught the counter and I steadied myself. The faucet leaked in a slow, steady rhythm like a drum beat into the stainless steel sink. Everything else sped away. The drip consumed me, cleansed my mind and opened the door for all sorts of previous transgressions to flow in. Things might have turned out differently had I taken Sadie's advice, but I chose a different road.

"Why do you hate me so much?"

She snickered like it was a joke. "What are you talking about?"

"What have I done, aside from being conceived, that you resent me so much for?"

She fidgeted in her chair. The first two fingers on her left hand came to life and tapped like pistons on her ten-dollar Salvation Army table. I settled my arms down at my sides, staying open, inviting an answer. But she didn't want to give one.

She stood suddenly, pushing her chair back like she was trying to get away from a giant cockroach. I didn't move. She whipped to the cupboard and grabbed a coffee mug. There was no room to set it on the cluttered Formica countertop; it was littered with dirty dishes and trash. She poured the used motor oil and drank it like it was water, then turned around to put the mug in the sink and stayed there. I could feel her thinking. Trying to figure out how to get out of this conversation.

I wasn't going to speak first. I'd asked the question. And I kind of wanted an answer.

"So I hear Dad's pretty sick," she said, still gazing into her sink.

Not exactly what I was expecting. Didn't really fit with the question. Or maybe it did.

"Are you going to answer me?" I said.

"No, 'cause it's a stupid thing to ask."

"Not really, when you think about the mounting evidence to support it."

"You are so spoiled, Kate."

"I'm sorry?" That was a new one.

"You get everything you want, everything always your way.

The one time somebody says no to you, you flip out."

"Everything I want? Really? Spoiled? Yes, I'm spoiled. Let's take inventory of all the things Kate's gotten in her life."

Uh oh. I was referring to myself in third person. I only did that when I was drunk or really riled up.

"Knock it off," she said, knowing she'd opened a super-sized can of worms.

"Let's see, we'll start with age ten. Her mother died suddenly leaving her with a non-existent father and crazy sister to take care of."

"Crazy?"

"Shush. I'm talking." This felt good.

"The next year her sister, the only potential for a positive female presence in her life now, ran away with the punk neighbor kid who got her pregnant and into drugs. Then—"

"That's enough, Kate." She was still standing by the sink, but at least she was looking at me now.

"Then her father really shut down because now both of his favorite girls were gone. And because she made the awful mistake of inheriting her mother's genes, reminding him every day of what he'd lost, he decided to go look for a new life with a little leg up from God."

"What?"

"Yeah, I didn't think you'd remember. I told you about it way back when, but you were too busy with your—whatever. You were fucked up."

"This little trip down memory road's been real great but—"

"Oh, it's not over yet. We've still got a couple corners to take.

After Dad got God, Katie got fucked." It was the first time I'd said it out loud in sixteen years. The words stopped us both. She held onto the counter, staring at the floor. The rhythm of the leaky faucet kept us from being absorbed into the black hole of silence.

"Dad?" she finally said. Her voice was small, like that of a child who's been punished asking to come out of her room.

"God no. A friend of his."

"Shit, you almost gave me a stroke."

"Well, as long as you're okay."

"Give me a break. I thought you were talking about Dad."

"I might as well have been."

"What's that mean?"

"Never mind."

She came to the table and sat down. I sat too.

"Why didn't you..."

"Tell you? I think you know the answer to that."

"Did you tell Dad?"

"Yeah. Went over really well."

"When? Who?"

"Doesn't matter. It's done. He's dead."

Her gaze pierced me.

"No, I didn't kill him! God. He did it himself."

"When? When did this happen?"

"Couple months after you left."

"Christ."

"Had nothing to do with Him." I picked up her pack of cigarettes and fingered the plastic wrap. I liked the crinkly sound it made.

"You were what, like twelve, thirteen?" she said.

"You were always shit at math, Chloe. I was eleven."

"Jenny's age," she whispered to herself.

"Yes."

There went the tapping fingers again. She stared at me. It seemed like she really wanted to hug me, but something was holding her against her chair. An invisible fence, like the ones people use for dogs that shock them when they try to go outside the bounds of their yard. My sister didn't dare expand the bounds of the cage she'd built around herself the day I was born.

"I was alone. I've been alone since Mom died. So please don't tell me how spoiled I am."

I considered popping a cigarette out and indulging myself, but decided against it. I played with the package, waiting for her to say something. She didn't. Just checked her watch and studied her tapping fingers that were set to break some kind of land speed record on the table. They were moving so fast now I couldn't see fingers anymore, just blurry pale skin. I reached out and covered her hand with mine. All motion stopped. The crinkling stopped. Everything was still, quiet. Even the sound of the television went away.

She looked at my hand like it was a poisonous alien tentacle then slid hers out from under it. She rested it on her lap and the tick transferred itself to her leg. It bobbed up and down like a sewing machine needle. I sat back, settling into my own cage and the world got noisy again.

"You said Dad was sick. What's that about?" I asked.

"Janet called a couple weeks ago. He's been in and out of the hospital. She asked me to come back, but you know..."

"No, I don't know."

"I can't really get time off work. They're not too easy down at the plant. My boss is an asshole."

"Is it serious? Is he really sick?"

"I don't know. I didn't ask."

"What the hell, Chloe? You were his fucking golden child and now you don't even give a shit if he's dying?"

"That's so dramatic, Kate. So you."

"What does that mean?"

Our hackles were rising again.

"It means you're a drama queen."

"Whatever." I stood, whipping my chair out from underneath me. It tipped over backward, smacking the linoleum. Nothing dramatic there.

"What? You can come into my house and tell me what to do, but I can't say anything to you?"

I went to the sink and picked up the mug she'd just used, filled it with coffee, took one swig, then spit it out. It tasted exactly like bile.

"That's nice. Spit in my sink."

"I wasn't telling you what to do. Trust me, I know how futile a thing that is."

"You trying to say something to me?"

I didn't answer. This was not going in the direction I'd hoped it would. I knew she might have a problem with taking us in, but not because she was trying to get her life straight. I thought she'd complain about Sadie getting in the way of her partying.

"Never mind," I said.

"So typical. Always starting shit you can't finish."

"Are you seriously still pissed? It was ten years ago. I did you a favor. I can't believe—"

"You're always sticking your nose where it doesn't belong, Kate, that's all I'm saying."

"I perjured myself for you. You'd still be inside like that shit-bag if it wasn't for me." I was standing at the sink talking to her ponytail. I wanted to grab it and wrap it around her neck.

"Yeah, well, neither of us would've gotten caught if you hadn't called the cops."

"Right. You're still—he was throwing you around the room like a fucking ragdoll, Chloe! What the hell was I supposed to do, let him kill you?" I'd circled the ponytail and landed in front of her. She held my gaze for a moment then let go, dropping her head to examine the floor.

"Oh my God. You wanted him to," I said to myself out loud.

"Just drop it."

I pulled the chair over and sat in front of her. She wouldn't look up at me. "Chloe—"

"I said drop it. What does it matter now?"

"Because it does. Why didn't you, I don't know, why didn't you tell me—"

"You were too busy running off to Atlanta with that douche bag to notice anything I had going on."

"Well, I learned from the master."

That didn't really help the situation any. She retreated further into her cage.

"Besides, would you have listened to me? Would you have cared?" she asked. Two excellent questions. I didn't know how to answer them. Well, I did know how. I just wasn't fond of my answers. I tried to rectify my past shortcomings.

"Do you still..." I fell off because I couldn't bring myself to ask.

"What? Want somebody to beat my skull in? Some days." Her eyes burned into mine. I didn't know what to do. My sister had never been this vulnerable in front of me before. I sat still, afraid to break our connection. I didn't know if we'd ever have another chance like this to be sisters. I took her hand in mine and held it. She tried to pull away but I held tight.

"I'm sorry," I said, but my voice didn't cooperate. It got stuck in my throat like a little rubber ball and I had to force it out. It made her nervous, I think, and she tried to pretend she didn't hear what I'd said. She chewed her lip and bobbed her leg faster and faster as she studied the table.

"Chloe. I'm sorry. For everything." I wasn't clear about who was talking. It sure as hell wasn't Kate. Must have been her five-year-old doppelganger.

Then all Chloe's movement stopped abruptly.

"That's real nice, but you still can't stay," she said, ripping her hand from mine. Her voice quavered. She was on the brink of something she wasn't up to emotionally, so she freed herself from the stimulus.

"I got to go to work." She waddled off through the kitchen door into a back room and left me sitting there, exposed. And pissed. I'd just shown her more concern in the last minute than she'd shown me in my entire life and she walks away? I guess I should have been used to it, but this time was different. I'd put myself out for her.

"Well fuck you very much," I hissed under my breath.

"I heard that."

"Well I've got more for you, then," I said, charging into her room. It was dark and musty like the rest of her place. This whole thing was not going to turn out the way I'd hoped, so I really had nothing to lose getting things off my chest.

"You should've stayed," I said, standing in her doorway.

"What?"

"You should've taken care of me."

"What's done is done."

"That doesn't even—I was eleven. *Eleven* Chloe!"

She rifled through her closet, a substitute for her other nervous ticks. "You're blaming me for what some pervert—"

"Jesus, you've never even acknowledged my birthday. Do you think I didn't notice how you were always conveniently absent?"

"Talk about tangents. What're you—"

"I remember the parties and the presents, before Mom died of course, I can even remember the cakes, but what I don't remember ever seeing was my sister's face."

"Maybe you blocked me out."

"No, Chloe, I think it was the other way around."

She rummaged through her mess, leaning so far in I was concerned she might get lost in the quagmire of her closet.

"Look, I'm sorry you...I mean it sucks you were..."

"Well, what's done is done. Right?"

She stopped rifling through her things and whipped around

to face me. My stomach flip-flopped itself into a mushy pretzel. I'd posed the question before not really believing the answer, but now I knew it was true. Her animosity was palpable. It shot through me like a thousand volts.

"Nothing is ever enough for you," she said. Again, a surprising observation coming from my ex-addict, ex-con, older sibling.

"I don't know how to respond to that."

"Course you don't. You only know how to take."

"I'm listening, Chloe, stop writing notes. Just say what you have to say."

"All I know is my life sucked after you came into it."

I should have been prepared for this, but I thought the whole family thing, sharing blood and all that, was supposed to provide a kind of buffer for those feelings. I always thought it was a requirement, like yearly head lice checks in grade school, for your family to love you. It's not pleasant; it's just what you do. I never realized when Chloe took her frustrations out on me it had more to do with me than the frustrations. *I* was her frustration.

"From birth on up, huh?" I rarely gave credence to the idea that she could truly hate me. I was a baby. What could I have— "Mom. It was Mom wasn't it?" I asked.

"Just drop it. Doesn't matter now."

"Yes it does, Chloe. Why do you always run away from everything?"

"You might want to ask yourself that question."

She made a valid point.

"What happened?" I said, stepping into her room. I moved toward her near the bed where she sat.

"I already told you."

"Tell me again. Sometimes I'm a little slow."

She glared at me. Felt like she was trying to burn right through my head with her laser beam eyes. "No, Kate. I am. And you know it. Before you came, I mattered."

She hauled herself off the bed like an old woman. Her bones were thirty-four, but her spirit was ancient. She plodded to the door and stopped, holding the casing for support. "I mattered."

She'd aged forty years on her trip to the door. She turned and spoke to the box serving as a nightstand behind me, "What's done is done."

I sat on the bed for a minute to gather my thoughts after she wobbled away. Was she right? Couldn't it be undone? I knew what one little person might think about that.

Chloe had picked up speed by the time I came back into the kitchen. She slogged back and forth between the stove and the fridge preparing her dinner.

"I'd ask you to stay and eat, but—"

"You're really not going to, we can't even stay a couple nights? Till I figure something out?"

"What car do you have, Kate?"

"Why?"

"Don't be an ass. Just answer me."

"A silver Volvo."

"Where's it parked?"

"Downstairs. I don't—"

"The one the cops are poking around?"

I don't remember the steps to the window or pushing the curtain back to look outside. Fight or flight kicked in and I shifted into autopilot. It was exactly what Chloe was looking for.

"See? I knew you were knee deep in some shit. You got to go, Kate. Now." There were no cops. The Silver Angel sat alone by the curb, waiting for her next adventure.

"And I don't want to know. Then I won't have to lie," she said with a full mouth. I let the curtains fall back over the window, enclosing us in Chloe's cave again.

"Right, you just leave that to everyone else."

She looked up from her enormous tri level pastrami sandwich mid bite. "Oh, get over it. It was one time. And it was the least you could do." Tiny bits of half chewed meat and cheese flew in arcs across the room toward me. Another way for her to keep me at a safe distance. Fortunately, I was far enough away to miss the incoming.

She'd never be grateful for what I'd done for her because she was too hung up on everything else. Everything else being my existence.

"So that's it? It's done? You're going to throw me out on the street with a child and no place to go? I don't have any money, Chloe. I'm broke. I. Have. Nothing." I thought I'd change course and go for the sympathy vote. Also it was mostly the truth. I had some money, but it was dwindling at a precipitous pace.

"Look, it's not my fault that—"

"You know what? Piss off about fault! Just be my sister for once. Please?"

"Telling me to piss off isn't going to get you what you want."

"What will, Chloe? What?" She didn't respond, just kept eating and staring at the table. "Great. That's just, yeah. You're not my sister. You're nothing." She'd shut down. Went further inside her cave. It was a hereditary trait. "Fine. We'll go."

I strode into the living room to fetch Sadie. She'd fallen asleep on her mother and the cracker wrapper had dropped to the floor, empty. I wasn't happy to wake her and take her away again. Where this time? I was exhausted by the chase. Running had transformed itself from freedom to prison for me. I didn't want to stop and think because if I did I knew I'd have to acknowledge just how terrified I'd become.

"I hope you really need me someday," I said with my hand on the doorknob. Sadie clung to me, barely conscious, resting her head on my shoulder.

"Bye Aunt Chloe. Thank you for the crackers."

I turned to look at my sister to see if Sadie had made an impact. She just chewed her sandwich and studied the table leg. I left silently and twisted the knob so the door closed without a sound. I didn't want to leave any trace of my existence there. No new grudges for her to cleave to.

Right before the door shut, I thought I heard something come from inside. A thin whisper of a voice saying, "you're welcome", but it was clear we weren't so I left the door closed.

I knew no one in Portland and didn't have enough money left for a hotel *and* gas. My options had dissolved to nothing, like my relationship with my sister.

I put Sadie in the front seat and tried to buckle her belt but my hand was shaking so much I couldn't fit the latch in the receiver end. The lava boiled up inside me. I was ready to blow. But just before I gave up and threw the seatbelt and another fit, Sadie put her hand on top of mine and helped me guide it down in.

The touch of her warm palm soothed me until I heard the click of the seatbelt. It sent a shockwave of panic through my whole body. In past lives it would have thrilled me. It had been the sound of adventure, new beginnings, reinvention. But in that moment all I heard was a jail door clanking shut, serving as a final punctuation to our trip. I stifled a scream and did everything in my power not to lose it in front of her again. I was a foot past complete exhaustion and it felt like I was shaking apart from the inside.

I climbed into the driver's seat and sat for a few minutes, trying to calm myself. I didn't even realize I was crying until I heard Sadie.

"Katie? Don't be sad, please."

From the side I saw a small white tissue float over my right arm, hovering there between her tiny fingers, waiting for me to take it. I glanced down and through my blurriness I saw her concern, but also the pride she felt for offering me the Kleenex, like a big person would.

"We can get chocolate. And we'll be together. It's—" I didn't let her finish. Just took her in my arms, with the Kleenex and seatbelt, and squeezed her. I buried my face in her hair like she'd done with Matilda and showed very little regard for her bones.

I was tired of feeling heavy and dull. Burdened with the weight of everything I couldn't let go. I'd realized in a very short time I was not so different from Chloe, though I needed desperately to believe I was.

I let go of Sadie and wiped her wet cheeks. I didn't mean to pawn my pain off on her; she had enough of her own.

"Thank you," I said, stuffed and snotty.

"Wowcome."

I gave her a kiss on the forehead and decided to curb my crazy in front of her from then on. The last thing she needed was me breaking apart. "We're going to be fine. Great. Better than great. We're going to be super-riffic."

"Supu-wiffic's not a word," she said, giggling.

"Oh, look who's so smart." I started the car and, with a million tiny shards of the past pricking my insides, headed for the highway.

"Where we going now?"

"North."

"Why come?"

I didn't want to tell her we had no other options, but I also didn't want to lie, so I compromised. "Because I want to introduce you to someone."

"Oh. Someone nice?"

"Yes, honey, someone nice."

Trindle's dolphin candle was in my bag on the back seat, waiting to be returned, and I thought she'd be happy to have it back. In fact, I counted on it.

FIFTEEN

Sadie's smile was the last thing I remembered cruising down the ramp onto the freeway in Portland. It was like the road had swallowed us there and spit us out almost two hundred miles north in Seattle. Everything in between was a dream. I awoke in Queen Anne idling in a parking lot that used to be Trindle's driveway, holding Sadie's hand in the glow of a red neon sign.

I'd tried to go home. They say it's where the heart is. My heart hadn't been with Gregory Denai at 519 Willow Way for a long time. It had been with the Kinrosses, Trindle's family, up until I left. They'd been my home the last few years of school while my father decided to drop God and pick up a bottle. They'd provided me with more support and good food than I could ask for. Even though I didn't actually live there until graduation night, I'd spent a good amount of time in the warmth of their everyday lives.

When I called Trindle's number and it was disconnected I wasn't shocked. I figured her parents had changed it, but I didn't realize until I was staring at the neon red *Hunan Wok* sign in the parking lot how much they'd changed everything. I was parked where their spare bedroom/my room used to be. You really can't go home. But apparently you can chow mein there.

My stomach twisted in knots and I thought I might get sick. I was treading water in the middle of an angry sea, alone. I didn't have Trindle's new number because I hadn't spoken to her in ten years. I was sad and ashamed for losing touch. At that particular moment more so than most days. She'd called and written me after I'd moved down to Chloe's in Portland, but I deliberately cut my ties with everything that reminded me of home. I thought I'd never come back.

And here I was, perched in a stolen Volvo next to a stolen mini-me, idling in front of a strip mall Chinese restaurant trying to remember how to swim. Even if I had pictured myself returning, this wasn't the snapshot I'd posted to my mental corkboard for the homecoming.

I knew Trindle would still be somewhere in Seattle as long as her parents were alive, so maybe they were gone. I was sure they wouldn't sell their house if all was well. It had been in their family for a hundred years. No way they'd take cash over family history. But maybe they'd expired and Trindle needed the money. I had no idea. I knew for certain only three things: the gas gauge was either broken or we really were close to empty, the Veggie Plate number two looked mighty tasty, and we had run out of options. And almost out of money. Okay, four things.

I dialed information but the closest I came to Trindle Kinross was Trundle's and More on King's Road. I'd lost my best friend and I wondered how much more I'd lose. Every little bit of this was my fault. An unfortunate detail I couldn't ignore anymore.

I felt the sparks shooting around in my gut again. The trembling beginnings of the flame working its way toward the inferno. But I'd promised myself for Sadie's sake I'd keep my shit in check. It took every ounce of the little self-control I'd cultivated on our trip not to beat my head against the steering wheel.

A tiny squeak, not unlike the voice of a mouse, came from the other side of the car. It was followed by sniffles and heavy breathing. I was grateful for it. I'd worked myself up into quite a lather considering all the things I wasn't going to do; it helped to bring me down.

The light from the sign washed over Sadie's cabbage patch face and reflected off the tributaries running down her cheeks. It looked like she was crying crimson tears. She embraced her backpack and stared straight ahead at the glove box.

"Honey, what's wrong?" She didn't move. "Sadie, what's wrong? You're worrying me." I shut the car off, unbuckled and turned to face her. She didn't look at me, kept her gaze forward.

"I miss her."

"Who? Matilda?"

"Mommy."

I knew this moment would come. I was just hoping to be somewhere different, a little less strip mall, a little more home, to have the conversation. Of course she missed her mother, but with the whole survival thing occupying most of my functioning brain cells, it wasn't always on my front burner.

I wasn't sure what to say. I only knew about my own grief and I didn't talk to anyone about it when I was young so I didn't have a quality example to emulate. I never put my pain on Trindle. We built forts and played Sardines with her neighbors and climbed trees. I kept her in the dark about a lot of things because I wanted her to be Switzerland for me. Neutral, unbiased. If she didn't know the facts about my life, then she wouldn't feel sorry for me. I'd know her friendship was real and not borne of pity.

She didn't know about Martin Flemming and I swore I'd never tell her. I'd already tried to tell my father a year after it had happened and it didn't go over well so I'd decided to keep the information to myself from then on.

"Of course you miss your mommy."

I wanted to ask, *aren't I a good replacement?* But I thought that might be crass. Didn't stand in my way of wanting to know the answer, though. And then I wondered if she had other people standing in line to be replacements too. I hadn't even considered the idea of other relatives who would be expecting to take care of her now that her mother was gone.

"Honey, do you have aunts or uncles or..." Anybody else I'm going to have to fight off to keep you?

Finally, after a long silence, she spoke, "I have a Aunt Betsy but she got hurt so she sleeps all the time. I never met her when she wasn't sleeping."

"Do you have any grandparents?"

"I never saw my grandaddy. And my granmommy was in the old people place but she didn't know who I was when my mommy took me to see her. I donwanna live with anybody else!"

The last part came out so fast I almost didn't understand what she'd said. But then I realized what her silence was about. Talking about her mother or the idea of having to live with an aunt in a coma set off another deluge.

"Don't worry, honey. I'm going to make sure you won't have to." A hefty promise. I intended to keep it.

"I'm sorry we've been on the go so much. We'll be settled soon." I cradled her in my arms and let her cry. Children craved stability. I figured the promise of it was a good start. And though there was no concrete evidence to backup what I'd just said, I found myself in an odd state, believing in the possibility of my own words, regardless of my previous indiscretions.

"My mommy likes the birdies at the water," she said, when the torrent had slowed to a trickle. She gazed at a drawing of a herring or egret or some other long-necked bird on the menu taped to the door of the restaurant.

"Do you like the water?" I asked.

"It's scary sometimes on the boat," she said, all goopy in the nose and throat.

"You went on a boat with your mommy?"

She nodded as the tears dribbled down her cheeks. "A sailboat. She likes the waves but they make me sick in my tummy when we tip."

"Me too."

A teenage couple left the restaurant, hand in hand, giggling and joking with each other. A female employee followed them and locked the door after they left. She flipped the OPEN sign over to CLOSED and walked away. I took it as my cue.

"Do you want to go on another boat? A big boat?" The words oozed out of my mouth like blood from a gaping wound. What was I saying? Why was I even considering it? I'd fled here for one reason only. To find Trindle and see if she'd help me. No extra-curricular activities allowed.

"Will I go on the boat with you?"

"Of course."

"Can we bring my mommy?"

"We wouldn't go without her."

Sadie smiled and threw herself on me, gripping my arms with her tiny fingers. It started to pinch a little, but I was preoccupied with discerning what demon had suddenly possessed me. My new doppelganger had taken over and I felt helpless to thwart her. She'd popped her ugly little head up in Portland with concern for a sick father. But Chloe was the one who was supposed to go see him before he kicked, not me. She was his favorite. He was already dead as far as I was concerned. Except he wasn't.

What did I think was going to happen? We'd have a snot drenched reunion, during which he'd implore my forgiveness and all would end in kisses and hugs and merry merry. He'd shelter us for as long as we needed and hire the best lawyers in town to plead my case when I decided to turn myself in a few years down the road.

"Stop." I didn't mean to say it out loud; it just flew out. Sadie thought I was talking to her, so she eased her grip on me. I couldn't believe I'd even contemplated going there. Nobody was going to tell me what to do. Especially myself. I'd be a stalwart soldier against my own will. That'd show me. Even if it meant sleeping in the car at the beach. Forever.

"I didn't mean you, honey. I'm sorry. Let's...you want to go to the beach?"

"Right now? To go on the boat?"

"Not yet. We'll wait a little bit to go on the boat. For now we'll just go look at the pretty lights of the city."

"They're at the beach?"

"Their reflection is."

"Can you read to me the rest of Clyde please?"

I pulled a flashlight from the glove box and pushed the button. A column of white light flew forth blazing against the padded car roof. Hopefully it would last us to the end of Clyde's amazing adventures. And our own. "Let's go find out what happens to Clyde," I said.

"And Clancy. Can't forget Clancy. She's special."

"Well, of course Clancy too. Without her, Clyde would be lost."

"Maybe she's an angel like Matewda."

"If she hadn't stowed away in his jeep he would've been blown straight out to sea."

"Clyde doesn't have a jeep."

"What?"

"Did you pay attention to the story? Are you making another one up?"

"What did I say?" I'd tuned out. Like a blackout, without the blacking out.

"That she sowed away in his jeep. But he doesn't have a jeep."

"Right. My bad. Let's get to the water, huh?"

"I don't mind if you make up a story too." She sat back in the seat and buckled herself up.

"I'll keep that in mind."

"Where we sleeping tonight?"

I wasn't prepared for twenty questions. "Um, I thought maybe we could camp out a little. We've got a blanket in the back and—"

"In the car?" I could tell from the thin, high note punctuating the end of her question the idea didn't much appeal to her. But who the hell was making the decisions around here? Right. Well, even still, I had a hand in things.

"Well, we'll see how it goes. It'll be fun. Our own adventure, just like Clyde's."

"Where will I go potty?"

Why was she always the one thinking the logical thoughts? If we hurried we could probably catch the last ferry to Bainbridge and be snuggled up in warm beds within an hour. Near a toilet.

"Don't worry. We'll manage." I had no idea how. But I still had some stubborn in me. Even if it was vastly misplaced.

We left Queen Anne and headed south into town. Cruising down through I suddenly became nostalgic for all the things I'd loved about the city in which I grew up. I wanted to share them with Sadie: the view from the Space Needle, the Lighthouse at Alki Point, the Arboretum. I hadn't been there since I was ten.

Nostalgia held me hostage and forced me down First Avenue to Pioneer Square; it had always been my favorite part of Seattle. Old brick and cobblestone, the rich history filling the air above and below the street. And though it was considered cheese by natives, I even wanted to take her on the Underground Tour to watch her gaze up through the thick bubbles of stained glass and see the people walking over her head on the sidewalk above. That would produce a squeal or two.

I passed the used bookstores I used to spend hours in, poring over titles. I'd go there to live in the scent of ancient pages, classic stories, to escape the pain of my own. *The Grotto* was my haven. They only sold used books so I was guaranteed that thick, musty aroma every time I walked through their door.

Trindle enjoyed reading as well, although not nearly as much as I did. On many occasions she'd leave me there when the boy of the hour came to whisk her away on some naughty adventure. My seventeen year old loins longed to have some of my own adventures, but my seventy-five year old mind reminded me I'd already had them and they weren't much fun.

I was content to stick my head back in the books and that's where it stayed till I graduated. Till my father was too incapacitated to give audience to his sublimely intelligent daughter making her valedictory speech in front of hundreds. Only the most important moment of her life. After that, naughty adventures were mine.

We headed across the bridge toward Alki Beach. I wanted to at least share that with her. The view from the northeast tip, just before you take the turn south toward Mount Rainier, was magical. The Emerald City glowed across Elliott Bay like it had lit itself on fire in a million different places, a universe in the black hole of night.

After we planted the crepe myrtle my mother took me there on nights she felt especially disconnected from herself, her life. It dawned on me much later these were the times her synapses weren't even in the same zip code together. So she went there to free herself from the cage she'd built at home. To feel all the things she couldn't allow herself to feel anywhere else. Get lost in something beautiful instead of a bottle and her own crazy. I wasn't sure why she took me with her, but I didn't care. I was happy to be there, even when she disappeared inside herself. And even when she came out. Many times I'd catch her wiping the tears away, hoping to erase the evidence before I saw them staining her cheeks.

"Are you okay, Mommy?"

"I'm fine. It's just so beautiful, that's all. Don't you think it's fantastic? The way the lights live on the water?"

I learned after a while to stop asking if she was all right because she never gave a real answer. Every time, she'd draw my attention away to the sparkly lights or an imaginary whale or school of flying fish. Some distraction to keep me preoccupied so I wouldn't witness her melting down.

I caught on after the first few questions. Don't ask. It's not polite to point out when someone is breaking up.

What I found fantastic about those times was not the reflection of the city on the water, not leaping fish, real or otherwise, but the reflection of the lights living in my mother's eyes. She was home to me, my sanctuary. Even on her dark nights.

She'd tell my father we were going out for ice cream or to the campus to get something she'd forgotten. I'm not sure if he ever believed her, but he never tried to stop us. Except the last time.

She'd been drinking again, though Dr. Greene had strictly forbidden it. Months before, she'd been hospitalized after suffering another acute attack of pancreatitis. Dr. Greene had warned her that alcohol was the likely cause and she'd need to quit drinking immediately if she wanted to get her health, her life, back. Of course, I didn't learn about that until after she was gone.

She and Dad had argued that last night, it was one of the few times I'd ever heard him raise his voice to her. Heated whispers emanated from the porch outside. The screen door was the only barrier between their anger and me so I turned up the volume on the Brady Bunch and did my best to concentrate on *Marcia Marcia Marcia*. I didn't like hearing them argue. It made my stomach cramp. But I didn't want to go to my room either. The thin door slammed, followed by my father's strained voice.

"Joanna, why are you doing this?"

"I'm not doing anything. Just leave it alone, Greg."

Feet scuffled across the tile of the kitchen floor. I wanted to go in and stop them, but I stayed in my chair while my heart leapt into my throat.

"What about what Dr. Greene said? Why would you—"

"What are you doing? Don't grab me."

"You're not going anywhere."

"Let go of me. Now."

It was the first time in my life I'd heard my parents argue at this level. It had never become physical before.

"Will you promise not to go?"

"You know I don't make promises."

That wasn't entirely true, she'd made plenty to me. Of course, in dying, she managed to break them all.

"Just stop, Jo."

"I'm not doing anything."

"You reek of it." More movement. It sounded like she'd freed herself from him and shuffled across the room. "Goddammit, Jo! Stop fighting me on this! Is it that bad? Am I, are we that bad you'd rather die?"

That was too much to handle, I had to see what was happening. My father had never sworn at her. And the idea that she was going to die was so unthinkable I needed some kind of visual re-assurance he was way off base for even thinking it, no less throw-ing it out there where it couldn't be put back on the shelf.

I moved to the stairs, teetering on the first step. Ready at any moment to bolt up, I peeked around the doorway into the kitch-en. My parents stood apart, facing each other. They were two Grecian columns, one on each side of the island in the middle, holding up the room. Both sides were aged and crumbling a little, for very different reasons, and I worried the roof might cave in around us all.

It wasn't long before it did. That was the night before Myrtle blossomed. And as always, with everything, my mother got her way. She didn't dignify his questions with a response, but instead called me out from my hiding place and took me with her one last time down to our spot. My father turned his back on us as we walked out past him.

"What daddy said before, he wasn't, you're not..."

We sat close on the break wall dangling our feet over the edge. The warm breeze flirted with the water, coaxing it over the rocks. The world was at peace, but fear swelled inside me.

"Don't worry about what Daddy said. He can be very dramatic sometimes. Overprotective. But it's only because he loves us."

It was August, a month before I would lose her forever. A chorus of crickets provided the background music for the city to dance to on the bay. Everything was as it had always been, but what she said next has haunted me ever since.

"You'll have to learn to forgive him for that and probably a great many other things. That's what love is, Bits." Her voice frightened me. It trembled and held in it fear and uncertainty. I knew then my father was not far off target when he'd dropped that bomb in the kitchen.

She put her arm around me and held me tight against her for a moment. Her sour breath hung heavy in the air above me. It was the same smell I used to walk into when I'd sneak up on her after school.

I was rather stealthy when I was eight. I'd come home in the afternoon and spy on my mother out in the garden or taking a bath or doing a crossword puzzle on the porch then I'd slink up and surprise her. She always screamed like I'd scared the bejeesus out of her, but I think she was just giving me what she knew I wanted. I'd giggle and she'd take me on her lap and tickle me silly for scaring her again.

If I didn't find her outside, I'd tiptoe up our spiral staircase, slip their bedroom door open and peek in, expecting to find her napping on their California king with one eye open, waiting for me to frighten her. But sometimes what I found frightened me. Those were the times she forgot all about my daily sneak attacks. Did her best to forget about her life entirely.

Sometimes she had Crown Royal, sometimes Absolut, and if the synapses were extra far apart, she went straight for the Everclear. For dessert, she always had the chocolate. More than a few times I caught her sitting on the floor in the corner of their room gorging herself on Pinwheels and Bon Bons.

My mother mixed her drinks with chocolate, made the depression go down easier, so I learned from a master how to deal with my own sadness. She tried to be discreet with her illness, but I caught her more than I liked to remember, more than she knew. And I never let on.

Joanna Denai had always felt like a caged bird, like my father was her keeper, her jailor. I know she loved him, and she loved her girls, but I think she also believed she was meant to live a different life. One with the same kind of freedom I'd experience after I ran away graduation night.

I hoped she was watching me with Sadie so she could realize how great she'd had it, how freedom can be as cramped and inescapable as any other cage when you're trapped inside yourself.

Also, stealing a car and going on the run with a child not your own can put up a few bars as well. I tried to stay away from public places as much as possible with Sadie, but when I passed the Admiral Market I had to stop for snacks. We hadn't eaten anything in hours and it was bound to be a long night so I wanted to stock up. I was a little worried I'd see someone I knew or be recognized, but it didn't happen. In a way it made me sad, like I hadn't grown up in this town. I had nothing left, no one to be attached to.

Except Sadie.

"Bubboos! Can I get the bubboos, please, please?"

We were in the checkout line and to our right was a shelf brimming with purple bottles of bubbles. Sadie had ants in her pants, she couldn't stand still she was so excited.

"Well, okay." It thrilled me to see her happy again.

When I handed her the bottle, she pondered it for a moment. Seemed like she was waiting for it to *do* something. Then she looked up at me. "Will you blow the bubboos with me? Please?"

She wore her expectation like a clown his big red nose, nothing subtle there. This meant something to her.

"Of course."

She unscrewed the top. Oh. This meant something to her right now.

"Honey, maybe it's not such a good idea right—"

Bubbles in the face. Sadie giggling her pants off.

"I got you in the face with the bubboos!"

"Yes you did." I looked around to see if we were drawing any unwanted attention but everyone in line behind us smiled politely, entertained by the cute little redhead spewing bubbles at her mommy.

"Can you get down here and help me blow them?"

I squatted down to put the basket on the floor and she blew them right into my mouth. I scrunched my face up and almost had to pull her off the ceiling she was so giddy.

"I got you with the bubboos! They taste yucky don't they Mommy!" She wasn't pretending. But I wasn't the mommy she was thinking of when she'd said it. It caught me off guard and I paused for one second, imperceptible to anyone but Sadie.

"Yes you did. And they do taste yucky."

She crashed like crystal on a cement floor. I tried to pick up her bits and pieces before we made a scene, but she wasn't interested in cooperating. She flowed without restraint from ecstasy into the fourth stage of grief. I found myself fighting back tears for the same reason she let them come.

"No, honey. Please don't." I took the bottle from her and put it on the shelf, then picked her up. She flopped her head on my shoulder, drenching it with tears. I rubbed her back and my hand got warm, like it was generating an abundance of energy. Or absorbing it.

What Sadie had done for me in the jeep after we broke down, I could feel myself doing for her now. Siphoning away her pain. Her back was warm and I suddenly felt sick to my stomach. I wanted to leave the store, to have a private moment, but we needed food and we were next in line so I stayed. I felt eyes on us from behind, so I faced forward and whispered to Sadie.

"Everything's going to be okay. Please know that. Everything's going to be good again for both of us."

I brushed her moist bangs out of her eyes. She didn't look up at me, just clung to my words and my shoulders. I wasn't sure what we were going to do when the sun rose the next morning. I couldn't think that far ahead, it made my body ache.

We bought our goodies and headed down to the water. I nestled Betty between two other cars on the main strip of Alki Avenue and turned her off. Sadie had come back from her dark place and was recouping quietly next to me in the co-pilot's seat. I was still loitering in my dark place. The exact significance of the bubbles wasn't clear, but I knew it was a matter of me trying to fill shoes that were too damn big. I sat quietly trying to reconcile myself with the idea of that.

A stiff wind blew across Elliott Bay, rippling and twisting the water so the lights from the city smeared and disappeared from its surface. A thin whisper of rain fell on the windshield, blurring our view into an impressionist version of Oz. We opened our Cupcakes and Snicker bars first. I bought sandwiches too, but I'd always been a firm believer in the Dessert First School of Eats. Especially following trauma.

Hopped up on sugar my thoughts bounced from big shoes to blue moons. I hadn't seen any more blue anything and I wondered if Sadie had given up on me. I'd gone too far stealing the car and she was done. The whole time I'd been with her I'd felt like a project, something to fix.

My dirty little doppelganger took over and I zigzagged back to the notion of Bainbridge Island and catching a ferry. Suddenly it felt like Sadie was doing the butterfly stroke in my noggin, digging in with both hands to clear a path and figure out what was going on in there. Oddly enough, I'd become comfortable with her swimming around inside me.

I finished the cupcake three-pack and moved on to the Suzie Q's. Always good to have a backup. She was still nursing her Snicker Bar. Amateur. The plastic wrapper crackled through the beautiful silence. Then Sadie did too.

"What's your Daddy's name?"

I took the mature approach to this question and ignored it. If she pursued it I'd bring her attention to the three hundred foot blue whale doing back flips in the middle of Elliott bay.

"He's sick, huh?" she asked.

"Did you see that? I think it was Moby Dick." She didn't get it, but it made me laugh. "My mom and I used to come down here a lot. Isn't it beautiful? Honey, you're not looking. See the way the lights live on the water? Isn't it—why aren't you looking?"

"Why don't you like him?"

Tit for tat.

"It's all very complicated and boring. Unlike the view. That's perfect. I'm pretty sure I just saw a whale."

"I don't like my new pretend daddy either. Sometimes he gets mean since Mommy went to Heaven."

What? Neglect and burned fingers were bad enough, enough for me to take her away, but if there was more to it, then he needed to be tattled on but good.

"What do you mean, 'mean'? Does he hurt you? Sadie?"

Now she was the one pretending. I waited for her to turn to me exclaiming she'd just seen King Kong riding Captain Ahab, look! But she held her silence. I curled her long spicy hair behind her ear so I could see her eyes. She had a strong profile, a survivor's chin. I knew she'd excel at whatever she chose for her life as long as she didn't follow in my spectacular footsteps. I too excelled at certain things, none of which I'd be inclined to share with anyone at a dinner party.

"I don't like it dark."

"Honey, please tell me what he did to you."

"'Member when the door was locked and you couldn't get in to me?"

"When?"

"In the dream."

"Sadie that won't happen, it was just a dream. You don't have to worry—"

"It did happen."

"What?" She didn't say any more. "Did he lock you in your room?" She shook her head. "But he locked you somewhere?"

She clutched her bag and nodded. I didn't need to know more.

In fact, I was worried if she told me I'd head south that minute and not stop till I ran through the bastard's living room.

"Can we finish Clyde?"

This had to stop: the distractions, the denials, the excuses. It seemed to me everything in my life for the last ten years, the last eighteen years, had been rushing toward this moment. I couldn't do that to Sadie. She was not going to live like I had. I was determined to give her more. And I'd do it the right way. Sort of.

"Not yet, honey. We have one more stop to make tonight. Do you want to go on the big boat now?"

"Does it rock side to side?"

"Nope. It's big and steady." No more rocking boats for Sadie.

"Yes please."

We got back on the road and headed toward Pier 52 and the Bainbridge Ferry. My father had moved from our family home on Alki to Bainbridge Island a few years ago. Aunt Janet had tracked me down like a bloodhound to give me his number and address "in case you decide you want to talk to him again before he dies." She was pure understatement.

Lining up behind the other cars to board the ferry I felt a little like a cow being herded into the slaughterhouse. They don't know exactly what's going to happen to them, but they have an inkling it's not going to be good. Most people probably didn't feel quite that sense of dread upon visiting their father, but under the circumstances it was all I could muster. I hoped there wasn't any basis for it in reality.

Here's to hoping.

SIXTEEN

"That's my mommy's new last name," Sadie said. We'd just passed the sign for Fletcher Bay, again. She'd woken long enough to read it then drifted off while I tried to pick my way around the mazelike innards of Bainbridge Island. It saddened me how she still talked about her mother in the present tense, as if she might return any moment from her fabulous vacation, tanned and gorgeous and ready to pick up Sadie's pieces.

Then it dawned on me. Fletcher must have been Chris's last name. And if it was her mother's new last name then they probably hadn't been married long. Sadie was still Beck. An interesting revelation, one I'd delve deeper into as soon as I stopped spinning in circles. We'd spent the better part of two hours getting lost on Bainbridge's winding back roads and I was convinced the anticipation of seeing my father again was going to give me a stroke. I was nearly ready to pull into the next person's driveway and camp out there for the night. It was a toss up, really, between a stranger's driveway and my father's which one would be more inviting.

I'd filed his address and phone number away in the back of my mind after Aunt Janet had called, thinking maybe I *would* want to see him or at least talk to him before he died. I actually dialed his number one late, drunken night in Los Angeles, but hung up after the tenth ring. I wondered if he'd fumbled from bed and scrambled out to the living room, groping at the receiver in the dark only to hear dial tone when he picked up. I pictured him stubbing his toe on a table or the couch on his way back to his room, screaming and ranting and mulling over the futility of life. A girl can dream.

I didn't call him now. Rejection was far too easy over the phone. It's much harder to turn a daughter away when she's standing on your porch holding your grandchild. Or something like that. Besides, we couldn't sleep in the car overnight. It was getting colder by the minute. It had been a foolish, selfish thing for me to even consider.

Either I was hallucinating, or I'd finally found the right road. I must have passed the sign at least a dozen times, but I just couldn't see it. I didn't want to approach the irony of it all. He lived at 922 Sweethome Road.

We pulled into his driveway and I felt my legs set up like cement. Or maybe that was my heart. I didn't move from the sanctuary of The Silver Angel until it had cooled enough to chill me. Just sat and observed the darkness.

There was no porch light. No light inside. Through the inky night I could barely make out the details of his house. It was a cottage, probably about a third of the size of our old home. A small part of me felt good for him. He'd moved to an island to start life anew. Put the past in its proper place.

I woke Sadie and brought her to the door. She clung to me, blowing her sweet, warm breath on my neck with each labored step I took. I found it odd my father would pave his driveway with foot thick pitch. Made the twenty feet from the car to the porch a bit tedious, but we finally arrived a few hours later.

"Where we go..." She yawned and the cutest little squeak escaped from somewhere in the middle of her. "Where we going?"

A question I was eternally unclear about in every respect.

"It's a surprise, honey." For one of us, anyway. Facing his door in the dark, a foot from the knocker, I found myself divided. Ninety-two percent of me wanted to spin on my heels and bolt for the car, never looking back. Five percent knew this was something I needed to do, for assorted reasons. And three percent was totally undecided.

I went with the five and used the knocker. The best way to get through the things we fear is to face them head on. Or bolt and crawl into a cave, but I'd been there and it was time for some light. Or at least some sparks.

The house remained dark, so I knocked again. This time with my fist. Then I had a thought. What if he was too sick to get up? I put my hand on the doorknob to see if it was locked and the window just off the porch to my right lit up. The knob turned white hot and grew spikes so I whipped my hand away.

The universe closed in on me. It was like the stars, so apparent in the midnight sky, were plummeting through a funnel straight into my head. I had to sit or I'd pass out and drop Sadie. Falling back asleep, she'd become a boulder in my arms. I turned to squat on the first step, then heard the suction of the door nudged open behind me.

"Hello?"

Smoking had damaged his throat, but remnants of his old voice sliced through the night air and straight into me. For an ephemeral moment I wanted to whip around and throw myself into him, but my feet waited out my desire and when they finally moved me around to face him, the feeling had passed.

And so, obviously, had time. For him at least. The dim lamp from the living room lit his profile and I saw great crevasses snaking through his forehead and cheeks. He'd aged forty years in the ten I'd been gone. It's shocking what the mind can do to the body when it implodes.

His face disappeared when he flicked on the interrogation spotlight mounted above the door outside. I almost fell over backward, blinded.

"Hi," I said. What was I supposed to say? *Hey pops. Long time. So. Good to see you're not dead yet.* I cleared my throat and tried again. The first one was anorexic. I wanted to appear strong and capable, like I hadn't messed my life up beyond repair since he saw me last.

"Hi. Wow. That's pretty bright."

He flicked the light off and then I was lost in the dark again. It took me a few seconds to return to my normal shapes-only vision, but I didn't need to see his expression to know he was dumbfounded by my presence in his world.

The door opened wider displaying the full picture of him in his threadbare old robe and slippers. The robe hung on him like it would a wire hanger. He was barely able to occupy the space his body filled inside his clothes.

Most of the hair on his head had crept down to his face. His pate shone in the light and I was shocked to see he'd cultivated lip fuzz Thomas Magnum would covet. I distracted myself with his whiskers so I wouldn't have to acknowledge the deep circles painted around his sunken black eyes.

I couldn't stay away from them. The azure I'd cherished for the first ten years of my life had been drawn out, leaving them nearly colorless. My nightmare had not been far off the mark from the reality standing before me. His frailty was shocking. It made me wonder if I'd knocked on the right door. Made me wish I hadn't.

"What...? What...?"

I didn't blame him really. It had been ten years. And I had run away while he was in the living room passed out drunk in his favorite chair. And we hadn't talked since. And I did have the upper hand with the element of surprise, and it was the middle of the night and I had woken him. A bit of shame nibbled at my insides for putting him in this position. Just a bit.

"Sorry for the short notice, the no notice really. I didn't, we got in a little late. I didn't think we'd be this late." I didn't think we'd be this *ever*. No need to share all information though, at least not right up front.

"Sorry for not calling first. I couldn't find your number." It was the only phone number I'd committed to memory in the last ten years.

He stood still, a sentinel stationed at the door. "We, Kathryn?" Ah, there it was. I did have the right house. Damn.

"This is Sadie. She's your, my...she's your granddaughter."

I waited for the jaw to drop and the eyes to widen with fatherly surprise. For the great wide grin that used to accompany our tickle sessions every weekend. I waited for legs to free themselves from the shackles of the past and race out to us. For arms to swallow me whole like they had so many times before our world stopped spinning. I waited.

A frigid wind blew and broke through the hot fury rising in me. In an instant I was an ice sculpture. I knew he'd never understand what it took to melt me.

"Did you hear—"

"Yes, Kathryn. What is it you need?"

Certain he was asking for the abridged version of the list, I put it to him straight. "Nothing. I don't need anything. I just wanted to see you."

"You don't show up at my door at this hour of night, with a child no less, after ten years of nothing simply wanting to see me."

Excellent point. He'd always been a quick one, mi padre. Obviously his mouth wasn't the least bit frail.

"Are you in trouble?"

Why did everyone keep asking me that? I felt like the Hester Prynne of River City. Instead of an A, I had a capital T, and that stands for Trouble, branded on my chest. Was it just so unheard of that I might want to visit my family? Yep, a big blood red T right in the middle of my chest.

My fingers were numb from the cold and the weight of Sadie.

"Can we come in?"

He studied his slippers like they were portals to some other world. An alternate universe where the answer to my question would be clear and he'd know exactly what to say.

Finally, he lifted his gaze to mine and held there for a month or so. I didn't want to seem impatient, but I was worried my hands would crack and break off, dropping Sadie to the porch on her head. I was certainly concerned about my appendages in that scenario, but she was my first priority. She shivered in my arms.

I wasn't going to speak first, though. No way.

"Please?"

Well, I certainly wasn't going to beg.

"We came all this way to—please, Dad." Wow. Dad even. I pulled out all the stops. He closed his eyes and if I'm not mistaken, made an awkward attempt to smile.

"Of course." He opened the door the rest of the way and moved aside for us to come in. I took a hesitant step forward. The moment I passed the threshold I was struck by the odor. It was as distinctive as a house full of cats. But this was the heavy scent of death, like the bones of the cottage were rotting from the inside out. Or his were.

I laid Sadie down on the couch and covered her with a plaid blanket crumpled in a ball at the other end. She woke briefly to snuggle up then drifted back to her dreams. Unfortunately, I had no dreams to drift off to. Just the reality of my nightmare standing next to me, wanting answers to questions I didn't know how to give.

"Be right back. I've got to get our stuff."

He nodded and stepped near the couch after I passed by him on my way to the door. I stopped and watched him stare at Sadie. It was like he was inspecting an alien life form that had just arbitrarily landed in his house.

I walked out thinking maybe things would be different than

I'd anticipated. Maybe this was a step in the right direction. When I returned, loaded with my bag and Sadie's mother, he was still standing in the same spot. I don't think he'd blinked the whole time I was gone.

"Where should I put these?" I said.

"There is fine." He pointed to the area next to the couch. By the door. I didn't want to read too much into it, but usually when you have guests, you put their things where they're going to sleep.

"There's only one bedroom," he said.

"So we'll sleep—"

"On the couch. I'm sorry, Kathryn. If I'd known you were coming, I would have made other arrangements."

I caught his irritation like a fastball without a mitt. I was sure those other arrangements would have had something to do with Aunt Janet and sleeping on her couch. He moved off from Sadie and into the small kitchen. His slippers scuffed along the hardwood and it took great restraint not to tell him to pick up his damn feet.

I sacked my irritation and followed him, leaving Sadie on the couch. If I'd learned anything from my experience with Chloe, it was to bide my time and unload the shit in increments.

He flipped the switch over the sink and a fluorescent light flickered and sparked and battled with itself. It couldn't decide whether it wanted to shine or sleep. Interesting how I could experience such affinity for a toilet and a sad little light all in the same week. Strange week.

After a few rapid flashes and ticks, shine won the war and engulfed us in a sour green glow that would have given Helen of Troy cause to pop a paper bag over her head.

"You hungry? Can I get you something to eat?"

I didn't understand the question. Had my father befriended some young African Masai refugee named Mopoko down at the local YMCA and learned his exotic tribal language? I knew he was asking me something simply by the inflection, but for the life of me I couldn't decipher what it was.

"Kathryn? Did you hear me?" Oh I heard him.

"Some water would be nice. Or whatever. I mean, whatever you have. Tap water's fine if you don't have any bottled or, you know, filtered. Or whatever you have. Milk is good. Maybe not if it's whole milk, 'cause I'd probably get hives or shingles or something. I haven't had milk in, like, a grillion years. Well, you know that. Or, I guess you don't. Anyway, lemonade's fine too. Or pomegranate juice. Would be perfect."

Well, he certainly heard me with my spectacular display of verbal incontinence. Way to appear solidly in control, Kate.

When I dredged up the courage to meet his gaze after derailing my own train I had to fight the urge to crash into him like I used to as a little girl. I'd start from across our vast living room and run as fast as I could into his outspread arms. He'd lift me up over his head and spin me around with my arms spread like I was flying till I couldn't stand it any longer. Then I'd drop down into the shelter of his embrace and he'd sway with me, balancing his chin on my little red head until I felt strong and unspun enough to stand on my own two feet again.

It had been one of my favorite Daddy activities and now,

standing so close, the urge to fly with him again rumbled deep inside me. "Water's fine. Any kind."

He nodded and opened the fridge. I was surprised by the amount of food in it, stocked, presumably, by Aunt Janet. I couldn't imagine him shopping, at least not in his current condition. I wondered who cooked for him, if she came over every day, or if he hired someone. There were so many things I didn't know. My head was chock full of questions about his life and my sudden interest staggered me a little. As did the biggest question of all: would he still be kicking around tomorrow?

He pulled a bottle of Evian out and handed it to me. Then grabbed a beer for himself. Still into it, I see. It had a twist off cap but he struggled with it. His hands obviously didn't get the message from his brain to twist. They were clumsy, useless paws. So I offered to help because when someone in a wheelchair is pushing himself up a steep hill, you help.

"I've got it."

But he didn't get it. Just continued to struggle. I moved to the table and sat so I wouldn't break apart watching my decrepit father toiling over a damn bottle cap. Had it really come to this? I was so ready to dump everything on him when we'd arrived. Spell out in specific and incisive terms exactly how he'd messed up my entire life. Now I had no idea what to say to him.

He finally got the cap off, using a towel for leverage, and sat down across from me at the table. We studied our bottles, our fingernails, the pile of mail in the middle, the dirty paper towel teetering on the edge, everything but each other.

He coughed and rattled everything loose inside himself. I

thought he might empty his entire contents into his hand. I'd wait for him to calm down then I would talk to him. I'd miraculously say the right thing. I'd take care of us, like Mom wanted. And I'd know how to answer the questions he had for me. Honestly. It would all be lovely.

He settled and took a swig of his beer. I waited till he swallowed it. Didn't want to start a conversation mid guzzle. He shifted in his chair; obviously he wasn't comfortable sitting on hard wood. I waited till he found a better position. Didn't want to start something while he was perched precariously on the edge of his seat. He might tumble off mid confession. He pushed back and relaxed against the chair. Now was the perfect—oh, he blinked. I didn't want to interrupt essential body functions. Especially one so important to the health of the ocular cavity. So I waited.

His interest floated down to something behind me and I felt the growing warmth of a tiny hand on my back. I hadn't heard her wake or move across the hardwood floor. A testament to the attention I'd devoted to my father. Or the attention I'd devoted to not attending to him.

"Well hi there, sleepy. When did you get up?" I said. She came out from behind the chair and leaned on me, resting her elbows on my lap. She was quiet. Unusual. She returned my father's gaze, twitching and balancing on one nervous leg. I thought for sure she'd reach out to him, but she didn't. Her default hug setting must have malfunctioned.

"So?" He was looking at me, through me, so I concentrated on the droplet dribbling down the side of my water bottle. "Kathryn."

Oh. Was he talking to me? Hard to be sure with a room full of people. I glanced up and met him in the middle; this was going to be the hard part. I'd never been good at lying to him. The only reason I could pull it off before was because we were out on the porch and not sitting at a table two feet away from each other. It was really all about distance and light. He couldn't see my eyes out there in the dark.

"Can we talk tomorrow? I'm beat."

"It is tomorrow, Kathryn. You come to my door after ten years. Ten years of wondering why you snuck out like a stinking worm just like your sister. Ten years of wondering, worrying you're becoming your sister. And then you show up at one o'clock in the morning, and 'oh by the way this is your grand-daughter. Isn't that nice?' You want to talk tomorrow? You'll talk now and you'll answer every question I pose to you."

Was that a no then? Difficult to discern through the barely reserved rage. Sadie gripped my leg with both hands and didn't let go. She beckoned me from below, so I focused on her and not bolting for the door or turning the table over on top of my father, or a billion other distractions to avoid this conversation.

"What do you want to know?" I was hoping my compliance would have the opposite effect than it did. Reverse psychology didn't work on my father.

"Who is that person standing next to you?"

"I told you, she's—"

"Don't make a mockery of my intelligence, Kathryn. I know that is not your daughter with as much certainty as I know you are in some kind of trouble."

"Why do you keep saying that?"

"It's the second time I've said it. Let's not play games. I realized a long time ago trouble would be the only thing to bring you back here. Either of you. So how much do you need?"

"I don't need money."

I'd be damned if I was going to tell the truth about that to prove him right. Boy was I on target about his mouth. As far from frail as my libido was.

He took another swig of his beer. It was almost gone, just like his patience for my bullshit. I didn't know how to tell him. Not because I thought he'd get angry or flip out. I could handle flipping out. But I realized when I first saw him on the porch, even after everything, I still couldn't handle disappointing him.

"Then what? What do you need? Why did you come here?"

Sadie reached out to me, so I lifted her onto my lap. She was a sack of Styrofoam peanuts, my floppy little Raggedy Anne. She embraced me, stretching her arms out on both sides like armor across my chest.

I suddenly felt like I could tell him anything because she was there with me. She'd promised me in the hotel and here she was, keeping her word. Maybe it should have been the other way around, but I'd become more and more comfortable with it being just the way it was.

But wait a minute, why was I on trial? Why wasn't he? Why wasn't I grilling him too? Or at least spewing all the shit I'd pent up all these years. He wasn't being very nice. Didn't even say I looked good.

I was glad for that though. Because then I'd feel obligated to say something about the way he looked and all I could think to say was, *Well, Dad, you don't look* exactly *dead.*

"Why didn't you look for me?" I asked.

"What?"

"When I 'snuck out like a stinking worm.' Why didn't you track me down? It really wouldn't have taken—"

"That's not what we're discussing."

"Why not? You wanted to talk. Let's talk."

He stood and hobbled over to the sink. The light bounced off his pallid skin and reflected his ghostly double onto the kitchen window. I could see neither of them was up for the fight tonight.

"You'll have to sleep on the couch. I don't have any other rooms." He turned away from the window toward me. "I'll get blankets," he said, shuffling off down the hall. I could tell by the way Sadie hung her head she was watching him go. She was curious about him, but wary as well. No different than her pretend mother.

I brought her to the couch and tucked her in under the blanket, then sat down beside her. She peeked out at me from under it. A hint of a smile curled the corners of her strawberry lips.

"What's that for?" I asked.

She smiled bigger still, but didn't answer me. Then she burped. I could tell it snuck up on her because her eyes widened with surprise and she threw her hands up over her mouth.

"I'm sorry."

"For what?"

"Sister Margaret says it's not polite to pass any kind of gas."

Sister Margaret was obviously of the Old School. I'd known

some young nuns in Atlanta, part of my Overeaters Anonymous group, who could fart any man under the table. Understandably, that's the last place you'd want to be if they were sitting at it.

"Then you should say excuse me." His voice startled me. I was still trying to get used to the idea of him being present at any moment. I'd lived so many years without that luxury, particularly the ones under the same roof. It was a darling irony I didn't let slip past my notice; this was the most we'd spoken in the last eighteen years.

"Scoos me." She sank under the blanket when he approached. Her eyes were wide, studying him. I was fascinated. It was like time had twisted around backward and I was an invisible by-stander watching a piece of my younger self interact with him.

He stopped and dropped a pile of blankets and a couple pillows at the other end of the couch, careful not to get too close to us.

"Thank you," Sadie said.

He peered out the window then turned toward his room and shuffled away again. Sadie wasn't having any of it.

"Scoos me."

"Honey, don't—"

"—scoos me. Scoos me Grampa!"

He stopped but didn't turn around to face us. I felt prickly all over, like someone had used me for target practice with a sack full of pins.

"Honey, he's tired. He wants to go to bed. You can talk to him tomorrow."

"I just wanted to say that when—" she whispered to me, but

then realized he had stopped to listen, even though he hadn't turned around. So she raised her voice for him to hear.

"I just wanted to say when somebody says thank you, it's polite to say wowcome. Like I told Aunt Chloe. That's what Sister Margaret says."

Shit. Now he knows I've seen Chloe.

"Right. Thank you. Now it's time—"

"Wowcome."

"Now it's time for us to sleep," I said.

He hadn't moved. She perched on her elbows and kept staring at his back.

"Lie down, honey."

"But—"

"Lie down."

He turned halfway around and looked straight at her.

"You're welcome," he said.

We watched him drag away. He didn't ask about Chloe or say good night to me. Right back where we started. I gave Sadie a kiss good night and headed over to the recliner with a blanket and pillow.

"Where you going, Katie?"

"To sleep. Same place you should go."

"Why don't you sleep here?"

"Because there's only room for one person on the couch. Don't worry. I'm right here."

"I don't like it."

"Well, maybe we'll figure something else out tomorrow."

"Promise?"

"I promise I'll try." I settled into the chair and raised my feet up. It was much more comfortable than the back seat of the car would have been and probably thirty degrees warmer too. This had been the right choice. Right choice. Right choice. It was good to keep reminding myself. I'd keep that mantra running through my head all night long so it would be fresh when morning came. The right choice.

"I still don't like it."

"Good night, Sadie."

"Night," she said, pouting. It was refreshing to see her act like a five-year-old for a change. Almost as satisfying as being needed.

I was on the border of sleep when the house settled. It creaked and groaned, hurling me back to consciousness. I looked out the living room window and the ground seemed much closer, like the house had sunk since we'd come. We were burying it. Of course I'd passed right through Creative Imaginings and directly into Coloring On The Walls with that one. It was an old house. Old houses settle in the middle of the night. It wasn't sinking, it was settling. End of story.

And yet, I couldn't shake the feeling there was something to the idea.

Sleep stole me from my father's living room and dumped me just outside the door to Martin Flemming's study on the last day I saw him. My small hand rested on the brass knob and I couldn't stop staring at it. Couldn't move, couldn't open the door.

I'd felt off that whole morning, my stomach had twitched and cramped all through our lesson and I didn't understand why. It had never done that before. I thought maybe I'd eaten a bad egg at breakfast, but I'd find out soon enough how little my pain had to do with edible eggs.

We'd been studying the Beatitudes and Martin decided to take a break a little over halfway through. We'd stopped after Verse Seven: *blessed are the merciful, for they shall obtain mercy.*

"Do you understand what mercy is, Katie?"

I nodded. But I lied. I knew it by definition only; I'd never known it personally.

"So why would the Lord want you to show it to those who are miserable and wretched?"

His leaky red eyes bored through me and I could tell something was about to break. He was different that day. More feral. His breath carried the stench of rotting flesh, the remnants of a steak he'd had for lunch before I'd arrived. And he must have been extra sore because the minute he opened the door to let me in, my eyes stung from the aura of Bengay wafting around him.

Everything about Martin made me sick, but I kept coming because I didn't think I had a choice not to. And because part of me truly believed this was my punishment for letting my family fall apart. Chloe leaving, my father crumbling, and on really bad days my mother dying, was all my fault and this was my cross to bear.

"Because it's the—"

"Katie we've been through this. Why must you make me correct you every time? You know how to answer the question properly. Do so now."

"I'm sorry. The Lord would want me to show mercy to the

miserable and the wretched because..." Because if I got the gun out of the top drawer of your desk, shot you in the crotch and watched your life pour away like I want to right now, I'd go to jail or at least a juvenile facility and it would really mess up the rest of my life. And God doesn't want me to do that. The latter part, anyway.

"...because it's the way into the Kingdom of Heaven."

"Close. It's one step. It's just one step on the path to the Kingdom of Heaven."

I wanted to ask him if verses eight, nine, or ten had anything to do with fondling little girls, and which step that was on the path to the Glory of God, but I just didn't have the courage. Even in my dreams. And I never learned the last three Beatitudes, that day or any other.

My twenty-eight year old mind tried to pull my eleven-year-old hand away from the study doorknob, but it was stuck. I felt a cool breeze snaking out from under the door and my younger self took over. I remembered that breeze. It was what made me think things might be different that day. And they were.

I opened the door. Martin stood across the room by the window holding the drapes aside to let fresh air and sunshine in. It was the first time I'd ever seen the glow of natural light in that room. The creamy curtains underneath the heavier yellow ones sprung to life in the breeze, dancing and swaying around his body. They were pregnant with warm air and the intoxicating aroma of the lilac trees in bloom just ten feet away in the front yard. Dust particles swarmed inside the column of light flowing around him and I stood mesmerized. Maybe God had spoken to him. Maybe he'd been struck by a miracle of conscience. Opening the window and letting in the light, the life of the world outside, was the first step in breaking his cycle. The first step in cracking my cocoon.

"Sit down, Katie."

That's what I'd hoped for anyway. The curtains died abruptly and so did my belief in better things when he slammed the window shut. He used such excessive force I thought it would shatter.

It didn't. I did.

I fought valiantly to preserve my last vestige of innocence, but in the end he was too big, too strong, too possessed of purpose. The only fortunate thing about my first experience with intercourse was that my rapist was so excited by the perversity of his theft it ended quickly. In real time anyway. In my head it went on for eons. Hasn't stopped.

"Oh God," he said, looking down toward our connecting points. No, I thought. Not God. If this was God, then I didn't want any.

"What in the devil...?" That was more like it.

"What have you, what is this?" he said, slithering off me. He stood up inspecting himself. He was covered in blood. Brilliant red female life force. His entire midsection, from the top of his pants to the bottom of his shirt, was stained crimson.

I wiped the rest of my tears away. I was afraid to look, but I had to see what he'd done to me. I knew it was my blood, I'd screamed when he ripped me open, but I didn't know why there'd be so much of it. I nudged my fingers down the insides of my thighs and back up my middle, inspecting the damage. The blood was sticky and warm and still coming out of me. I pulled my hands up and nearly passed out. I was shocked by the color, the immediacy of it. Then I remembered something Chloe had said to Mom when I was younger about her stomach hurting around that time of the month. I'd never had that time of the month before, but it suddenly became clear to me why I'd had stomach cramps earlier. I'd become a woman in more ways than one that day.

I froze there, sprawled on Martin's soiled white couch, staring at the evidence of my wounds. I didn't know how to stop it. How to clean myself up. I didn't know how to move, or if I ever would again. But Martin did. He pulled his pants up and held them around his waist with his forearm because he'd gotten blood on his hands too. Boy had he.

"Jezebel! Get out of my house. I don't ever want to catch you here again!" As if I'd try to sneak *in*. He was belligerent and incoherent, spewing scripture, and without another word to me he careened out of the room, and my life, forever. So much for cracking the cocoon. He'd just sealed it shut for good.

My mind bumped up against consciousness and the cool November night then swerved back down and skidded to a halt in a different nightmare.

It was another beautiful sun-filled day. Not unusual for Seattle in the summer. My father sat at the kitchen table reading the Sunday paper and I strolled by behind him with no particular destination in mind. He'd wrapped the paper around the corners of his face, so I couldn't see his features at all, just the back of his head. He didn't make any effort to acknowledge me on my first trip past, so I sauntered back around him the other way. Still not so much as a glance. I skipped past him, but this time I flicked his paper on my way. Not even a sigh. I wasn't worthy of a second of his attention, especially now. Now that I was used. Dirty.

I stood right behind him, staring at the back of his head, whistling as loud as my little lungs could, and to a degree of obnoxiousness that even irritated me and still got nothing in return. His hair had turned salt and peppery shortly after Mom had died the year before and on that particular day I was fascinated by the gray. I stepped closer to him, just a foot away, and picked the gray hairs out of his head. One at a time. Plink. Plink. Plink. Not even an irritated headshake. Desperate times call for drastic measures.

"Father, I have something to tell you about Martin Flemming."

He shook the paper and turned the page. Then gasped.

"Martin Flemming is dead," he said. His voice was distant, like he was talking through a PVC pipe a mile away. "He jumped off the back of a ferry and was lost."

He was lost way before he jumped off the back of a ferry.

"Good," I said.

"What do you mean, good?"

At least I was getting something now.

"I just mean, well, maybe he should have. Maybe it's what he needed to do to atone for his sins."

"Atone for what sins?"

I took a deep breath and held it till I nearly fell over, then fired it out in high staccato notes.

"He did wrong bad things to me at my lessons."

I danced around the room, spinning, pirouetting and hopping from one foot to the other. A moving target is hard to hit.

"What are you talking about?"

As if saying it once wasn't hard enough, I pushed it out again. It had sharper edges the second time through. "He did wrong bad things to me and I let him and I'm bad too."

"Martin Flemming was a good man, a just man who took the time to teach you the word of God and now, after you find out he's dead you want to what? Defile his memory with specious stories about wrongdoings? What is the matter with you, girl? Are you that starved for attention?"

"Yes."

"I'm sorry, I don't understand what you're saying to me. Whatever language you're speaking isn't English." He continued to read, but his hands began to shake and the paper rattled like it was being blown in the wind. "He's survived by no one," he said.

I included myself.

"Do you really think I'd send you into a lion's den every week to be fondled and raped?"

I stopped dancing. Nowhere in there had I given him the details.

"You knew?"

"Of course I didn't know! There's nothing to know. You're making it up."

I sidled up next to him. Nothing but a thin piece of newspaper separated his face from mine, but I couldn't see through it. I was calm, like I hadn't just been called a liar by my own father. I took a breath and exhaled. It set the paper on fire. Maybe I wasn't that calm.

He lowered the paper like it wasn't burning. Slow and calculated, it dropped to reveal parts of a face. Eyes without lids, a maniacal grin with no lips, and the cavities of nostrils. Other parts had already slipped off the bones underneath leaving gaping black holes.

"Do you really think I'd send my little girl into a lion's den every week? Every week? Every week!"

He pounded his quaking skeletal fist on the table and it broke apart, causing a domino effect. The rest of his decaying body shattered in an explosion of bones and flesh. The burning paper floated down over the pile and set it all on fire, cremating him.

I woke, disoriented, with Sadie wiping sweat from my forehead. She was snuggled up beside me in the chair.

"It was just a dream, Katie. The bad man's gone. He won't get you." I wasn't sure which bad man she was referring to. I hadn't seen her in there anywhere with Martin or my father, but still, she knew what was going on in my head. It was difficult to breath. When I tried to move my body was stuck, like I was strapped into the chair by tie downs. Sadie brushed the hair out of my eyes and kissed my clammy cheek.

We snuggled for a few minutes while I dragged myself out of the nightmare and into the sounds of the waning night. Angry waves tumbled to the shore out back and the revelation of water surprised me. I hadn't heard it when we came in before, mostly because I was so focused on not passing out when my father opened the door. I was happy to have something else to concentrate on. It was odd my father bought waterfront property, such an optimistic thing to do.

The wind picked up and the Evergreens rustled against each other outside the living room window. The whole world was restless.

Sadie fell asleep quickly, but I was awake. After the lead drained from my veins I extracted myself from her embrace and headed to the bathroom. When I passed my father's room, the floor creaked like I'd cracked its bones. I was trying to be quiet and not wake anyone, but the house didn't want to cooperate with me.

I shuffled into the bathroom and closed the door. Nothing but darkness met me, but I didn't know if I was ready for light, so I fumbled my way to the sink without it and turned the water on. It took a minute to warm up and while I waited, with one finger in the stream, I looked at my reflection in the medicine chest mirror. My eyes had acclimated to the room but they were playing tricks on me. I could barely see my face. All I saw was my mother's. I looked away and back again, then splashed warm water on her but she didn't want to go away. A towel hung on the rack next to the sink and I used it to dry myself off. When I glanced back she was still there staring back at me.

"Why am I here, Mom? Why?" It was my voice, not hers, filling the room. I waited for her brilliant answer, but nothing came. "Right. I didn't think so."

I found the light switch and flipped it up. The room erupted in golden brilliance and I staggered back to the mirror. Though bits and pieces of me were particularly similar to her, my eyes, the shape of my nose, my full lips, it was wholly my reflection in the glass. Including the crow's feet that had developed virtually overnight. Just like hers had right before she died.

I killed the light and made my way back out into the dark hall. Even at that age I would have appreciated some kind of night-light to guide me. I neared my father's room and my wish was granted. The gap under his door lit up, splaying light out into the hall in a golden fan. It startled me, so I tiptoed through it and over the grouchy floor. My palms moistened and I sped my pace to get to the end of the hall before he could catch me in it. I failed.

The click of the door latch released the barrier between us. He had been waiting for me this time.

"Kathryn, come here." I tried to continue through it, but his voice was frigid, freezing me mid step.

"Please."

I'm sorry. Did my father just ask nicely? I turned to face him, half expecting the thing from my dream to be staring back at me, but it was just him. What was left of him. He used to be so much bigger, more imposing. Now he couldn't intimidate his own shadow. Yet he still held a mysterious power over me. A force too strong to deny when I was in his presence, and strong enough to keep me away for so long.

"Please come here."

The idea of him spanking me was absurd, mostly. I mean he

could barely lift his arm, how would he contain me if I wanted to run? Of course, I knew he had no intentions of spanking me, but the thought of it was a fun way to pass the time it took to walk down the hall to him.

I arrived at his door, two feet from where he stood, about three hours later. Give or take. Things had slowed down for me the minute I'd stepped onto his driveway. I looked at him, then the doorway, then back to him, then my knees, then the ceiling. Six and a half days later, he spoke.

"I...is the situation suitable for you in the living room?"

Was he talking to an employee or his daughter? *Ah, sir, the living room is acceptable, although the lumbar support in the La-Z-Boy leaves something to be desired.*

"It's fine. Thanks."

"Good."

Was that it? His gaze wandered off down the hall into darkness. I waited and waited, then turned away. He grabbed my arm before I could make a full rotation and pulled me back toward him. I looked up into his eyes and nearly fell over. I'd never seen my father cry. Not once. Not even when Mom died. I'm sure he had, but he never did it anywhere I'd catch him at it.

And here he was, standing naked in front of me, wrapped in his robe and slippers, at three o'clock on a Thursday morning. His eyes were glassy and moist and it seemed by the way his teeth clenched inside his cheeks he was using every ounce of his waning strength to keep himself together. The warm light reflected off the tears damming up in the center of his eyes, ready at a blink to fall, to give in to gravity and years of guilt.

Well, that wasn't quite what I was expecting. Hoping for? Maybe. I didn't know what to do with myself. I certainly wasn't going to be a big crybaby too. At least not in front of him. There would have been a glut of vulnerability swirling around that hallway if I'd given in.

He looked a little constipated, like he needed to say something but didn't know how. Part of me wanted to stick around and find out what was on his mind, but a much larger part wanted to scurry out to the recliner, bury myself under some covers, and wake up when everybody was mean and cold again. That was much easier to deal with. This? This was *intimidating*.

"Are you...all right, Kate?" He asked the door hinge to my right, but it echoed off the metal and plunged straight into me, shaking my core. My father had not inquired about my well be-ing in eighteen years, not with any true interest anyway. I had no idea how to respond. About sixty-three percent of me wanted to shout the roof off. *No, mother-fucker! I'm not okay. I've gotten myself into a right fucking mess this time and it's all your fault! Thanks for asking half a lifetime too late.* The other thirty-seven percent was totally on the fence about the whole thing.

I realize in polite society when a person asks you a question like that, you're supposed to answer them with the best version of the truth, or at least your most creative. Something they want to hear, because they're not asking you how you really are. But from my father, after ten years, at three a.m. with tears, this was no ordinary question. It would be like Judas asking Jesus, "Hey J.C., not much wiggle room up there, eh? You need anything?"

Well, maybe not exactly like that. I certainly wasn't Christ, and though I'd felt betrayed, I didn't consider my father Judas. Just broken. But the question had the same weight in my eyes.

"I'm fine." I tried to smile to really drive home how I wasn't making it up for his sake, but my lips wouldn't cooperate. My whole body began to quiver and I knew I was on the verge of breaking open down the middle if I stood there any longer, so I spun around and left him in the doorway, obviously needing something from me I couldn't give. I didn't want to stick around for either of our tears to drop because I knew if I did, that would be it. I'd throw myself into him, a wailing mess, and I couldn't let him off that easily. So I held onto my shit and ran away. Again. He didn't follow. Again.

I scurried back out into the living room and waited for the click of his door. When I saw the light die under it I knew it was safe to pillage. I'd pushed the tears back and everything that came with them, holding it together long enough to get away. The burning in my head and eyes had passed. I was on a mission now.

Sadie slept in the chair and I didn't want to wake her, so I crept over to the liquor cabinet like a cat. A blind, three-legged cat. I stubbed my wounded toe on no fewer than three corners and legs of things getting to it on the far end of the living room.

I stuffed my fist in my gaping mouth so the screams were muffled and continued till I made it. I'd noticed the cabinet before, when we went to sleep, but didn't have any desire to inspect its contents till now.

I knelt next to it, massaging my toe. The door didn't give at first and I thought it was locked, but then it opened with a yank. Silly to think it'd be locked. He certainly wasn't expecting me.

It was dark, I couldn't tell one bottle from another and I didn't want to turn the light on, so I shuffled over to my bag and grabbed the flashlight. Came in handy after all.

The column of light spread over the inside of the cabinet. It was chock full of half empty bottles: Dewar's, Skyy, Johnny Walker, Ketel One. The Ketel One was in the back so I cleared a path to pull it out. I slid the bottles to the side and cringed when they clinked and clanked against each other, a glass symphony of self-destruction. Not as quiet as I'd hoped.

I reached in and the light landed on something that took my breath away. I yanked my arm out and fell back on the floor. My God, it had been ten years. I hadn't seen it out where he used to keep it in our old house, so I assumed he'd finally just gotten rid of it somehow. I didn't want to think about how.

I got up on my knees, grabbed the light in my unsteady hand and went back in after it. After her. My mother. He'd hidden her urn in the back of his liquor cabinet. I pulled on her, but she was heavier than I remembered and the bottom scuffed along the particleboard so I put the flashlight down, picked her up in both hands and carried her the rest of the way out. I didn't want to wake Sadie or telegraph what I was doing to my father.

I sat against the wall next to the window and cradled her in my lap, tracing the curves of the ceramic pot with my fingers. A cold draft snuck through the corner of the window and whispered over the back of my neck. It didn't do much to calm me. I was still reeling from her being stuffed in the back of his liquor cabinet. I couldn't decide if it was apropos or perverse. Maybe the line was too thin to draw between the two at that point.

302 | KELLY BYRNE

I found two spots where the urn had been chipped and pulled it up closer to inspect it. It had been perfect, pristine when I'd left. It must have been damaged in the move. Or maybe after I left he tossed her around the living room like a football on lonely Saturday nights.

"Hi, Mom," I whispered. I flitted from one memory of her to the next, like a butterfly zigzagging from bush to bush, never alighting for more than a few seconds. Never planting roots. The way I'd lived my life since she'd fallen from it. Fleeting memories flashed around inside me and disappeared before I could catch hold of them. As ephemeral as sparks.

Then suddenly, one ignited. I was in my parent's room again, helping her get ready for my big fifth grade graduation dinner. Watching her dress, apply her makeup, move. I studied her, hoping someday I'd possess the same innate grace. Hoping it would rub off on me if I stayed close enough, something like osmosis.

Then another memory caught fire. The day I snuck into her lecture on Milton. I was eight and I'd had a half-day at school, but instead of going home I took the cross-town bus all the way over to the university by myself. I knew I wasn't supposed to and I was pretty sure I'd get in trouble, but I was so proud of myself for being a big girl and figuring out which line to take and doing it all on my own with my own allowance money.

When I got there, I sat way in the back of the lecture hall. It was one of those raked, fan shaped rooms with about two hundred seats, so I lost myself on a step behind a linebacker wearing a University of Washington football jersey. I just wanted to listen to the smooth, chocolaty velvet of her voice. To see her in action in front of all those students eager to absorb her brilliance. Every one of them rapt by her, gleaning inspiration and knowledge from everything she said. Just like I did.

Of course she knew I was there, but she didn't let on until the very end when she saw me trying to sneak out in the middle of the crowd. It was one of the only times she'd scolded me with that kind of intensity, punctuating every word. Each one felt like a slap.

"Don't you ever do that again, Bits. Something could've happened to you. Anything could've happened."

"I'm sorry, Mommy," I said to the carpet. She hugged me when the lip quivered and squeezed the tears out of me.

Later that night I overheard her telling my father about my adventures across town and I saw her smile when she told him about me getting there all by myself. I knew then at least a little part of her was proud of me for doing it.

Since she'd died I'd been waiting for her essence to blossom inside me, for her brilliance to shine from my eyes. But clearly, in the past week alone, I'd fallen miles short of the perfection she'd attained. I couldn't imagine my exceptional mother setting her ex's garage on fire, getting accidentally naked in the process. Or kidnapping a child, by accident or not. Or stealing someone's car. Or any of the other stupid things I'd done prior to the last week. She was refined and level headed and put together.

My hands rested on the side of the urn with the biggest piece missing. I ran my fingers over the divot, slowly taking in the shape of it. Then went to the next. And the next. It was riddled with nicks and cuts and missing pieces and I remembered then that it had been for a long time. Since long before I left. It had been perfect and pristine when we'd brought her home, but over the years it had succumbed to the friction of life, especially in my care, chipping and scarring just like anything else that lives un-protected. Just like the person it was made to hold.

Why had I spent so much energy ignoring this? My mother had never been perfect. She was a beautiful disaster. Chipped and scarred and coming apart at her seams. For Christ's sake, the woman couldn't even decide on a dress without me there to help her.

I'd been desperate to hold on to my own personal version of the truth for so many years, but now I saw it for what it really was.

The day I went to her lecture I listened to her repeat the same thing three times before she moved on to a different thought. She was stuck, like a skipping record. And her students knew it. At one point she stood silent, staring up at all the faces in her audience, ready to erupt in a big mess of tears and confusion. I'd seen her do it at home when she thought she was alone. I just held my breath and hoped she'd work through it, at least till the end of her class. She did. But it was still in her.

Since she'd died I'd been holding on to this image of her as unattainable goddess. Why do we do this with our dearly depart-ed? Remembering them as saints, instead of human with the same frailties and flaws we all possess. When a beloved dies, we wipe their slate clean, creating ideal memories that may or may not have existed in reality the way they do in our minds. In reali-ty, my beautiful mother had been just as messed up as I was. In different ways, of course, but the end result was the same. I didn't want my end result to be the same as hers.

I thought about how she'd encouraged her own death and anger swelled in my belly. I had to control a sudden urge to hurl her across the room. I was pissed at her for leaving us, for making me responsible for her selfishness. For being my mother in the first place and making me want so desperately to emulate her. There. I'd blame her for a little while. But that didn't feel good either.

I knew something else too. Sadie had brought me here. None of it was an accident; there was purpose in this.

"Katie, where you going? Don't leave me alone." She'd snuck up behind me at the back door, the youngest spy in the history of the world. I looked down at her, she was still heavy with sleep, and her immaculate beauty struck me. Her perfect porcelain skin, so young and blemish free. No chips, scrapes or scars. No damage, yet. I wanted to protect her from all the things that would ever wound her.

"Go back to bed, honey. I'm going outside for a minute."

"Can I go?"

"No. Not now."

"You'll be back, right?"

"Yes. I'll be back." I wondered if that was completely true.

"What awe you holding?" The shiny blue ceramic of my mother's urn glistened like water in the moonlight coming through the kitchen window.

"Go to sleep, okay honey? I'll be back in a little while."

She shuffled back to the chair and snuggled up. I opened the door and the West Wind welcomed me out. I guess I should have

306 | KELLY BYRNE

been concerned about being cold, but the air was warm like a summer night. I didn't know if it was real, if any of this was, but I didn't question it anymore. It was time for silence.

I marched across the beach toward the neighbor's dock guided by the moon lighting my path. It was full again, which I found strange since it had been waning the night before. Had it somehow derailed from its orbit and gone backward, like Superman spinning the world into the past to bring Lois back?

A sailboat was moored toward the end of the dock. When I passed by on my way to the end, its hull tapped against the rough water and I thought about Sadie's mother. How she liked the waves and sailing. But they made Sadie sick to her stomach, and that's how I felt then. Like I was manning a tiny sailboat in the middle of an angry sea, pitching back and forth, but not tipping over yet. Not giving in. The air was still warm, but I was suddenly chilled. I didn't know if I could go through with this.

I sat on the end of the dock, dangling my feet over the edge like we used to at the wall across from the city. There were no lights to reflect off the water, but the moon made up for that. Its glow stretched across the bay, an unblinking beacon, and landed on me, warming my face like the sun. I lay back on the dock, not ready yet, and stretched my arm up in front of me. The moon bounced off the silver of my bracelet and lit the charm. My butterfly glowed from the inside.

"Mom." My voice was unsteady. Almost didn't sound like me at all. I ran my finger over the surface of the charm's ceramic. It was warm too, like a living thing.

"Thank you."

"Wowcome."

Damn it. I whipped up, spun around and there was Sadie, holding her mother in her arms.

"Sadie, what are you doing? You shouldn't be out here."

"I thought you might be lonely."

She wasn't wrong. "You're just going to get sicker, honey. You need to get back inside."

"But I feel good." I felt her forehead. Cool to the touch. She wasn't chock full of phlegm anymore either and I hadn't heard her cough all night.

"Huh. That's weird."

"Are you looking at the kisses?" She sat down next to me, dangling her legs over the end like I was, and put her mother next to mine. I'd forgotten about the kisses, but it was as good a reason as any to be out there at three o'clock in the morning.

"Yes, I was looking."

"Did you see them?"

"No, honey. I didn't. I don't think I can."

"Yes you can. You just have to look up."

Just have to look up. The same thing my mother had told me that day under Myrtle. *Everything around you is from God.* I didn't know if I believed in God, but I believed in my mother and I believed in Sadie and maybe that was the same thing. So I laid back and gave it a shot. She followed right after me.

I can't say with any certainty that I saw the kisses on the mooner, but when I looked at the little girl beside me on that dock, I saw a reflection of myself in her essence. Her innocence.

"No silly, you have to look at the mooner."

"Right, sorry. Oh my goodness, there they are! Wow, look at that." She didn't see me staring at her again. Maybe the kisses look different to everybody.

"I told you."

Yes, she did. I was beginning to think there was something to my loony idea about Sadie being Chief Red Hair Knows-A-Lot. I wondered if she knew anything about trees. If she'd fall in love with the Crepe Myrtle someday and not fully understand why.

I was ready to do it. Even more so with Sadie by my side. I sat up, pulled the urn onto my lap, and held my mother for a minute longer. Sadie mimicked me, scooping her bag up and cradling it on her lap.

A great wall of emotion rushed in and I let my dam break. Everything I'd held onto and pushed back for the last eighteen years came charging out of me. The guilt over my family disintegrating, the shame of Martin, the men, the failures, everything that wanted to hold me in my prison thrust forth and I let it go.

Sadie scooted closer and took my hand. I put my arm around her and we sat in silence for a while. The night was quiet again, and so was I, finally. When I was ready, I stood and took the top off the urn.

"Maybe we don't have to." She stood next to me holding her mother. Her hand on the zipper.

"Honey, no. You don't have to. But I do."

She wasn't ready to release her mother. She hadn't had enough time. And maybe I hadn't either, but this wasn't for me. This was for Joanna. I tipped the urn over and the breeze picked her up and carried her into the smoky water. Into her freedom.

The rip of a zipper plucked me from my memorial. I looked down in time to see Sadie doing her best to empty out her backpack. All I can say is thank God for Clyde the Cloud. The book was blocking the opening and she was having a hard time getting it out of the way.

"No! Honey, no!" I yanked the bag away and zipped it up. I think my intensity frightened her, but I couldn't let her do it.

"You did," she said.

"I know. It's just not time for you yet."

"Why?"

I hoped she'd never need to, but I didn't know how to explain it. The feeling was back in my gut again. Wanting to keep everything bad away from her. To keep her luminous spirit intact, never letting the monsters in to wear it down or dull it up. Our appearances were so similar, but I wanted to be sure we'd always be different in that respect.

Then it hit me. Shook me like a million volts of reality. I wouldn't be able to. *I* wouldn't be able to. I felt sick, like all my insides were coming out. My whole body trembled and I wondered if I was going to break apart again.

If this was what they called enlightenment, I didn't want any of it. Suddenly things with Sadie were clear to me. And just as suddenly, the air around us lost its heat and became frigid again, like a normal November night. The wind picked up and pushed the clouds around the moon, plunging us into a hazy darkness. I tossed the bag over my shoulder, took Sadie in my arms and ran back to my father's house. We stepped inside just as it started to rain. My summer vacation was over.

We lay down in the chair with her bag and snuggled up together in the blankets. Her teeth chattered as she spoke. "Will you look after me for always, Katie?"

"I'll make sure you're always taken care of." I kissed her cold cheek and tucked the blanket up around her chest. It had been a rough night. One of many lately. We both fell asleep quickly, sliding off into dreams we'd forget in the morning.

I was finally ready to stop. To turn around and face my shit head on. Funny how that's telegraphed to the universe. Then, when it gives you exactly what you asked for, you wonder why you were crazy enough to send the memo in the first place.

SEVENTEEN

Life would be fine if we didn't have to live it every day. If we could do every third day, or maybe even every other day, it would be far less troublesome. On the off days we'd just fall into a delightful coma, letting the world go on around us, ignorant of it all.

If I'd had my way, that Thursday would definitely have been a coma day. I woke to the sound of nothing. It was heavier and more deafening than lightning striking the roof. At least any roof I shared with my father.

It used to suffocate me after Mom died. Ours was a house filled with perpetual morning breath, unused from the day before. I'd tiptoe around him, not making a sound, not disrupting his precious solitude. Only when I couldn't stand it any longer did I manufacture my coincidental meetings in the hall. Those were endings of particularly empty days.

I'd come to know the danger of quiet. How it can eat you from the inside. I never said anything to my mother when I caught her destroying herself. Never told her how it hurt me to see her doing it. A home becomes a tomb with too much silence. I needed to break it.

But not until I had some coffee. Couldn't face the storm without a pick-me-up. And since vodka was out of the question at nine in the morning, I went for a more reasonable choice. Also, it would give me an excuse to stall more because I'd have to make a pit stop in the toilet after the first cup.

I stumbled into the kitchen, passing my father at the table. I didn't realize he was there till I got a whiff of the sour bubble surrounding him. From the strength of it I figured either he was fermenting or whatever was in his coffee mug was not coffee. Apparently it was never too early for my dad.

I should have known he wouldn't have a coffeemaker. What would he need it for? His drink of choice was much stronger and easier to fix. Pour and serve. No messy filters. No waiting. I rummaged through cupboards hoping to find something helpful. I'd even settle for tea, the liquid equivalent of Melba toast, but I was out of luck. So I grabbed a glass and filled it with refreshing bubble filled tap water and stood at the sink sipping it, surveying Fletcher Bay.

The sky was bleak. Growing up in Seattle, home of the nine-month permacloud, sometimes I wondered if Mother Nature had thrown out all her other Crayolas and kept only her gray, timberwolf, and manatee. All possessing varying shades of the same personality: cold, detached, dismal. Pretty much summed up the atmosphere in my father's kitchen that morning.

We still hadn't spoken. He came to the sink to rinse out his mug, or maybe just to be close to me. I turned away and took a seat at the table. He moved to the cupboard next to it. I'd never waltzed but I imagined this was similar, without the nasty business of actual contact. He pulled a box of Life cereal out. Ironic. From the faded colors I placed it circa '74, somewhere right after Watergate. Surely it would be fresh and tasty, like this whole experience. He pulled two bowls down from another cupboard and two spoons from the silverware drawer.

"You still like Life, yeah?"

There he goes again, speaking that damn Afrikaans or Swahili or father. All Greek to me. I think it was a rhetorical question anyway, because he didn't wait for a response. Just poured himself another mug of muscle-relaxant and sat down at the table across from me. We played hide and seek for a couple hours until I was thoroughly exhausted. I began to think it might be easier to face it than to run. Less taxing on my creativity anyway. You really have to plumb the depths of your inner resources to hide from someone sitting three feet away.

"So, I was hoping we might be able to stay with you for a bit."

He finally looked at me. Seemed like he had something to say, but he held back. He wasn't going to let me off that easily, I could see it in his eyes. He knew there was truth somewhere in me and he wasn't going to respond until he'd heard some of it. Or maybe he was just drunk. Speculation is always tricky business.

Either way, I knew there was truth in me and I finally felt like it needed to surface before I imploded and made a mess of myself on his kitchen floor. I stood and moseyed back to the sink.

"Sure looks cold out," I said, peering through the window. "Also, Sadie's not quite my daughter." The words sprang from my mouth. I couldn't look back at him, but I felt the air across the kitchen thicken, like batter. Or cement.

He cleared his throat like he was preparing to speak, then decided against it. Nothing but silence setting up between us again. I turned around and found his glassy gaze. His intensity startled me. I wanted to look away, but he held me there with it. "I, well, she, see she got in my car, my jeep, and, I, I didn't know she was there the first time. And then, you know, I almost bludgeoned her with my bat, but luckily I didn't."

When the floodgates opened, they opened.

"And then she did it again after I set the fire and I didn't know until I was, you know, a long way away. I mean not too far to go back, I was going to take her back, but then she showed me her fingers and the blisters from the stove and then I couldn't take her back. And I mean, she grew on me. Kind of like fungus at first, but then she just, you know, she got in. She gets in. She does. Tiptoes around in your head. You'll see."

I had his attention now. Felt good, like how a cutter must feel after a fresh wound.

"And after we broke down, Carolyn picked us up, but then I had to borrow their car to get to Chloe's because of the scanner. I just needed to stop for a minute and figure out a game plan, but then she wouldn't let us stay 'cause she's all reformed now, but I don't think she would've even if she was still messed up. She's carrying around a lot of baggage. Literally. So then we came here 'cause, well, because..."

"You didn't have anywhere else to go."

Backed myself right into that corner.

"Yes and no. Mostly yes."

He studied his mug, scraping off some invisible crud to keep himself from what? Screaming? Kicking me out? Showing any signs of life?

This felt just like the day I'd told him about Martin. He was unreasonably calm, until he wasn't. Until he threw the blame back on me.

I waited for the rage, but it never came. Instead, a great sadness pulled his face to the ground, like I'd really done it this time. There was no redeeming me, even after he knew it wasn't my fault. His voice was the color of the sky when he spoke.

"What did you do with it?"

I was thrown. Granted, he didn't know her like I did, but calling Sadie "it" was cold, even for him.

"I don't understand—"

"What. Did. You. Do. With. It?" The voice shot from gray to blood in a blink. He fixed his eyes on me like a laser on a sniper rifle, ready to pull the trigger.

"Dad, I don't know what you're talking—"

"Your mother. What did you do with her?"

Shit! I'd forgotten the urn out on the neighbor's dock. I couldn't believe I'd forgotten it. Her.

"I took a walk with her last night. Just wanted to...never mind. I'll go get her."

Hopefully the urn was still there. I couldn't discount the possibility that the wind had blown it into the bay where it was on its way to Bremerton. I kept that to myself and put my shoes on.

He must have seen she was missing when he took his bottle out this morning. Why hadn't he said anything before? Why did he let me spew my guts first? Damn it, I felt duped. And why hadn't he said anything about Sadie?

"Where you going, Mommy?" I stopped with my hand on the doorknob. She stood behind me all sleepy, cute and well heeled.

"Honey, you don't have to call me that anymore."

"But I want to." She smiled and threw herself into me. I saw him watching us out of the corner of his eye, like he didn't want to get caught.

"I want to go with you."

"No. You..." Then I rethought it. When I left, she'd be alone with him and I think the idea of that frightened her. I didn't blame her, not even a bit. "Get your shoes and coat."

She brought her things back to me and I got her all ready to go. Felt like we belonged at the zoo. He watched us with the same detached curiosity he might a mother chimp picking nits off her little one's noggin.

I was still waiting for some kind of response about Sadie. He was quiet, unmoving. Was this the calm before the storm or was it his new level of apathy for everything in his life? I had a niggling feeling I'd find out soon enough.

I took Sadie's hand and led her out the door into the gray abyss. Her bells jingled as we walked down to the shore. It wasn't raining anymore, just cold and windy. The water was the color of charcoal. My stomach rippled and curled into wavelets just like the bay. I'd laid myself bare and he hadn't heard anything.

We neared the dock and I saw the urn sitting at the end of it. Relief swept over me. At least I hadn't totally screwed things up. I just didn't want to be around when he found out my mother had a new address. I wasn't about to tell him what I'd done. It would be the one surefire thing to drag him screaming from his apathy.

The dock was slick from the rain. So was the urn. It nearly slid out of my hands when I picked it up. It was cold and I wanted to be back in the warmth of the house. I turned and walked away embracing the urn, but Sadie didn't follow me. She squatted at the edge of the dock peering down into the water, like there was something there.

"Sadie, honey, come on. Let's go." She ignored me. Giggled and waved to what would have been her reflection had it been a calm day.

"Sadie. That's not..." I stopped myself. I didn't want to bring attention to the fact that she was in danger of falling into the water because it might have made her nervous. Whenever I became aware of imminent peril I'd lose my balance or do something stupid. Joe and Carolyn could attest to that.

"Honey, what are you..." I bent down next to her, searching the water to see what she'd been so fascinated with. There was nothing there.

"Did you see a fish?"

She looked at me and smiled. I'd never seen anything so beautiful in my life. In the middle of that dreary day, Sadie Beck glowed just like my mother had the morning Myrtle blossomed. A crazy thought popped into my head, so I took Sadie's hand and pulled her away. I couldn't handle confirming my suspicion that she was waving to someone.

Marching back to the house Sadie squeezed my hand. I glanced down at her and stopped. The color had drained from her face like someone had pulled her stopper out.

"What's wrong?"

"My bumper feels funny."

I put my hand on her chest and felt her heart. It was racing.

"Does it hurt? Are you hurting?" I didn't know what to do. What if there was really something wrong with her heart? I'd have to take her to the hospital, but I didn't have any insurance, or money for that matter. I couldn't imagine my father helping me out considering what I'd just told him.

"Something's wrong."

"Can you tell me what it feels like? Is it sharp or dull or—"

"My bumper feels funny—"

"I know, honey, I'm trying to figure out—"

"My bumper goes funny when something's wrong. I think something's wrong."

"So you're not...you're okay? It doesn't hurt?"

"I'm okay."

I put the urn down and hugged her. Something being wrong I could deal with. Something wrong with her? Well. Not prepared to go there. I'd felt the same withering feeling in my stomach on our walk back. Something was rotten in my Denmark.

"No matter what, everything will be all right. I promise."

"Kay."

"You believe me?"

"Yes."

At least one of us did.

"How's your bumper?"

"Better."

I kissed her nose. When I stood I felt the weight of someone watching me. Glancing toward the house I caught my father turning away from the kitchen window. When we went back in the room was empty.

"I'm hungry."

I put the urn on the counter next to the cereal and helped Sadie out of her coat. She put it on the back of a chair then climbed up to sit.

"Do you want cereal?"

"Yes please."

I prepared our breakfast and we ate in silence, softly clinking our spoons against the bowls with every scoop. I think we were both waiting to hear scuffing across the wood floor.

Careful what you wait for, you just might get it.

He'd changed into a pair of baggy jeans and a t-shirt and wandered out holding the cordless phone. It was like he'd had a stroke or a lobotomy. His eyes were glassy and distant. Halfway to the kitchen he decided against it and detoured into the living room, stopping in front of the television. He turned it on loud enough for me to hear. There was no mistaking that. And boy did I hear.

The anchor's voice was deep, foreboding, as he spoke of a reckless redhead named Kate, possibly dangerous and definitely unstable, who had torched her own jeep on the interstate and stolen a car with her child in tow. But where was the Amber Alert I'd been expecting to hear? They said nothing about the fact that I'd stolen Sadie too. I didn't possess the mental clarity at that moment to truly comprehend what it meant. My head spun and my body barely had time to catch up to my feet as they flew out of the seat into the living room.

My father was crumpled up on the couch fully rapt by the story Carolyn and Joe told the field reporter. Given that I'd been there, I wasn't as interested in that as I was in his reaction. I felt Sadie's tiny hand worm itself into mine and tried to move away from the TV and the sketch artist's rendition of me, but I was glued to the floor. Sadie stayed right by my side.

When the report was finished, he turned the television off but continued to stare at it like it would give him the answers he needed. When it didn't, he turned to me.

"What did you do, Kate?"

I couldn't respond. Had to remember how to speak first, how to formulate a thought. So Sadie took over for me.

"It's not her fault. It's mine."

I couldn't believe what I'd just heard. I squatted down in front of her and took her by the shoulders, because that's what other parents do when they're serious and want their kid to listen.

"It is not your fault. Do you hear me? Sadie?" She wouldn't look at me, so I lifted her chin with my finger because she needed to hear this. If I did nothing else right, this was something she needed to understand.

"Honey, none of this is your fault. Do you hear me?"

"But I got up into the jeep."

"Doesn't matter. You did nothing wrong."

Her face crumpled up and she threw herself into me. I lifted her and held her in my arms. The room hushed into a heavy silence. I heard someone sniffle and thought it was Sadie, but when I turned to face him, I saw tears streaking down my father's pasty face. He was staring at the phone cupped between his hands and I knew then he'd done something awful and I couldn't bear to be near him.

I took Sadie into the kitchen to get her coat and he followed us in, stopping at the doorway. He wiped his tears and looked at me. I stood still, in the middle of the room, not knowing what to do with myself.

"Katie, listen to me. If you—"

"No, you don't get to call me that. It's way too late for that."

"It's not too late. If I'd done it for Chloe she never would've...it's not too late."

"I'm pretty sure we're talking about two different things here."

I tried to zip Sadie's coat for her but my hands were shaking and the zipper got stuck. "Damn it." It wouldn't budge. And he'd stepped into the kitchen near us. I could feel him staring a hole in my back. Sadie's eyes shot up toward him but she kept her face close to mine.

"You want me to try?" she said.

"No, honey, I got it. Just hold still."

"What are you doing, Kate?"

"Trying to zip a zipper."

"Why?"

"Because we're leaving. I thought that would be fairly clear—"

"You're on an island. Where are you going to go? It's time to stop. Just stop."

He was right, of course, and I'd decided to do exactly that the night before. But boy it pissed me off he was telling me what to do. He had no right. Not after everything he'd put me through, everything he continued to put me through. So I decided to take my chances. I knew what I had to do last night; I just didn't plan on doing it this quickly. I needed a little more time.

"When did you call them?" I asked. He backed away and stood propped up against the counter by the sink.

"Six minutes ago."

Something about his answer set me off. Maybe it was the precision of the word six, as opposed to rounding down to five like most normal people. Maybe I didn't like the color of his t-shirt. Or maybe it was because he'd called the cops on his own daughter. Whatever it was I snapped and went for the jugular.

I took two steps over to the counter and hurled the urn to the floor right in front of him. It broke into a thousand pieces and Sadie screamed when it hit. I didn't mean to frighten her, but I needed some kind of release.

He didn't react the way I'd expected. He didn't try to stop me and when it landed at his feet, he didn't bend to gather the pieces. He just looked at me. He looked at me. For the first time in eighteen years, my father looked at me. And he didn't look away. Even when I did.

Sadie ran over and grabbed my leg. I embraced her, but honestly, she was the one holding me up. We had things to do, but I couldn't bring myself to move away from him. The cops were going to be breaking the door down in approximately two minutes and my feet wouldn't budge. I looked up at him again and found his gaze steady on me still. I couldn't tell if he'd fallen deeper into his trance or if it had shattered along with the urn.

"Why do you hate me?" I said, trying to sound very matter of fact, very Sunday afternoon brunch, but I'm pretty sure it came out pure bile.

"Katie." His intonation said, *don't be a moron.*

"It's a simple question. Answer it simply."

"You know the answer."

"No, I really don't. And I'm a little pressed for time right now, so if you could just, you know—"

"I'm trying to help you."

"Right. Like you helped with—you know what? Never mind. I don't know why I'm wasting my breath. We've got to go."

I picked Sadie up and carried her past him into the living room to gather our things. He stayed in the kitchen for a minute, no doubt inspecting the ruins at his feet. I turned to open the front door and I heard him scuff across the floor.

"What did you do with her?" he asked. I wanted to hurt him with my answer, slice him down the middle with the sharp edges of my words. Especially since he wasn't nearly as frantic as I'd imagined, hoped, he'd be when he discovered she'd gone missing. He seemed more relieved than anything. That might have been nice at a different time, no harm no foul kind of thing, but at that particular moment his reaction really pissed me off. At the very least I deserved a little hysteria for the shit he'd caused me.

Then Sadie diffused the situation with one touch. Except this time she didn't touch me. She let go of my hand and walked with measured steps over to my father across the room. When she arrived, she motioned for him to bend down to her. To my great surprise, he did.

"She's not sad. She still loves you," she whispered.

I didn't understand why she'd said that to him. Of course I was sad. And mad. And I wasn't positive I loved him, so what was she—oh. She wasn't talking about me. My suspicions from the dock had been confirmed. She *had* been waving at someone in the water. And, somehow, he understood what she meant. He crouched down as low as he could and took her in his arms. She looked back at me to make sure she had permission to hug him. I wasn't thrilled with the idea, but I wasn't going to stop her.

I'd spent a good deal of my adolescence hating my father. If we were moving and he'd suddenly dropped dead in the corner of a room I would have stepped over his body and told the movers, "Don't take *that*." But looking at him then with Sadie I realized this might be the last time I'd ever see him alive. It was such a left field thought, but I was struck by its power. By its possibility.

Then the weirdest thing happened. Like coming home to find Brad Pitt in your bed, kind of weird. The hate that had swelled and swirled around in my belly for so many years and had just had a grand resurgence, drained. My sink had been backed up with an enormous, bitter hairball for over half my life and it had just been unclogged. I didn't know if it was Sadie's doing or my mother's and maybe that was the same thing, but in one swift moment I finally knew what mercy was.

"I ve ou, ad," I squeaked out. Then I cleared my throat and tried again. This time, with a lot more breath and a little more conviction.

"I love you, Dad."

Isn't that funny? I still love you even after this. Now that was true mercy. True something. He looked over at me. I didn't want to cry in front of him, too vulnerable, but saying those words and actually meaning them hit me like the last half hour of *Beaches*.

He stood and Sadie raced over to me and grabbed my hand. I

felt like I was going to shake apart. This time Sadie wasn't enough. I was a junkie; I needed more. Something stronger. More potent. But I'd be damned if I was going to cross the desert of that living room to get it. I'd already given too much with nothing in return.

"Katie..." He had something to say and I was going to let him, but I put my trembling fingers back on the doorknob so he was aware of my intentions.

"I'm...I'm sorry. For everything."

It was what I'd needed to hear for half a lifetime. But it wasn't my father who'd said it. It was me. I didn't think he'd be able to bring himself to it and I needed to hear it in his presence. I guess it didn't matter whose mouth it came from.

I gave him time to reply to any of the varied things I'd just said to him, but he couldn't find the words. And he hadn't brought any water for the thousand-mile trek across the living room, so I did the only thing I could do to live with myself later.

In five strides and two seconds I embraced Gregory Denai and all his shortcomings as my father. Engulfed in a wave of shocking and riotous self-awareness I acknowledged my own part in them. Not vocally of course, but it all screamed inside me. And then I let it, and him, go.

Before we left I pulled the "Blue Moos" picture from my bag and propped it up on the couch for him. He bowed his head when he spoke, "I told them you wanted to turn yourself in. They'll go easier on you. Please, Katie. Don't run."

We left without another word. Traveled approximately one minute down Sweethome road before I switched direction and pulled back into my father's driveway. I turned the car off and took the key from the ignition. The sudden calm was a relief.

"Why did we come back?"

I unbuckled Sadie's seatbelt and pulled her close to me, resting my cheek on her head. "I'm going to keep my promise. I want you to know that now. I'm going to do whatever I can."

"What do you mean? Why is the police here? Katie?"

I didn't have time to answer because the cruisers had pulled in behind us, flashing lights, sirens and all. I caressed her hair, wet with my tears, and kissed her cheek one last time before they took her from me.

My father disappeared from the living room window when the patrol car escorted me away. It wasn't an optimistic thing he'd done, buying a cottage on an island. He'd moved there to disappear, and maybe he would have if his daughter hadn't shown up in the middle of the night. Or maybe he still would. Regardless, I'd made an impression on someone in the house that day.

Now I had to worry about other impressions, those of a judge and jury. I was happy to be done running, but in my stillness I'd lost my little girl. There was no relief in that.

EIGHTEEN

Sadie had screamed when they took her from me and that wretched sound echoed in my head all day. At least it blocked out the incessant blathering of the other prisoners around me. I sat chewing my nails on the lumpy sandbag bed in the holding cell, inhaling the vile scent of humanity, wondering what had happened to her. Where she'd been taken. If she was all right. No one would tell me because they thought I'd kidnapped her and was a horrible person for it, even though I explained over and over what had happened.

It had been the second time in less than a week someone had taken her away from me. She certainly wouldn't be sneaking into my cell to see me this time. Being without her made my head throb.

That night I tried to sleep, but couldn't. I was so exhausted, even the lumps in the bed wouldn't have prevented me from falling unconscious, but the lumps in my stomach were relentless. It twisted and knotted and I knew she'd been sent back to Chris. I couldn't help but speculate how his anger at her running away would color his treatment of her now.

Friday morning, when the guard came to fetch me for my one call I was at a loss again. I hadn't used it the day before because I had no idea who it should be used for. I didn't know anyone in Seattle anymore and I'd let my eyeballs rot out of my head before

I'd call Aunt Janet. No doubt she supported every move my father made. Chloe was out too. I had no one.

"How's Sadie? The little redhead," I asked when the guard approached.

"I'm not allowed to discuss that with you."

"I just want to know she's all ri—"

"Do you wish to use your phone privileges today or not?"

"I don't think I—I don't..." And then I remembered a card someone had given me days before. I also remembered what he'd said when he'd handed it to me. So I used my call to convince the one person who might be able to help me that my inherent goodness was still alive. Scratched and chipped, but still in me.

"Patrick? Hi, it's Kate...Denai. I don't know if you rememb—"

"Kate, you've been a busy woman." I guess he remembered me. Would have made me feel a little better if I hadn't been handcuffed to a chair.

"Yeah. Well. Yeah."

"Why are you calling me? How are you calling me? You're in custody." His voice was tempered with equal parts fire and ice. Obviously I had some work to do.

"My one phone call..."

"Listen, I don't know what you want, but I don't think I have anything to say. Kidnapping, Kate? I mean...what...what were you..." Even his bewilderment was hot. I imagined his eyes. "Why did you do it?"

"I admit it seems a little off center, but when you hear why, I think you'll under—"

"Tell me then."

"Okay, but I'd just ask that you keep an open mind, please."

"On second thought, don't. I can't help you, Kate. Not with this. Kidnapping. Grand theft auto. Arson. I mean, come—"

"When did you get the report that she was missing?"

Silence on the other end. I hoped he wasn't upset I'd interrupted him, but I had to go with my hunch. Like Sadie's heart, my gut told me when things weren't right. He still hadn't answered but I could hear him breathing. I did my best not to find it sexy.

"Yesterday afternoon, why?"

"We've been gone since Monday night. The people I borrowed the car—the people I used—the people I stole the car from can corroborate. We were there on Tuesday."

It had taken Chris three days to report her missing after she ran away. Why? He was new to being her stepfather and obviously didn't appreciate the job, but why would he take so long to tell the cops she'd gone missing? I felt Patrick mulling over this new information. He was silent for a few more seconds. Then it dawned on me.

"That's why there was no Amber Alert. He didn't report her missing until we'd already been taken into custody. He must have seen the news about me stealing the car with my daughter and put two and two together. Why would he do that?"

"I don't know, Kate. Tell me what happened."

"I'll tell you everything, just, I need your help. You said you'd do anything you could to help me. Did you mean it?"

"I want the truth first."

I only had a couple minutes left on my call so I gave him the abridged version of our adventure, making sure to include as much of my responsibility in it as I could handle. I nearly passed out when I told him how we stole the car in the middle of the night. He didn't need to know every ugly detail. Like how I'd made Sadie my accomplice or how I'd lost her at the motel.

I wanted him to understand I was willing to atone for my sins, willing to do whatever was necessary to make things right. Sadie was my first priority.

"I think she was sent back to him yesterday. Can you please look into it?"

"I'll see what I can do."

"Thank you, Patrick. I know I don't have a right to ask this, but there's something else I need."

"What?"

In the end, he offered me a miracle. He promised to do what I'd asked of him.

A few days later, I had visitors. I was taken to a small, gray interrogation room with the typical two-way mirror in the center. I wondered who we'd be entertaining on the other side.

I looked down at them sitting at the metal table. Neither of them acknowledged me right away. They inspected their own hands, neatly intertwined on the top of the table, instead. Carolyn was wounded, disappointed, peeved. Joe was just peeved.

They both glanced up at the same time. It was difficult to look either of them in the eye. And boy did they make it difficult not to, focusing like eagles on their prey.

"Ten minutes," the guard said and closed the door.

My arms began to hurt, pulled together behind my back in the handcuffs.

"Hi," I said. Still spectacularly inadequate.

"How's your mother, Kate?" This from Joe. His voice tasted like bile.

"Joe," Carolyn warned.

"Actually, she died when I was ten. So my guess is, she's still dead. But thanks for your concern." I'd never outgrown my knee jerk reaction to return sarcasm with its twin.

"We didn't come here to exchange insults," Carolyn said. Good thing someone was an adult.

"I'm sorry," I said.

"Yeah," Joe said, obviously not interested in my mea culpa.

"For everything."

They were quiet. Studying me, I think, to see if I was being sincere or if this was just another lie. Another con.

"We came to get our car back," Joe said, all business. They both stared at me like I had Betty in my back pocket and that had been my cue to yank her out and hand her over.

"Honey, give me a minute, please?" Carolyn whispered to Joe.

"Why?"

She gave him a look I believe all women have mastered. The "You're not getting any later unless you do what I ask now," glance. Subtle, but unmistakable.

"I'll be out there."

"Thank you." She gave him a peck on the cheek to let him know there would be future nooky then refocused on me.

"We talked to Officer West, but I needed to hear it from you. We believed you. I believed you. And you did an awful thing. So I don't know how I'm supposed to believe anything else. I'm not sure why I'm here, honestly. I guess, I thought we'd connected on some level. I—"

"We did. I didn't mean to interrupt, but I want you to know how sorry I am. I fully intended to bring your car back to you. I want you to know that."

"It's not about the car, Kate."

Lately, I'd struggled with nearly everything in my life, but what I wrestled with most was my place in it. Was I going to be a spectator, a bystander, a victim of myself?

The last week with Sadie had shown me there might be a different path, a different choice to make. I hadn't fully grasped that until I faced Carolyn. Until she was sitting in front of me awash in my betrayal.

"I'm so sorry," I choked out just before I dissolved into myself. The release felt good. I was surprised at how capable of apology I'd suddenly become.

"Why'd you do it?"

"I don't know. I—I don't know."

"Kate, why did you do it?"

"I was afraid. I was, I figured if you knew, I couldn't tell you. I needed to protect her and I didn't want to involve you."

"You didn't want to involve me or you thought I'd turn you in?"

"A little of both, I guess. You were good to us. Kind, and I—I didn't want to let you down. I know that sounds really stupid considering what I did, but I thought I was protecting you too. I'm so sorry."

Carolyn looked at me and smiled. I knew I wasn't in the same place I'd been before I stole their car, but hopefully we could move forward to something good. Maybe there was still room for me to use my life well.

"I don't fully understand what happened. Or why you asked us here. Was it for this?"

"Sadie."

"She's not your daughter."

"No." The truth of it hit me then. She had been mine. I wanted her to be mine. But that was fantasy and I was in jail. Didn't get much more real for me than that.

"Will you tell me what happened?" she said.

"Do you believe in God?"

"Well that's—where did that come from?"

"I just want to know."

She contemplated her will, her faith. Could she believe in God, in life, when hers had crumbled down around her and kept on crumbling? What did it take to believe in the face of any parent's worst nightmare?

She glanced over at me with tears brimming her eyes and when she blinked they streamed down her cheek. She didn't need to answer; I knew what she was going to say. And I knew what I would say if she'd asked me the same question.

I told her everything, exactly as it had happened since Sunday evening. I wasn't afraid of the truth anymore or who was hearing it through the glass.

"I need to talk to Joe, all right?" she said, after I'd finished.

"You know where to find me."

"Are you sure about this, Kate? I mean, you could try—"

"No. It's the best thing for her." And it would be the hardest thing I'd ever have to do.

Carolyn raced out to consult with Joe and I sat there in the stillness of the empty room wondering what would come of all this. There were so many variables, so many things I didn't know. It surprised me how much I missed Sadie. It had only been a couple days, but not seeing her or hearing her voice drove me crazy. I needed to hold her. To feel her strength.

"Are you serious about this, Kate? You're not messing with us again?" Joe asked. They'd come back in with the guard. Our time was nearly up.

"I don't know what's going to happen, Joe, but if I don't try to help her now—"

"What can you do from here?"

"Nothing. That's why I need your help."

Carolyn studied Joe mulling it over. First he had to wrestle his ugly pride and accept my apology for duping him. In the end compassion, and his own desires, won out.

"What do we do?"

Carolyn and Joe dropped the charges against me, but I had two other major ones to worry about. So they contacted Patrick and asked him to pull some strings. They were more like hunks of rope, but two days later I was on a plane heading back to Salt

Lake City. One giant step closer to Sadie. What I didn't realize was the rope he'd tugged was attached to the District Attorney, Charles Schaffer. Randy's father. He'd only agreed to such a speedy return because he couldn't wait to prosecute me to the full extent for my crimes. The biggest in his mind, I imagined, was endangering his son's virility. Of course, he wasn't aware of the videos in junior's closet, but I'd worry about that when the time came.

Seeing Officer Patrick West in uniform for the first time didn't even keep me from needing to see Sadie. He met me at the airport terminal to be my personal escort to jail.

"Thank you, sir, I've got her from here," he said to the police escort I'd flown in with. Patrick signed my papers and the other officer handed me over to him then disappeared into the airport to catch a plane back to Seattle.

Thankfully Patrick had been able to keep my return quiet so there were no press hounds sniffing around the airport waiting to get first dibs on my story.

"Is she with them? Is she safe?" I asked. He helped me into the back of his cruiser, taking care to cover my head as he eased me down in. His touch felt safe. Like I was protected now. He left my hands cuffed. "I'm sorry. I just—I really need to see her."

"I checked in on her Friday after we talked. He said she was upstairs sleeping."

"And you believed him?"

"No." He closed the door and climbed in the front. His partner wasn't with him. Maybe he just wanted to do this alone. I could tell he was torn about the whole thing. Probably felt like he was aiding and abetting. I hoped to convince him otherwise. We left the airport and headed for my new temporary home at the Salt Lake jail.

"And?"

"And she's safe. That's all you need to know right now," he said, peering at my reflection in his rear view mirror. I really didn't appreciate sitting in the back of his car, separated from him by metal mesh. But I suppose he had to keep up appearances. After all, I was a criminal until proven otherwise.

"Can I see her?"

"She can visit you."

"No. Not in jail. I don't want her to see me there."

"I don't know what to tell you, Kate."

"Tell me you'll take me to her."

"You know I can't do that." Officer Patrick West was a meticulous driver. He followed the speed limit in every zone, in fact, he traveled even slower than the signs dictated on the surface streets.

"Where did you find her?"

"I can't tell you that. It's an open investigation."

"Did she have her bag?"

"Kate, please with the twenty questions."

I wasn't letting him off the hook. "Did she cry for me when you took her out of the basement?"

He was silent. Still. His gaze reached up to the rear view mirror and caught mine staring back.

"She's safe now?"

"She's safe," he said.

A relief. I'd been so concerned with Sadie's wellbeing I forgot to ask about my own.

"Am I still being charged?"

"I'm working on that."

"Why am I in handcuffs?"

"Protocol. Charges haven't been dropped yet."

"Protocol. Great."

"And you have others pending. You must've really messed with Randy Schaffer. His father's out for blood."

And he would get some before this whole thing was over.

A week had never felt more like a lifetime, but at the end of it, thanks to Carolyn and Joe posting my bail, I was a free woman, at least until my hearing. Patrick picked me up. I was finally going to see Sadie.

"Thank you. For everything," I said. He didn't answer. Just smiled at the corners of his mouth and kept his eyes on the road. His hand gently rested on mine. It was a beautiful gesture.

I was chock full of confusion about seeing Sadie again. I didn't know if I wanted to do this or not. If it would make everything harder. Maybe it was best to leave things the way they were.

We pulled up and parked right in front of a large, brick house. There was a sign with a Christmas tree carved in it on the front lawn and it read "Children's Shelter—The Christmas Box House." I had a good feeling about this place. She'd be taken care of here, at least until Carolyn and Joe's paperwork went through. Because Sadie had no other living relatives capable of taking care of her, and given that she loved being with them, they were able to file for adoption without hassle.

"There she is." Patrick's voice startled me in the silence of the car. I'd been gazing at the statue of the bronze angel in the front yard. She looked a lot like Sadie.

But then I saw the real thing charging out the front door holding Matilda. I didn't see Carolyn or Joe until a while later when I could focus on something other than that ray of light blazing toward me. I'd never seen her happier. Part of me wondered if it was because of me or if it was because she knew things were going to be different for her now. Maybe a little of both.

"Katie! Katie! Katie!"

I sprung from the car and held my arms out for her to jump into. Even though she was tiny, she threw herself with such force we almost tipped over backward.

"Hi," I whispered into her.

"Hi," she whispered back. I noticed it immediately. It was stronger than ever. Sadie got her strawberries back. I didn't know if it was her doing or mine, but it didn't matter. I knew then I'd made the right decision.

"I miss you. Will you stay with me now? Look, I have Matewda. And Joe and Cowlin are here and that's the policeman who got me. And there are lots of nice people in the house and guess what my roommate's name is? It's Katie like you. Will you read the rest of Clyde for me? We have to read the rest of Clyde."

This was all I'd wanted. Just to hold her one more time, to know she was all right. To know she would be all right. I didn't know how to tell her I wouldn't be part of her life anymore.

"Honey, I'm...I..." I put her down and squatted next to her, straightening her dress. Carolyn must have put her hair in ponytails, just as she liked it. The ginger ringlets spiraled down on both sides of her freckly, cherub cheeks.

I looked back at Patrick sitting patiently in the driver's seat watching us. I could see he understood now, why I'd needed this. It was a strange kind of validation, but it made me feel good. Like I was finally on the right track with him.

"I'd love to see where you live and meet all your new friends."

"Kay, let's go, let's go!" She took my hand and dragged me toward the door. I glanced over my shoulder and waved to Patrick. He waved back and drove off.

We met up with Joe and Carolyn just inside the lobby. "Everything's all set at my sister's for you," Carolyn said, hugging me. "You can stay as long as you need to." Her hair tickled my cheek. It was soft and still smelled like roses.

"I can't thank you enou—"

"Don't. You've given us a tremendous gift." That gift yanked on me to go see her new Spongebob bedspread and meet her friends. It was glorious to finally see her be exactly what she was, a five-year-old child.

I spent the next week and a half with Sadie. Joe and Carolyn respected my time with her and kept themselves scarce. They were also taking the month long course required for adoption so they didn't have much spare time anyway.

The day of my hearing was one of the most difficult of my life. "Honey, I have to go now." I stood and closed the book.

"Are you coming back tomorrow?"

"I can't."

"Why?"

"I'm not...I probably won't see you for a while."

Her face turned red again and began its journey to Crumple-land, but this time she tried to hold it in. It was adorable.

"How come?"

"I have to go away for a while, but I want you to take good care of Matilda and Joe and Carolyn."

"And The Boys?"

"And The Boys."

She went quiet for a minute. Hung her head and tried to compose herself. "Will you kiss her for me?"

"Matilda?" She nodded. "Of course."

She held Matilda to her heart and when I leaned in to kiss the doll, Sadie's tears rolled down her cheeks and landed on mine. Angel's tears.

I took my charm bracelet off and put it in her hand. "I want you to have this. Remember when you asked me if it was special?" She nodded and looked up at me. "It's special because my mommy gave it to me. But now I want you to have it. That'll be our tradition. And if you miss me, just hold it close and you'll know I'm with you."

She kissed the butterfly then wrapped Matilda in my arms. "Whenever you miss me, you just hold her and I'll be with you."

"No honey. I can't take Matilda."

"Yes you can." It was that simple for her. And so I did.

Nothing held my words back now. "I love you, Sadie Beck." I took her in my arms, squeezing her like a teddy bear.

"I can't breathe."

"Sorry."

I loosened my grip. This whole thing was loosening my grip.

She hugged me again and whispered in my ear, "She said it's not your fault."

I pulled away and looked at her, shocked.

"What..."

"At the water. She wanted me to tell you it's not your fault."

This time *I* crumpled. I'd needed to hear that for eighteen years and there it suddenly was.

"Thank you." That was all I managed to say, but it was everything I needed to. I squeezed her tight to me for the last time.

I was afraid if I stayed any longer I'd either spontaneously combust or do something stupid like try to disappear with her again. Neither option was likely to make anyone happy, so I kissed her on the nose and gave her back to the ground.

"I'm pretty sure Clyde makes it to Los Angeles," I said. We still hadn't made it to the end of his story. Too many distractions at the shelter.

"He does but then he misses his home. He misses his family."

She'd known all along what happened in the story. She'd probably read it a million times over with her mother. She just wanted to return to something normal, familiar. I was positive Carolyn and Joe would wear the ink off the pages reading it to her now.

"I'm going to miss you," I said, hugging her one more time.

"I love you and I want you to stay with me."

"I know, honey. But I can't."

It was that simple. I just wanted her to get back home.

After they took Chris into custody, I found out he'd had a record of spousal abuse in Arizona and there was a warrant for his arrest there. Could have been one reason he didn't run to the authorities to report Sadie missing. I don't wish to think about what might have happened to her had she not hid in my jeep that night.

And even though my lawyer argued the kidnapping charges away, with the aid of Patrick's testimony and my intent to protect, I still wound up serving five months in the Utah State Penitentiary for the basket of goodies I'd perpetrated against Adam and Randy, with an additional two years of parole tacked on as an extra-special bonus. Randy's daddy managed to stick me despite the naughty tapes.

My father passed away while I was inside, and I was never more grateful for Sadie than when I received the letter from Aunt Janet. Without her I wouldn't have said goodbye.

I took my punishment as a blessing. It was my gestation period. And now I'm ready to spread my wings. After much deliberation I've decided when I get out of here today, I won't go see Patrick West just yet. Instead, on my way home to the house I'll be renting with three other ex-penitentiary darlings, I'm going to stop at the local gardening store. I'll buy one tulip bulb, take it to my new backyard and plant it. And maybe, just maybe, I'll stand still long enough to see what grows.

Acknowledgments

I'm so grateful, Lindsay Brooks, for the lovely lunch and the brilliant seed that grew the idea for this book. Thank you.

Kate would still be a three-chapter Word file on my old Macbook Pro if not for the constant, unwavering support and cheerleading of Jay Garrett. Thank you for your belief in me, for always reading a new chapter with excitement, and encouraging me to just keep going. I really needed that.

Julie Shimer Lawrence, Scott Ritchie, and Natascha Corrigan Aldridge, you were the best, most enthusiastic beta readers any writer could ask for. Julie, the fact that you risked getting in trouble for reading my book at work (in two days!) because you *just couldn't stop* was the most encouraging feedback I've ever received. Thank you for your notes and your great enthusiasm for this project. Scott, your thoroughness was exactly what I needed to make *Kate* better. I'm eternally grateful for your time and your honesty. Tashi, thank you, you know, for everything, always.

I bear a great debt of gratitude to my agent, BJ Robbins, for your notes and your tireless efforts on behalf of *Kate*.

Mom, for your eternal belief in me and my dreams regardless of how they're taking shape, and your instant and undying love for Kate and Sadie.

And Tony, my Magic Man, my hero. Thank you for lending your incredible talents to help bring this book to life in paper form, and for all you do for us every single day.

CONNECT WITH THE AUTHOR

Website: http://authorkellybyrne.com

Twitter: http://twitter.com/KellyByrneCA

Facebook: http://facebook.com/authorkellybyrne

Google+: http://plus.google.com/+KellyByrne/

If you'd like to know when Kelly's next book is coming out, please subscribe to the *Book Club* on her website for project updates and great book recommendations.

One last thing before you go...

PLEASE HELP SPREAD THE WORD

Without supportive friends like you, indie authors wouldn't be able to do what they do, so thank you!

If you enjoyed *Chasing Kate* there are two ways you can help others do the same if you would be so kind.

<u>Recommend it</u>: Please tell your friends and/or book club how much you loved the book. An easy way to do that right now is to share it on Twitter and Facebook.

<u>Review it:</u> If you loved it, please tell other readers why by reviewing it on Amazon and Goodreads (you can copy and paste one review to both sites). Reviews help other readers decide which books to purchase and they help indie authors gain visibility in a congested marketplace.

If you recommend it or write a review, please connect with Kelly through email at: authorkellybyrne@gmail.com or social media and let her know so she can personally thank you and tell you what a superhero you are to her.

Made in the USA
San Bernardino, CA
24 November 2015